'I must tell you that I myself would have accepted her. We may be mistaken. I am not giving it as my opinion that she is Anne — not yet. But do you not think it at least possible that the mistake is yours, and that it was Annie Joyce who died in the boat?'

'It was Anne.'

'You certainly thought it was Anne. It seems to me it would be much easier to make a mistake about a dead person than about a living one. The arrangement of the hair makes a great deal of difference to a likeness. Annie Joyce's head was tied up in a scarf. If that scarf had come off, as I suppose it might very easily have done, may not the family likeness have been intensified sufficiently for you to mistake Annie for Anne — especially after death, when personality and expression are withdrawn and only the features remain?'

'I agree that it might happen. I don't agree that it did happen.'

2

The Traveller
Returns

Patricia
Wentworth

CORONET BOOKS
Hodder and Stoughton.

Copyright © 1948 by Patricia Wentworth

First published in Great Britain 1948 by
Hodder and Stoughton Limited

Coronet edition 1968
Third impression 1978

British Library
Wentworth, Patricia
   The traveller returns.
   1. Fiction in English
   I. Title
   823'.9'1F   PR6045.E66S/
   ISBN 0–340–02932–3

Printed and bound in Great Britain for
Hodder and Stoughton Paperbacks, a
division of Hodder and Stoughton Ltd.,
Mill Road, Dunton Green, Sevenoaks,
Kent (Editorial Office: 47 Bedford
Square, London, WC1 3DP) by
Richard Clay (The Chaucer Press) Ltd
Bungay, Suffolk

I

THE air in the Food Office was cold and stuffy. It would be nice to get out into the fresh air again. It would be nice when this business was over. She hadn't really been waiting for so long, but she felt an angry impatience. To go through all she had gone through, to come back quite literally from the dead, and to be wasting time standing in a queue for a ration card was, at the very least of it, an anticlimax. She was Anne Jocelyn come back from the dead, and here she was in a queue, waiting for a ration card instead of ringing up Philip.

The people in front of her moved on slowly. She began to think about Philip. Three years was a long time to have been dead. Philip had been a widower for more than three years, and in about half an hour somebody would call him to the telephone and a voice—her voice—would impart the glad tidings that Anne Jocelyn wasn't dead. It gave her a good deal of pleasure to think about telling Philip that he wasn't a widower after all.

Suppose he wasn't there. . . . A curious tingling ran over her from head to foot. It was exactly the feeling she might have had if her next slow step forward had shown her the floor broken away and her foot poised above a descending emptiness. She had a moment of vertigo. Then it passed. Philip would be there. If he had had no news of her, something of his movements, his whereabouts, had been conveyed by careful, circuitous channels to those who had helped her on her way. He had been in Egypt, in Tunisia. He had been wounded and sent home. He was to have an appointment at the War Office as soon as he was able to take it up. He'd be there all right, at Jocelyn's Holt—sleeping in the tower room, walking up and down the terrace, going round the stables, thinking of all the things he'd be able to do with Anne Jocelyn's money now that she was dead. Of course he would have to wait until the war was over. But it would take more than a world war to stop Philip planning for Jocelyn's Holt. Oh, yes, he'd be there.

She moved up one in the queue and went on thinking. Suppose he had married again. . . . Something pricked her sharply. She bit her lip. No—she would have heard, she would have been told, warned. . . . Would she? *Would* she? Her head came up, lips parted, breath quickened. No, she couldn't reckon on that, she couldn't reckon on anything. But all the same she didn't think that Philip would have married again. She shook her head slowly. She didn't think he would. He had the money, he had the place, and she didn't think he'd be in too much of a hurry to tie himself up again. After all, it hadn't gone too well, and once bitten twice shy. A faint smile just touched her lips. She didn't think Philip was going to react very pleasurably to the idea that he was still a married man.

There were three people in front of her—a very stout woman with a basket full of shopping, a little dowdy creature with a string bag, and a stooping elderly man. The stout woman was explaining at the greatest possible length how she had come to lose her ration card. . "And I'm not one to do that in a general way, Miss Marsh, though I suppose there's nobody that doesn't lose things sometimes, and I don't set up to be better than anyone else, but many's the time my husband's said, 'Give it to Mother—she's as safe as a church'. So I don't know what come over me, but put it down somewhere I must of, for when I got home there was Father's, and Ernie's, and Carrie's, and my sister-in-law's that's on a visit, but as for mine I might never have had one. So I went back and round to all the shops where I'd been, and there wasn't nobody had seen it. . . ."

The woman behind the counter dived and came up with a book in her hand.

"You dropped it in the High Street," she said in a resigned voice. "Good afternoon."

The little dowdy creature moved up. She leaned on the counter and whispered.

Anne stood there, tall, fair, and thin. She looked over the stooped shoulders of the elderly man, shivering a little and drawing her fur coat about her. Her hair hung down over the collar in a rough bob. It had a dull, neglected look, but it was thick, and with a little care it would be bright again. Just now it might have been a light brown burned by the sun, or a much fairer shade dimmed by neglect. She was bare-headed. A long straight lock fell forward on either side, framing a thin oval

6

face, straight nose, pale well-shaped lips, very deep grey eyes, and fine arched brows much darker than the hair.

The coat which she drew close was a very handsome one. The soft dark fur would be flattering when she had got something done to her face and her hair. That was the next thing. She buoyed herself up with the thought. In about ten minutes this ration card business would be over and she could go and have her hair cut and waved and see what was to be had in the way of face-powder and lipstick. She was perfectly well aware that she was looking a mess, and Philip wasn't going to see her like that.

Less than ten minutes now . . . less than five . . . The little whispering woman had gone, and the elderly man was going. She moved up into the vacant place and set down her bag on the counter. Like the coat, it was or had been very expensive, but unlike the coat it showed signs of wear. The dark brown leather was rubbed and stained, a piece of the gold initial A had broken off. Anne undid the clasp, took out a ration book, and pushed it across the counter.

"Can you let me have a new book, please?"

Miss Marsh picked it up, brought a colourless gaze to bear upon it, raised her eybrows, and said,

"This is a very old book—quite out of date."

Anne leaned nearer.

"Yes, it is. You see, I've just come over from France."

"*France?*"

"Yes. I was caught there when the Germans came. I've only just managed to get away. Can you let me have a new book?"

"Well, no—I don't see how we can——" She gave a fleeting glance at the cover of the book and added, "Lady Jocelyn."

"But I must have a ration book."

"Are you staying here?"

"No—only passing through."

"Then I don't see what we can do about it. You'll have to get your ration book wherever you're going to stay—at least—I don't know—have you got your identity card?"

"Yes—here it is. I was lucky—a friend hid it for me—and some clothes, or I should be in rags, and one would rather not come back from the grave in rags."

Miss Marsh's pale eyes stared. She said nervously,

"I think I had better ask Miss Clutterbuck." She slipped down from her chair and vanished.

About ten minutes later Anne emerged into the street. She had filled in a form, she had been given an emergency card for a fortnight, and the old identity card to keep until such time as a new one should be issued.

She crossed the road and entered a telephone-box.

II

MRS. Armitage looked up from the Air Force pullover she was knitting and immediately dropped a stitch. She was large, fair, and extremely good natured. She wore aged tweeds and a battered felt hat which was generally over one ear. A spare knitting-needle of a horribly bright pink was thrust into a thick disordered fuzz of hair. Once almost too golden, it was now in a streaky half-way stage which probably went better with the freckled skin, light eyes, and wide genial mouth. The tweeds were, or had been, a regrettable mustard. She would have been the first to admit that they clashed with the room. It would have been quite in character if she had said, "But just think of a room that wouldn't clash with me!"

This particular room had been decorated for Anne Jocelyn when she married. It was pretty, conventional, and eminently suitable for a bride of twenty, with its flowery chintzes, blue curtains, and old china. The Four Seasons stood in graceful poses on the white mantelshelf. In a corner cupboard the bright colour of a tea-set in *bleu-de-roi* caught up and repeated the shade of the curtains. The mustard-coloured tweeds were certainly a mistake, and she was as certainly quite unperturbed about it.

Mrs. Armitage leaned towards her niece Lyndall, who was sitting on the hearth-rug dropping fir cones on a reluctant fire, and said in her usual irrelevant manner,

"There's one good thing about the war anyway—if we had to sit in that awful purse-proud drawing-room I should want to scream, like the girls who wrote to the *Daily Mirror* the other day."

Lyn wrinkled her nose and said, "What girls?"

Mrs. Armitage dragged the knitting-needle from her hair.

"Three of them," she said. "They were bored with their job, and they said they wanted to scream every so often.

8

Well, I should if I had to sit in a room with seven chandeliers and about fifty mirrors."

Lyndall blew a kiss.

"Only six, darling—I counted them yesterday—and three chandeliers. And I quite agree, but why purse-proud?"

"Because Sir Ambrose Jocelyn, who was Anne's grand-father and Philip's great-uncle, built it on with his wife's money. I expect he did it to annoy her—they didn't get on, you know. She left him, but he managed to build the drawing-room and that awful north wing first, and I suppose she felt she just couldn't bear it and cleared out before he spent it all, or there wouldn't have been anything left to come down to Anne, and Philip would have to sell Jocelyn's Holt. So it's all for the best. Oh, lord—I've dropped a stitch!"

Lyn giggled. She was a little thing, slim and pale, with rather nice grey eyes and a lot of soft dark hair in a bush of curls. She reached for the pullover.

"Two, darling. You shouldn't take your eye off the ball. Better give it to me."

"No—I'll pick them up myself—I can if I put my mind to it. Yes, I suppose it was lucky for Philip that Anne and the money were there. Of course people aren't keen on cousins marrying now. Funny how fashions change, because in the Victorian novels it was quite the thing—even firsts, which is a bit too near. Anne and Philip were only seconds, and as he came into the title and the place, and she had the money to keep them up, everybody said it couldn't have been better— except that I don't know how they would have got on if it had lasted, because of course Anne—well, Anne——" Her voice trailed away. She pursued the lost stitches.

Lyndall's colour rose.

"Anne was *sweet*," she said, her voice quick and warm.

Mrs. Armitage coerced a stitch into its place on the pink needle and said vaguely,

"Oh, yes. Anne was sweet."

Lyn's colour brightened.

"She *was*!"

"Oh, yes, my dear." The light eyes blinked. "Of course I remember you had a—what do you call it—a crush on her when you were a schoolgirl, didn't you? I had forgotten. But you didn't see much of her after that—did you?"

Lyndall shook her head.

9

"Only at the wedding. But I've never forgotten the summer holidays the year before the war, when Anne and her aunt were here on a visit. I've often thought since how easy it would have been for Anne to be horrid about it. You see, there was you and Mrs. Kendall, and Philip and Anne. Anne was nineteen and quite grown up, and I was only sixteen and a horrid little scrub. I must have been an awful nuisance, but Anne was wonderful. Lots of girls would have been horrid and high-hat, and not wanting to be bothered with a flapper, but she was wonderful. She took me everywhere and let me do everything with them. She was *sweet*. And if Philip didn't get on with her after they were married, it must have been his fault."

Mildred Armitage looked across her dishevelled knitting.

"They both liked their own way," she said. "They were both only children, and Anne was very pretty, and she had a lot of money, and she hadn't found out that it's not all jam holding the purse-strings when you're married to anyone as proud as Philip."

Lyn's eyes came to her face with a wondering look.

"Is Philip proud?"

"Oh, my dear—*proud*!"

"Well, is he?"

Mrs. Armitage shrugged her shoulders.

"Well, well——" she said. "Anyhow there wasn't a great deal of time for things to go wrong, was there? And perhaps they wouldn't have gone wrong at all—or perhaps they would have gone wrong and come right again. It's no use worrying about it now—she's gone, and there it is. You can think about her as kindly as you like."

"She was wonderful to me." The three times repeated phrase had the effect of a response in some private litany of loyalty and regret. "It was lovely of her to have me for a bridesmaid."

She got up and went back to the middle of the room, tilting her head and looking up at the full-length painting over the mantelpiece. It was Amory's famous *Girl with a Fur Coat*, and it had been painted from Anne Jocelyn a few weeks after her marriage. Soft dark fur over a thin blue dress, pearls hanging down, a smiling oval face and rosy lips, gold-tinted hair in a cluster of careless curls, the soft bloom of youth and happiness. Anne Jocelyn looked out of the picture as if she was alive. A young girl, bare-headed, drawing her coat about her, smiling

10

as if she was just starting off for a party—smiling at all the pleasant things that were to come. And a year later she had died in the dark on a Breton beach to the rattle of machine-gun fire.

Lyndall's eyes widened. She went on looking at the picture, all its colours bright under the electric light. Anne's room— Anne's picture. And Anne dead at twenty-one! The anger in her leapt up. She turned on Mildred Armitage.

"Why weren't you fond of her?"

The knitting sank in a heap on the mustard-coloured lap. The pale eyes blinked as if with surprise.

"My darling child, I hardly knew her. Anne's mother didn't cotton to the Jocelyns very much. You've got to re-member that Marian was old Ambrose's daughter and she was brought up to look upon him as a monster. He took another woman to live with him, and they had a boy—and you can imagine that didn't go down very well. So Marian grew up hating the Jocelyns, and she brought Anne up to do the same. It wasn't until she died that her sister-in-law Mrs. Kendal— quite a sensible woman—allowed Anne to meet any of us. Not, of course, that I'm a Jocelyn, but when my sister married Philip's father we were just lumped in with the rest. So I didn't see Anne till she was turned nineteen."

Lyndall went on looking at her with those wide, accusing eyes.

"Why didn't you like her?"

She said like, but she meant love. How could anyone have known Anne without loving her? There wasn't any answer to that.

Mildred Armitage made a small vexed sound.

"How on earth do I know! One doesn't get fond of people in a hurry like that—not at my age. She was young, she was pretty, she had pots of money, and Mrs. Kendal obviously meant her to marry Philip. Well, she married him, and it didn't last long enough for anyone to know how it would have turned out."

"But you didn't like her!"

At the angry quiver in Lyndall's voice Milly Armitage smiled her wide, disarming smile.

"Don't get in a rage. You can't help your feelings. Jane Kendal wanted her to marry Philip, and I didn't."

"Why didn't you?"

"Because they were cousins, for one thing. I didn't think two of a trade would agree. Jocelyns have all got a perfectly lethal streak of pride and self-will."

"Anne hadn't!"

"Hadn't she? She wanted to marry Philip, and she married him."

"Why shouldn't she?"

"No reason at all except that her mother would rather have died than let her do it. I don't blame Anne about that—I don't blame either of them. There wasn't any reason why they shouldn't marry, but if there had been it wouldn't have made a ha'porth of difference. Jocelyns are like that. Look at Theresa Jocelyn, going off and living in a Breton château. And why? Because she took up with old Ambrose's illegitimate granddaughter and had a furious row with the family on her account. Joyce—that was the name—Annie Joyce. Ambrose called the woman Mrs. Joyce—as near to Jocelyn as he dared go—and the son, Roger, carried it on. Annie was his daughter, and there wasn't a bean, because Ambrose never signed his will. So when Theresa, who was only an umpteenth cousin, came blinding in and wanted the family to take Annie to their bosom and give her an income, there weren't any takers, and she quarrelled with everyone and rushed off to France and rented a château. She had quite a lot of money, and of course everyone thought she would leave it to Annie. But she didn't, she left it to Anne, who'd got plenty already. Sent for her to come over and told her she was going to have the lot, and she must always be kind to Annie because the poor girl was an orphan and had been done out of her rights. Philip said it was indecent, and of course it was. After all the fuss she'd made about the girl!"

Lyndall's eyes were stormy. She hated injustice. She loved Anne. The two things struggled in her. She said like an abrupt child,

"Why did she do it?"

"Theresa? Because she was a Jocelyn—because she wanted to—because her crazy fancy for Annie Joyce was over and she'd taken a new one for Anne. She came over to the wedding and fell on their necks. A dreadfully tiresome woman, all gush and feathers. To be quite honest, I'm surprised that she had managed to keep out of having a finger in the family pie for as long as she did. The wedding was a perfectly splendid excuse, and it's my belief she jumped at it. She was probably

12

sick to death of her precious Annie Joyce and all set for a new craze. I believe she would have come back to England for good, but she got ill. By the time she'd sent for Anne it was too late to move her, and things were hotting up in France. That's when the rows began. Philip put his foot down, and Anne put hers down too. He said she wasn't to go, and she went. I don't think I've ever seen anyone so angry."

"He'd no right to be angry!"

"My angel child, when married people begin to talk about their rights, it means something has gone pretty far wrong between them."

Lyndall said,

"Did they make it up?"

"I don't know."

"It would be dreadful if they didn't."

Milly Armitage had her own ideas about that. Philip had certainly not been in any mood for reconciliation when he left England. She had never seen an angrier man in her life.

It would have been better if she had kept her thoughts to herself, but she was really incapable of doing so. She said,

"He was in a most frightful rage—and for the lord's sake, why are we talking about it? It was a horrid tragic business, and it's over. Why don't we leave it alone instead of screwing our heads round over our shoulders and looking back like Lot's wife? Uncomfortable, useless things, pillars of salt. And I've dropped about fifty stitches with you glaring at me like a vulture."

"Vultures don't glare—they have horrid little hoods on their eyes."

Milly Armitage burst out laughing.

"Come and pick up my stitches, and we'll have a nice calming talk about natural history!"

III

PHILIP Jocelyn rang up at eight o'clock.

"Who's that? . . . Lyn? . . . All right, tell Aunt Milly I'll be down to lunch tomorrow—or perhaps not till after lunch. Will that disorganize the rations?"

Lyn gurgled.

"I expect so."

"Well, I shan't know until the last minute. Anyhow I can't make it tonight."

"All right. Just wait a second—someone rang you up this morning."

"Who?"

"I don't know. She didn't give any name—only asked if you were here, and when I said you were up in London she wanted to know when you would be back. I said perhaps to-tonight but most probably not till tomorrow, and she rang off. It was a long distance call and the line was awfully faint."

She heard him laugh.

"The Voice on the Telephone—our great serial mystery—to be continued in our next! Don't be apologetic—I expect she'll keep. Give Aunt Milly my love. I kiss your hands and your feet."

"You don't do anything of the sort!"

"Perhaps not—it's a sadly unpicturesque age. Good-bye, my child. Be good." He hung up.

Lyndall put down the receiver and came back to the fire. She had changed into a warm green house-coat, and Mrs. Armitage into a shapeless garment of brown velveteen with a fur collar which was rather the worse for wear.

Lyndall said, "That was Philip."

"So I gathered."

"He doesn't know whether he'll be down for lunch to-morrow."

Things like that never worried Mrs. Armitage. She nodded, and said with what appeared to be complete irrelevance,

"What a good thing you and Philip are not really cousins."

Lyndall bent forward to put a log on the fire, her long, full skirt flaring out from a childish waist. The glow from the embers stung her cheeks. She murmured,

"Why?"

"Well, I just thought it was a good thing. Jocelyns are all very well, and poor Louie was very happy with Philip's father. He was a most charming man. But that's what it is with the Jocelyns—they're charming. But you can have too much of them—they want diluting."

It was at this moment that the front door bell rang.

Anne Jocelyn stood on the dark step and waited for someone to come. The taxi which had brought her from Clayford turned noisily behind her on the gravel sweep. Then it drove away. The sound receded and was gone. She stood in the dark and waited for someone to come. Presently she rang again, but almost at once the key turned in the lock. The door opened a little way and a young girl looked round it. When she saw that it was a woman standing there she stepped back opening the door wide.

Anne Jocelyn walked in.

"Is Sir Philip back?"

Ivy Fossett was a little bit flustered. Visitors didn't just walk in like that after dark, not these days they didn't. But it was a lady all right, and a lovely fur coat. She stared her eyes out at it and said,

"No, ma'am, he isn't."

The lady took her up sharp.

"Who is here then? Who answered the telephone this morning?"

"Mrs. Armitage, and Miss Lyndall—Miss Lyndall Armitage. It would be her answered the phone."

"Where are they? . . . In the Parlour? You needn't announce me—I'll go through."

Ivy gaped, and watched her go. "Walked right past me as if I wasn't there," she told them in the kitchen, and was reproved by Mrs. Ramage, the rather more than elderly cook.

"You should have asked her name."

Ivy tossed her head.

"She never give me a chanst!"

Anne crossed the hall. The Parlour looked out to a terrace at the back. The name came down, with the white panelling, from the reign of good Queen Anne. The first Anne Jocelyn had been her god-daughter.

She put her hand on the door-knob and stood for a moment, loosening her coat, pushing it back to show the blue of the dress beneath. Her heart beat hard against her side. It isn't every day that one comes back from the dead. Perhaps she was glad that Philip wasn't there. She opened the door and stood on the threshold looking in.

Light overhead, the blue curtains drawn at the windows, a wood fire glowing bright, and over it the white mantelshelf with *The Seasons* looking down, and, over *The Seasons*, *The Girl with a Fur Coat*. She looked at her steadily, critically, as she might have looked at her own reflection in the glass. She thought the portrait might very well have been a mirror reflecting her.

There were two people in the room. On the right of the hearth Milly Armitage with a newspaper on her lap and another sprawling beside her on the blue carpet. Untidy, tiresome woman. Never her friend. Of course she *would* be here. Well dug in. *Nous allons changer tout cela.* Down on the hearthrug, curled up with a book, that brat Lyndall.

The paper rustled under the sudden heavy pressure of Milly Armitage's hand, the book pitched forward on to the white fur rug. Lyndall sprang up, stumbling on the folds of her long green skirt, catching at the arm of the empty chair against which she had been leaning. Her eyes widened and darkened, all the colour went out of her face. She stared at the open door and saw Anne Jocelyn stepped from the portrait behind her— Anne Jocelyn, bare-headed, with her gold curls and her tinted oval face, pearls hanging down over the thin blue dress, fur coat hanging open.

In the same moment she heard Milly Armitage gasp. She herself did not seem to be breathing at all. Everything stopped while she looked at Anne. Then irrepressibly, incongruously, there zigzagged into her mind the thought, "Amory painted her better than that." When this came back to her later it shocked her horribly. After more than three years of privation, suffering, and strain, who wouldn't look different—older? A rush of feeling blotted out everything except the realization that this was Anne and she was alive. She ran forward with a half articulate cry, and Anne opened her arms. In a moment Lyndall was hugging her, saying her name over and over, the tears running down her cheeks.

"Anne—Anne—*Anne*! We thought you were dead!"

"I very nearly thought so myself."

They came across the room together.

"Aunt Milly! How good to see you! Oh, how very, very good to be here!"

Milly Armitage was embraced. Struggling with a horrid rush of completely disorganized emotions, she kissed a cheek which was thinner and considerably more made-up than it had been three years ago. She couldn't remember ever having been embraced by Anne before. A cool kiss on the cheek was as far as they had ever got or wanted to get. She stood back with a transient feeling of relief and endeavoured to find words. It

16

wasn't that there weren't plenty of things to say, but even in this moment of shock she had a feeling that she had better not say them. Philip—she mustn't say or do anything which would hurt Philip. A sense of immeasurable disaster hovered. Three and a half years was a long time to be dead. Anne had come back. Awful to come back and feel that you weren't wanted any more. "The living close their ranks." Who said that? It was true—you had to. Under this high-flown strain, something quite homely and commonplace. "Gosh! Why did she have to come back?"

Lyndall was saying, "Anne darling—oh, Anne darling! How lovely that you are alive!"

Mrs. Armitage remembered that she had been brought up to be a gentlewoman. With grim determination she set herself to behave like one.

IV

It was getting on for four o'clock of the following day before Philip Jocelyn came home. He was intercepted in the hall by Milly Armitage.

"Philip—come here—I want to speak to you."

"What's the matter?"

She had him by the arm, drawing him down the hall towards the study, which balanced the Parlour on the opposite side and was comfortably far away from it. Like most rooms of the name it had never been much studied in, but the walls were lined with books and it had a pleasant lived-in air, with its rust-red curtains and deep leather chairs.

When the door was shut, Philip looked curiously at his Aunt Milly. He was very fond of her, but he wished she would come to the point. Something had obviously happened, but instead of getting on with it and telling him what it was, she was just beating about the bush.

"We tried to get on to you, but they said you'd left the club."

"Yes—Blackett asked me to go down to his place. What's the matter? Where's Lyn? It's not got anything to do with Lyn?"

"No."

17

Milly Armitage said to herself in a distraught manner, "You see, he thought about her at once. He's fond of her—he's been getting fonder of her every day. What's the good of it now? I'm a wicked woman. . . . Oh, lord—what a mix-up!" She rubbed her chin with a shaking hand.

"Aunt Milly, what is it? Anyone dead?"

Mrs. Armitage restrained herself from saying, "Worse than that." By making a tremendous effort she contrived merely to shake her head.

He said with some impatience, "What is it then?"

Milly Armitage blurted it right out.

"Anne's come back."

They were standing close together beside the writing table. Philip had his coat over his arm and his hat in his hand. He stood there, fair and tall like all the Jocelyns, his face longer and sharper than the type, his eyes the same dark grey as Anne's, the eyebrows marked like hers but crooked where hers were arched, his hair burnt almost flaxen by the Tunisian sun. After a moment he turned, dropped his hat into a chair, laid his coat across the back, and said softly,

"Would you mind saying that again?"

Milly Armitage felt as if she was going to burst. She said it again, separating the words as if she was speaking to a child.

"Anne—has—come—back."

"I thought that was what you said—I just wanted to be sure. Would you mind telling me what it means?"

"Philip—don't! I can't tell you if you're like that."

His crooked brows went up.

"Like what?"

"Inhuman. She's alive—she's come back—she's here."

His voice grated for the first time as he said,

"Have you gone out of your mind?"

"Not yet, but I expect I shall."

He said quietly, "Anne's dead. What makes you think she isn't?"

"Anne. She walked in on us last night. She's here—she's in the Parlour with Lyndall now."

"Nonsense!"

"Philip, if you go on saying that sort of thing to me, I shall scream! I tell you she's alive—I tell you she's in the Parlour with Lyndall."

"And I tell you that I saw her die, and I saw her buried."

Milly Armitage checked an involuntary shudder. She said in an angry voice,

"What's the good of saying that?"

"Meaning I'm telling lies?"

"She's in the Parlour with Lyndall."

Philip walked over to the door.

"Then suppose we join them."

"Wait! It's no good taking it like that. It's happened—better let me tell you. Someone rang up in the morning—yesterday morning. Lyn told you on the telephone."

"Yes?"

"It was Anne. She had just landed from a fishing-boat. She didn't say who she was—only asked if you were here. Last night at about half-past eight she walked in. It was a most frightful shock. I don't wonder you can't believe it. Lyn had been looking at Amory's picture of her only a little time before, and when the door opened, there she was, just as if she had stepped out of it—the blue dress, the pearls, the fur coat. It was *the* most frightful shock."

He turned away and opened the door.

"Anne's dead, Aunt Milly. I think I'd like to go and see who it is in the Parlour with Lyn."

Neither of them spoke as they went across the hall. It was Philip who opened the door and went in. He saw Lyndall first. She was sitting on the arm of one of the big chairs on the left-hand side of the hearth. She jumped up, and he saw behind her in the chair the blue dress of the portrait—Anne Jocelyn's going-away dress—Anne Jocelyn's pearls hanging down over the stuff—Anne Jocelyn's curled gold hair, the oval face, the dark grey eyes, the arching brows. He stood looking for a time that none of them could have counted. Then he came forward in a quiet, deliberate manner.

"Very well staged," he said. "Let me congratulate you on your make-up and your nerve, Miss Joyce."

V

She got out of her chair and stood facing him.

"Philip!"

He nodded briefly.

19

"Philip. But not Anne—or at least not Anne Jocelyn. I suppose Annie Joyce was christened Anne."

"Philip!"

"That doesn't get us anywhere, does it? May I ask how you thought you could get away with a fraud of this kind? Very ingenious of you, but perhaps you thought I'd be abroad—or better still a casualty, in which case I suppose you might have brought it off. It seems to have gone down with Lyn and Aunt Milly, but it doesn't go down with me, and I'll tell you why. When Anne was hit I picked her up and I got her into the boat. She died there. I brought her body home."

She kept her eyes on his face.

"You brought Annie Joyce home. You buried Annie Joyce."

"And why am I supposed to have done that?"

She said, "I think you made a mistake. It was Annie who was hit, but I screamed. She was holding on to my arm. You had gone ahead towards the boat. The bullet went between us—I felt it go by. Annie let go of me and fell down. I screamed. Then you came back and picked her up. You may have thought it was I. You may have made a mistake in the dark—I don't know—I don't want to say. It was dark, and they were firing at us—you *could* have made a mistake. I thought you would come back for me, but you didn't."

Philip said softly, "So that's your story—I left you on the beach?"

"I think—no, I am sure—you only thought that you were leaving Annie Joyce."

"That's a pretty damnable thing to say——" He checked himself. "This is what happened. I carried Anne to the boat. There were those other people who tacked on—the Reddings." He turned to face Lyndall. When he went on speaking it was to her. "Murdoch and I took his motor-boat over. When we got there Theresa Jocelyn was dead and buried and the Germans were in the village. I went to the château whilst Murdoch stayed with the boat. I gave Anne and Miss Joyce half an hour to get any valuables together, and Anne said there were some other English people hiding at a farm, couldn't I take them too? She said Pierre would go and tell them. I said how many were there, and she wasn't sure—she thought two of them were children. She sent for Pierre—he was Theresa's butler and factotum—and he said there was Monsieur and Madame, and a son and daughter not quite grown up. The farm belonged to his cousin, and he seemed to know all about them. I said all right, they could come, but they must be down on the beach within the hour. Well, they were late—they were the sort of people who would always be late for everything. We waited, and by the time they turned up the Boche had spotted us and the balloon was going up. I was a little way ahead, when Anne screamed. I went back and managed to get her into the boat. It was pitch dark and there was a lot of shooting. I called out to Annie Joyce, and got no answer. Murdoch and I went to look for her. By this time the Reddings were calling out to us. Murdoch came past me carrying someone—I thought it was Miss Joyce. When we'd got everyone in we counted heads. There was Murdoch, and myself, a man, a boy, and four women. And that was right—another of the women had been hit. We pushed off. Anne never recovered consciousness. She was shot through the head. We were half way over before I found out that Miss Joyce wasn't there. We'd got our six passengers all right, but the Reddings had brought their French governess along. She had a bullet in the chest and she was pretty bad. We couldn't go back. It wouldn't have been any good if we had. Anyone on the beach would have been picked up by the Boche long ago—he's thorough. Well, there you have it." He turned back to Anne. "That is what happened, Miss Joyce."

She was standing against the mantelshelf, her left arm carelessly laid along it, the hand drooping. There was a platinum wedding-ring on the third finger, and, overlapping it, the big diamond-set sapphire that had been Anne Jocelyn's engagement ring. She said in a frank voice,

"I am very glad to know. It has hurt all this time not knowing how you could have left me. Because it wasn't Annie Joyce you left—it was me. You can imagine what I felt like when you didn't come back. I couldn't understand it, but now I see that it could have been the way you say—you *could* have mistaken Annie for me in the dark. I believe you when you say that you thought it was I whom you carried to the boat. I don't know how long you went on thinking that. I suppose you could have gone on for a long time—in the dark. I suppose——" She broke off, dropped her voice, and said with distress, "Was she—much disfigured?"

"No."

21

"And in the morning you still didn't recognize her? I suppose—well, I suppose it's possible. There was a strong likeness. It must have been possible, because it seems to have happened. I won't think, or let anyone else think, of the only other possibility."

Philip said, "You know you interest me very much. Won't you be a little more explicit? I'd really like to know about this other possibility."

"I'd rather not put it into words."

"I'm afraid you'll have to."

All this time Milly Armitage had been just inside the door. She came forward now and sat on the arm of her usual chair. She really felt as if she couldn't stand any more. Her head was buzzing and the furniture had begun to flicker. Lyndall hadn't moved. Her hands held one another tightly. There was no colour in her face. Her eyes had a horrified look.

Anne said, "Very well. I didn't want to say it—I don't ever want to think it, Philip—but the other possibility is that you buried Annie Joyce as Anne Jocelyn because you would be pretty sure that I was dead, and if you had to admit that you left me behind, it wasn't going to look too well, and the death wasn't going to be any too easy to prove. It might have been years before the legal question could be cleared up. There would have been quite a strong temptation to take a short cut —wouldn't there?"

Philip was grey under his tan. His face had sharpened, his eyes were cold and angry. Milly Armitage found herself wishing that he would swear, or shout. Her father and her husband had always made a lot of noise when they were angry. There was something homely about it. She wished that Philip would make a noise.

Instead he said quite softly,

"So that's the line. I see—I mistook Annie Joyce for Anne in the dark, and when I saw what I'd done I stuck to the mistake so as to be able to get my hands on Anne's money. Is that it?"

She looked away. Those icy eyes were hard to meet.

"Philip—don't! I didn't want to say it—you know I didn't —you made me. But it's what people will say if you stick to this impossible story. Oh, don't you see I'm trying to help you? Don't you see that for both our sakes we've got to put some sort of face on it? It's got to look like a genuine mistake.

22

Do you think I want to believe it wasn't? It *must* have been, and that's what people have got to believe. You hadn't seen me for three months—I'd got thin with all the worry—the likeness to Annie was confusing, and a dead person—" she gave a sudden violent shudder—"a dead person doesn't look like any living one. Philip, please don't take it like this! We're saying all the wrong sort of things to each other. I'm saying all the wrong sort of things—just because it's so important—just because I want to say the right ones. Philip!"

He stepped back a pace.

"You're not my wife."

Milly Armitage couldn't hold her tongue any longer. It was a wonder that she had held it so long. Her eyes on the hand with the sapphire ring, she said,

"Anne's wedding-ring had an inscription inside it, hadn't it? I remember you told me."

"A.J., and the date," said Philip.

Anne slipped off the sapphire, slipped off the platinum ring beneath it, crossed to Milly Armitage, and held it out on her palm.

"A.J., and the date," she said.

There was a moment of silence. Nobody moved. Lyndall felt as if her heart would break. The three people she loved most in the world were there in that silence together. It wasn't just a silence. It was cold, it was suspicion, it was distrust—and that icy anger of Philip's which cut to the bone. She wanted to run away and hide. But you can't hide from a thing which is in your own mind. It goes with you. You can't hide from it. She stayed where she was, and heard Philip say,

"Anne took off her wedding-ring when she went to France. We quarrelled about her going, and she took it off."

Anne stepped back.

"I put it on again."

"I've no doubt you did—when you made up your mind to this impersonation. Now perhaps you will give us your story. You've had mine. I suppose you've got one ready. You had better let us have it."

"Philip——" Her voice broke a little on the word. She slipped the ring back on her finger and stood up straight. "I'm very glad to tell you my story. Aunt Milly and Lyn have heard it already. Pierre helped me to get away from the beach. There was a cave—we hid there until the shooting was over. I had

23

sprained my ankle very badly. The Germans came down and searched, but they didn't find us. When they had gone away we went back to the chateau. I was very wet and cold, and I was beginning to be ill. By the time the Germans came to search I was in a high fever. Pierre told them that I was Annie Joyce, and that I had been living there for ten years with my old cousin who had just died. He said there had been another English lady there, but she had gone away when she heard that the soldiers were coming. They sent a doctor to look at me, and he said I had double pneumonia and couldn't be moved. I was ill for a long time. They left me alone. When I was all right they sent me to a concentration camp, but I got ill again and they let me go back. That's all. I just lived there with Pierre and his wife. Fortunately Cousin Theresa always kept a great deal of money in the house. We kept finding it in all sorts of places—lavender-bags, pin-cushions, between the pages of books, rolled up in the toes of her slippers. When it seemed to be coming to an end I began to feel desperate."

"Why did you never write?"

"I was afraid. They were leaving me alone, and I didn't want to do anything that might stir them up. But I did write—twice—when Pierre said there was a chance of getting a letter smuggled across."

"Are you very surprised that these—letters never arrived?" She met his look with an open one.

"Oh, no—I knew it was only a chance. Then a week ago I was offered a chance of getting over myself. I had to put up all the rest of Cousin Theresa's money, but I thought it was worth the risk. I landed with nothing in my purse except a five-pound note which I had taken over with me. There isn't a great deal of change left out of it now, so if you're thinking of turning me out, I'm afraid you will have to provide me with funds until Mr. Codrington has handed my own money over to me again."

Philip considered this in a cold fury. He couldn't turn her out penniless, and she knew it. But every hour she spent under his roof was going to help her claim. If he turned out himself. . . . He was damned if he would turn out of Jocelyn's Holt for Annie Joyce.

There was hardly any pause before he said, "*Anne's* money." And none at all between that and her reply, "*My* money, Philip."

24

VI

"A most extraordinary situation," said Mr. Codrington. "Awkward—very awkward. You know, it would have been better if you had left the house."

Philip Jocelyn smiled.

"Leave Miss Annie Joyce in possession? I'm afraid that doesn't appeal to me."

Mr. Codrington frowned. His father and he between them had known four generations of Jocelyns. They were an intractable family. He had attended Philip's christening and known him ever since—liked him a good deal, and was not at all sure that he wasn't the most intractable of the lot. Lawyers see a good deal of human nature. He said,

"These identity cases are always ticklish, and they attract a most undesirable amount of interest."

"An understatement, I should say."

Mr. Codrington looked grave.

"If she brings a case——" he said, and then broke off. "You know, I couldn't go into the box myself and swear she wasn't Anne Jocelyn."

"You couldn't?"

"No, I couldn't."

"You think she'd win her case?"

"I don't say that. She might break down under cross-examination. Short of that——" He shrugged his shoulders. "You know, Philip, the resemblance is amazing, and the trouble is we can't get at the people who know Annie Joyce, and by the time we can get at them—if there are any of them left—accurate recollection will be dimmed. She's been over there in France with Miss Jocelyn ever since she was fifteen, and that's getting on for eleven years ago. I saw her just before she went—Miss Jocelyn brought her into my office. She was a year or two older than Anne, and thinner in the face, but there was quite a likeness—you've all got the same eyes and general colouring. But there it ended. Her hair was darker and quite straight—none of Anne's wave."

"Hair can be tinted and waves induced."

"That, I think, would be susceptible of proof."

Philip shook his head.

"Aunt Milly raised the point last night. Miss Joyce had her answer ready. Three years of privation had spoiled her hair dreadfully. She had had to have a permanent wave as soon as she landed. She said she had found a very good hairdresser in Westhaven—spent her last penny on it. And as to the colour, all these fair girls use a brightening wash, you know. Anne did herself, so there's nothing in that."

Mr. Codrington slewed round in his chair.

"Philip," he said, "will you tell me just why you are so sure that she isn't Anne? When I went into the room just now and saw her standing there under the portrait—well, you know——"

Philip Jocelyn laughed.

"She's very fond of standing under Anne's portrait. It's a pity she can't wear the fur coat all the time. She made a most effective entrance in it, I understand, but she can't very well go on wearing it in the house. Everything else is most carefully reproduced—the hair, the dress, the pearls—Anne to the life at the time the portrait was painted. But don't you see how that gives her away? Why should Anne dress to a portrait that's four years old? Do you see her doing her hair the same way for four years? I don't." He gave a short laugh. "Why should she bother to reproduce Amory's portrait, or to stop in West-haven and have things done to her hair? If she was Anne she wouldn't have to bother. She could come home in any old rag, with her head tied up in a scarf like half the girls do anyway, and it would never occur to her that she could be taken for any-one else. It's the woman who's putting on an act who's got to dress the part and be particular over her make-up. Why should Anne think that her identity would be questioned? The bare possibility would simply never enter her head."

Mr. Codrington nodded slowly.

"That's a point. But I don't quite know what a jury would think about it. Juries like facts. I'm afraid they don't care about psychology."

"Well, it's one of my reasons for being sure she isn't Anne. Here's another—but I'm afraid you'll call that psychological too. She's astonishingly like Anne—as Anne might have been if she had lived to be nearly four years older—astonishingly like to look at. But she's not Anne, because if she were, she'd have flared back the moment I gave her the rough side of my tongue. I didn't mince words, you know, and she turned the other cheek. I don't see Anne doing that."

26

"Three and a half years under German rule might very well have taught her self-control."

Philip got out of his chair with an impatient movement.

"Not Anne—and not with me." He began to walk to and fro in the room. "You've got to consider the way those two girls were brought up. Anne was the charming, spoiled only child of an heiress. At eighteen she was an heiress herself. She had such a lot of charm you wouldn't find out she was spoiled unless you crossed her. I found out when I said she couldn't possibly accept Theresa Jocelyn's bequest. We had a very bad row about it, and she went to France. If this were Anne, she'd have simply boiled over when I said she was Annie Joyce. This is somone older, toughter, warier."

"Nearly four years of German rule, Philip."

"It would take more than four grown-up years to produce this woman who is pretending to be Anne. Just take a look at what has produced her. Her father was old Ambrose's illegitimate son. But he only just missed being legitimate. If Anne's grandmother had died a month sooner, there's no doubt at all that Uncle Ambrose would have married his Mrs. Joyce, and young Roger would have been Sir Roger. As it was, the old man didn't even bother to sign his will, and Annie didn't inherit anything except a grievance. When she was fifteen Theresa tried to foist her on the family. I don't suppose their very natural reactions helped the grievance to fade out. For the next seven years or so she was at Theresa's beck and call. Very unstable sort of person, my cousin Theresa—the wretched girl would never know where she was with her. She'd be petted one minute, and snubbed the next—she'd always have to watch her step—she'd always have to think before she spoke—she simply couldn't afford to lose her temper. She served a seven-years apprenticeship for Theresa's money, and Theresa diddled her. Don't you think the original grievance must have done some growing by the time it came to that? Don't you think you'd get just the kind of woman who might think up a plan for getting her own back?"

"Quite persuasive. But it's not an easy job impersonating someone. Of course it's been done, and it will be done again, but there are a lot of pitfalls. In this case Annie Joyce would, of course, be quite familiar with all the family history, and with all the family photographs. Miss Jocelyn was an indefatigable gossip. She probably knew as much family tittle-tattle as anyone, and what she knew Annie would know. They stayed here too, didn't they?"

"They did—for a week. Theresa insisted on bringing her. I was in my last term at school, so I missed the row, but I gather that Theresa surpassed herself. My father was livid, and my step-mother spent all her time picking up the bits. In fact, a pleasant time was had by all."

"Quite so—rather hard on the child."

Philip smiled, not too pleasantly.

"Well, there you have it. She had a week to memorize everything—the first big house she had ever been into, the first time she had ever been in the country. I remember my step-mother telling me that. Well, don't you suppose it would stick? Those sort of impressions are strong, and they last. Miss Joyce finds her way with perfect ease all over the house and garden."

"Oh, she does, does she?"

"That impresses you? It doesn't impress me. I stayed with the McLarens in a shooting-box in the Highlands when I was fifteen—the same age as Annie Joyce when she came here. I'd back myself to find my way over it blindfold now, and I haven't had the advantage of a refresher course—Annie Joyce has. Anne was three months at the château. I don't say this was planned then—it couldn't have been—but if you remember Theresa, you can imagine how she would have pumped Anne about everything."

Mr. Codrington nodded.

"I agree that Annie Joyce would be in a better position to produce corroborative detail than most of the classic claimants have been. I gather that she is in possession of Anne's fur coat and going-away dress, her pearls, wedding and engagement rings, also her passport and identity card. How do you account for that?"

Philip continued to walk up and down.

"I told them to get their valuables. Anne came down with the handbag that woman has got—it was one of her wedding presents. The papers and the jewellery must have been in it. One of the girls was carrying the fur coat—I ought to be able to remember which of them, but I can't."

"Unfortunately." Mr. Codrington's tone was dry.

Philip swung round on him.

"Look here, if I was lying I'd say Annie had it, wouldn't

I? I just can't remember. All I do know is that Anne hadn't got it when I carried her to the boat. If Pierre or Annie had it they could have got it back to the château. If Annie was as cold as she says she was she probably wore it. Pierre had a couple of suit-cases. I don't know what happened to them. It was pitch-dark, and the Boche shooting at us. Anne was hit right away. Annie may have picked up the handbag, or she may have had it all along—I can't say."

"I see. There's really no evidence there. It would cut either way. What about handwriting?"

Philip said gloomily, "She's had three and a half years to practise Anne's writing. It looks pretty good to me. I don't know what an expert would say."

"Juries don't like experts."

Philip nodded.

"I've always thought they did a good deal of hard swearing myself."

"Juries distrust technicalities."

Philip came over to the writing-table and sat down on the corner.

"For God's sake don't go on talking about juries! This woman isn't Anne, and we've got to get her to admit it. She is Annie Joyce, and I want you to tell her that as Annie Joyce she is in my opinion entitled to Theresa Jocelyn's thirty thousand pounds. I told Anne that I wouldn't let her keep the money, and I told you after Anne's death that I had no intention of keeping it myself unless I was sure Annie Joyce was dead. Well, she isn't dead—she's in the Parlour with Lyndall. They are probably going through Aunt Milly's collection of snapshots."

Mr. Codrington exclaimed, and Philip laughed. "They started on them last night. It was most tactfully done. 'Dear Aunt Milly, have you been able to keep up your photography at all? Oh, yes—do let me see! You don't know how starved I've been for a familiar face!' And if they weren't familiar before, you can bet she's getting them by heart as fast as she can."

Mr. Codrington said quickly, "Why did you allow it? It shouldn't have been allowed."

Philip shrugged.

"A good deal of it happened before I came. Lyn's following her round like a dog. Thinks I'm——" His voice changed, dropped almost to inaudibility. "I don't know what she thinks."

29

Mr. Codrington drummed on his knee.

"Mrs. Armitage ought to have had more sense."

Philip got up and walked away.

"Oh, you can't blame Aunt Milly. She and Lyn hadn't a doubt—until I came. Aunt Milly is shaken now—at least I hope she is. But Lyn——" He turned round and came back. "We've got right away from the point. I want you to go into the Parlour and tell Annie she can have Theresa's thirty thousand down on the nail for a nice safe legal receipt signed Annie Joyce."

VII

LYNDALL came out of the Parlour and shut the door behind her. For a moment there was a little relief, an illusory feeling of escape. And then Philip came down at the top of his angry stride and took her by the arm and marched her off.

When he had slammed the study door he leaned against it and said,

"Now you're for it! What are you playing at?"

"Nothing."

"You're making a damned fool of yourself!"

Words sprang to her lips but were not allowed to pass them. They horrified her so much that she turned even whiter than she had been before, because she had so nearly said, "I wish I were." Philip had said she was making a fool of herself, and she had almost said, "I wish I were." And that would mean she wished that Anne had not come back to trouble them. She couldn't wish that—she couldn't ever wish that.

Philip looked at her with what she thought was contempt.

"You're a damned little fool!" he said. "You've done your level best to queer my pitch, you know. What are you doing it for?"

She stood in front of him like a grieving child.

"What have I done?"

He laughed.

"It's more a case of what haven't you done. If there was anything she didn't know, you've been down on your knees handing it to her. Haven't you?"

"You mean about the photographs?" She spoke in a slow, troubled voice.

Philip took her by the wrists.

"Look at me! She isn't Anne. Anne is dead. No—go on looking at me! Why do you think she is Anne?" His grasp tightened. "Do you really think so?"

She went on looking at him, but she hadn't any words. He let go of her and stepped back laughing.

"You're not sure, are you? You stand there and you don't say a word. Where have they all gone? You'd find them quick enough if you were really sure. Shall I tell you some of the things you can't find those words for?" He drove his hands into his pockets and leaned against the door. "At first you were sure—you hadn't a doubt. It was all 'Oh, let us be joyful! Anne isn't dead—she never has been!'"

She hadn't looked away. She said,

"Yes——"

"And then it wasn't quite so joyful, was it?" His eyes narrowed as he watched her. "Not—quite—so—joyful. You had to whip it up a bit. That meant tumbling over yourself to do anything she asked."

"Yes——" again, but this time it wasn't said by the pale lips. It was the eyes which said it, wincing away from Philip's.

He said, "If I didn't love you like hell I'd knock your head off!"

If it was possible to turn any paler, she did so. It may have been only a tensing of the muscles, giving that drawn look to a skin already blanched. Her hands took hold of one another and clung rigidly. She said,

"You mustn't——"

Only very keen hearing could have caught the words. Philip's hearing was keen. He said,

"Which?" Then, as her eyes came back to his face in a look of tragic reproach, "Mustn't love you—or mustn't knock your head off?"

"You know——"

His smile came, and went again. Just for a moment you could see how it would warm and soften the Jocelyn type. Just for a moment the hard lines about the mouth relaxed and a gleam of humour changed the eyes. It was a very fleeting affair. Before Lyndall could take any comfort from it he was saying,

"You're quite right—I know. I mustn't love you because Annie Joyce is putting up an act and pretending to be Anne. That's it—isn't it?"

31

"Because of Anne—because Anne is your wife." A little louder this time, but the lips hardly moving.

Philip said in an icy, exasperated tone,

"That woman isn't Anne, and she certainly isn't my wife! Don't you suppose I should know? You can't be married to a woman for a year and not know her. Anne and I knew each other very well. Every time we quarrelled we knew each other a little better. This woman doesn't know me any better than I know her. We don't meet anywhere—she is an utter stranger."

Lyndall's eyes had been blank with pain. Something stirred in them now—some thought, some consciousness. Then the pain swamped it.

Philip said roughly, "You want to be a little martyr—don't you? Just because I love you—Anne is alive. Just because she's going to come between us—Annie Joyce has got to be Anne. Just because it hurts like blazes—you've got to do everything you can to put her between us. And I suppose you think I'm going to back you up. Well, I'm not." He put out a hand. "Come here!" he said.

She came, moving slowly until the hand fell on her shoulder.

"Did you think I didn't know what you were up to? First of all, you were sure she was Anne. Then, when you weren't so sure, you thought how wicked it was—how wicked you were to have any doubts about it. And from there you got to thinking you had the doubts because you didn't really want Anne to be alive—and after that of course you just had to do everything you could to show her and everyone else how glad you were. I don't know how much damage you've done—quite a considerable amount, I should think. And I hope it'l be a lesson to you not to try and hide things up, because you'll never make a good liar, and I should always find you out." He pulled her up against him and held her there, an arm about her shoulders.

She drew a long breath.

"Have I done a lot of harm?"

"I expect so."

"I'm sorry—I didn't mean to."

"My child, 'Evil is wrought by want of thought as well as want of heart.'"

"You're being horrid."

"That was my intention."

"Philip—how much harm have I done?"

"We shall go on finding out—or, *qui vivra verra*, if you'd rather have it in French. I expect you've probably told her quite a lot of things she ought to have known and didn't, and wouldn't have known if you hadn't been there to oblige."

"What sort of things?"

"Family things—but she'd have heard most of those from Theresa. Things about the neighbourhood—that's where she'd have been most likely to slip up, and I expect that's where you came in."

Lyndall turned in the circle of his arm.

"Philip, that's not fair. You've got to be fair. If Anne had been away all this time and then come back, wouldn't it be natural for her to ask about everyone—how they are, and where they are, and all that sort of thing?"

"It depends on how it was done. I'd like you to tell me how she did it. Cleverly, I've no doubt. She's a much cleverer person than Anne. Anne wasn't clever at all. She knew what she wanted, and generally speaking she got it—if she didn't there was a row. All quite honest and open. She had never had to be anything else. Annie Joyce had. If she wanted to get her own way she had got to be clever about it. I expect she's had plenty of practice. Now suppose you tell me just how clever she was about the neighbours."

Lyndall bit her lip.

"Philip, it's so horrid when you put it that way. It was all quite natural—it was really. She wanted to know which of the places round were empty. Wouldn't Anne have wanted to know that? And who had lost anyone in the war, and what everyone was doing—well, Anne would have wanted to know all those things."

"And then you got on to the photograph albums?"

"Philip, that was quite natural too. She asked me why I hadn't been called up, and I said I was a Wren, but I'd been ill and was having sick leave, and she said she'd love to see a photograph of me in uniform—did Aunt Milly still take her snapshots? And I said she did when she could get the films. And—well, you see——"

Philip saw. The milk was spilled and couldn't be picked up again. No good crying over it.

She was looking up at him.

"Philip——"

"What is it?"

"Philip——"

"What else have you done?"

"Nothing. I want to say you mustn't think I agree with what you said. I don't think anyone could know the things she knows unless she was Anne."

His brows lifted ironically.

"But then you hadn't the advantage of knowing my cousin Theresa. I assure you she made it her business to know everything, and Annie Joyce lived with her for seven years or so."

Lyndall shook her head. She looked as if she was shaking something off.

"You've made up your mind. Philip, you mustn't do that. It makes me go the other way, because somebody has got to be fair. I can't help thinking about Anne. I loved her very much. I thought she had come back. If she hasn't, it's a dreadfully cruel trick. But if she has—if it is really Anne—what are we doing—how are we treating her? I keep thinking of that all the time. To come back home and find that nobody wants you—to find that your own husband doesn't want you—it's—it's the most dreadful thing. I keep thinking about it."

Philip stepped away from the door, stepped away from Lyndall.

"Stop harrowing yourself. She isn't Anne."

VIII

Mr. Codrington's interview was not going according to plan —at least not to any plan of Philip's. The offer of the late Miss Theresa Jocelyn's thirty thousand pounds in return for a receipt signed Annie Joyce had been as lightly and smilingly refused as if it had been a cucumber sandwich.

"Dear Mr. Codrington—how could I! It wouldn't be legal —I mean, I couldn't sign poor Annie's name——"

"Philip never intended to keep this money——" He bit his lip. He ought to have said Sir Philip—if he was talking to Annie Joyce he would certainly do so. He found it impossible to believe that he was talking to Annie Joyce. He found it impossible to believe that he was not talking to Anne Jocelyn.

She sat just across the hearth from him, her long slim legs stretched out to the fire, her head with its bright curls thrown

back against a cushion which repeated the blue of her dress—
a very pleasant picture, softened by the faint haze of her cigarette. She held it away from her in the hand which rested on
the arm of her chair and smiled.

"No—Philip never meant me to keep it. That's what we
had the row about. You know, I don't believe he has got over
it yet. That's why he is being so horrid now. We both lost our
tempers—said we wished we hadn't married each other—"
she waved the cigarette—"things like that. Of course he was
quite right—Cousin Theresa hadn't any business to leave me
the money after practically adopting Annie. And I wouldn't
have taken it, Mr. Codrington—I really wouldn't—but there
was Philip putting down his foot and saying I wasn't to, and
all the rest of it, and naturally I wasn't going to stand for that.
You do like to refuse your own legacies!" She laughed a little.
"Philip was very, very tactless, and of course I wasn't going to
give in, so we had our row, and I dashed off to France. And
now—well, I've got over it, but I don't think he has. I don't
see how he can really believe that I am Annie Joyce. It's silly.
He's just being stiff-necked and obstinate. You know what
the Jocelyns are like."

Mr. Codrington found himself every moment more convinced. The changes which he noticed were those which were
only natural in the circumstances. It was just on four years
since he had seen her. She was older, she was thinner, she
looked as if she had been ill. She had a little more manner, and
there were signs that it had been acquired amongst foreigners.
Well, she had been living amongst foreigners, hadn't she?
There was nothing in that.

He said, "What do you want?"

She had her cigarette at her lips. She drew at it without
hurrying herself. The haze between them deepened. Then
she said, looking away from him into the fire,

"I want a reconciliation."

"I'm afraid that won't be easy."

"No. But that's what I want. I don't think I ought to let
our marriage break up without trying to save it. Philip cared
for me enough to marry me, and we had some happy times. I
have learned a lot since then—I've learned to keep my temper,
for one thing. I suppose he has put that up to you as one of the
reasons why he thinks I'm Annie Joyce. Well, if I hadn't
learned how to keep my temper out there under the Germans I

35

really should have been dead by now. You can tell Philip that." She leaned towards him, the cigarette in her hand. "Mr. Codrington, do help us. Philip's angry because I've come back. He's imagining himself in love with Lyndall, and he doesn't want me. I want to save our marriage if I can. Won't you help?"

He made no reply in words, only lifted his hand and let it fall again upon his knee. He was actually a good deal moved.

After a moment she said in a different tone,

"Mr. Codrington—what am I to do? I haven't any money. I can't sign that receipt, but can't you let me have some of the money? You see, it's really mine whichever way you look at it."

"Not quite, I am afraid."

"Well, what happens next? It's all so strange. I never thought of anything like this, and I don't know what to do. Is there anything I could do in—in a legal way?"

"You could bring a suit against Philip in respect of Anne Jocelyn's property."

She looked distressed.

"Oh, I wouldn't do that."

He was watching her keenly.

"Or Philip might bring a suit against you in respect of those pearls you are wearing, and any other jewellery which belonged to his wife. In either case the verdict would depend on whether you were able to establish your identity as Anne Jocelyn."

The look of distress deepened. She drew at her cigarette.

"Would Philip do that?"

"He might."

"It would be horrid. It would be in the papers. Oh, we couldn't do anything like that! I thought——"

"Yes? What did you think?"

"I thought—oh, Mr. Codrington, couldn't it be settled privately? That's what I thought. Couldn't we get the family together and let them decide? Like the *conseil de famille* in France."

"There would be no legal value in such a decision."

Her colour had risen. She was pretty and animated.

"But if we were all agreed, there would be no need of any legal decision. You do not have to go into a court of law to prove that you are Mr. Codrington. It is only because Philip keeps on saying that I am not his wife that there is any talk about going to law."

36

Mr. Codrington put up a hand and stopped her.

"Wait a minute—wait a minute—Anne Jocelyn is legally dead. Even if Philip recognized you, there would be certain formalities——"

She interrupted him eagerly.

"But you could see to all that. There wouldn't have to be a case about it, and a lot of publicity. It would just be that I came back after everyone thought I was dead."

"Something like that—if Philip recognized you and no one else raised the question."

She said quickly, "Who else would be likely to raise it?"

"Philip's next of kin—the next heir to the title and estates."

"That would be Perry Jocelyn. Would he be likely to do that?"

"I can't tell you what anyone would be likely to do. It would depend upon whether he believed that you were Anne." In his own mind he didn't see Perry raising trouble for anyone, but it wasn't for him to say so.

She was asking with some anxiety,

"Where is he? Can you get at him? He's not abroad?"

"No—I believe he's somewhere near London. He is married, you know—two years ago, to an American girl. So you see he is a good deal concerned."

She nodded.

"I see—— It would be to his advantage if Philip was married and separated from his wife."

Mr. Codrington said drily, "I really can't imagine such an idea coming into Perry's head."

She said, "Oh, well——" There was a graceful movement of the cigarette. She laughed a little. "I thought we were talking from the legal point of view. You mustn't make it a personal matter. Let us get back to the family council. Get all the family together—Perry, and his wife, and anyone else you can lay hands on, and let them say whether they recognize me. If they do, it seems to me there's an end of it, and I think Philip must stop being so obstinate, because no one in any case would believe him against all the rest of the family. But if they are on Philip's side, well, then I will go away and call myself something else. But I will not call myself Annie Joyce, because I am Anne Jocelyn and no one can take that from me!" Those very fine eyes were proudly lit.

Mr. Codrington admired and approved. He was more sure

than ever that she was Anne, and that she had developed from being a charming impulsive girl into a no less charming woman.

After a moment's pause she went on speaking in a softened voice,

"Mr. Codrington, won't you help me? I'm only asking for a chance to save my marriage. If there is a court case, it would all be over so far as Philip and I are concerned. It wouldn't matter which way it went, we'd never be able to pick up the bits again. He's too proud——" She paused and bit her lip.

Mr. Codrington agreed with her. All the Jocelyns were proud. He thought of headlines in the papers and their probable effect on Philip Jocelyn's pride. He did not speak, but he very slightly inclined his head.

She went on,

"It would be fatal. That is why I would never bring a case against him even if he turned me out without a penny. Will you tell him so? I don't want him to think that I'm putting a pistol to his head or anything of that sort. I want you to tell him that in no conceivable circumstances would I bring an action against him. I do him the justice to believe that he wouldn't bring one against me. But a family council would be quite a different thing—there would be no publicity, no outsiders. I would do my best to satisfy Philip's doubts. I don't see how he can really think I'm anyone else, but if he does, I'll do my best to satisfy him. If the family is satisfied, I want Philip to let me stay here. I don't ask him to live with me, but I want him to be under the same roof as much as he would be if things were different. If he has to live in town, I'd like to be there too. I just want a chance to set things right between us. I know it won't be easy, but I think I ought to have the chance. If I don't pull it off in six months I'll clear out and give him his freedom. If it comes to that, I'll leave you to make any money settlement you think fair. Meanwhile I must have something to go on with—mustn't I? Will you arrange that with Philip, please?" She broke suddenly into a laugh. "It's too stupid, isn't it, but I'm an absolute pauper—I can't even buy a packet of cigarettes!"

IX

"I EXPRESSED no opinion," said Mr. Codrington.

"You mean you expressed no opinion to her." Philip's tone was dry in the extreme. "You're making it quite clear to me that I haven't got a leg to stand on."

"I haven't said that. What I do want to put before you is the undoubted advantage of a private settlement. This sort of case brings down the maximum of notoriety upon the people who engage in it. I do not know any family in England who would dislike it more."

"I don't propose to accept Annie Joyce as a wife merely to avoid seeing my name in the papers."

"Quite so. But I would like to point out that those are not the alternatives. I made no comment on the suggestion of a family council, but I think you would do well to consider it. Quite apart from its being desirable to avoid washing the family linen in public, the plan has other advantages. A private enquiry of that nature could be held immediately—a dishonest claimant being thereby deprived of the opportunity of gathering information and getting up a case. Then at a private enquiry the claimant would not be protected, as in court, by the strict application of the rules of evidence. Anybody will be able to ask her anything, and the fact that Anne is not only willing but anxious to submit herself to this test——"

"Anne?" Philip's voice was bleak.

"My dear Philip, what am I to call her? If it comes to that, both the girls were baptized Anne." The words came out a little more warmly than he intended. He checked himself. "You mustn't think that I don't feel for your position. I feel for it so much that I am bound to hold my own feelings in check. I would like your permission to discuss the whole matter with Trent. You haven't met him, have you? He came in as a partner just before the war. Some kind of connection of old Sutherland, who was the senior partner in my father's time. Rather remote, but it is pleasant to keep up these old ties." Partly in order to relieve the tension he continued to talk about Pelham Trent. "A very able fellow—I'm lucky to have him. Not forty yet, but he's in the Fire Service, so he hasn't been called up. Of course he is only available every third day—

they do forty-eight hours on and twenty-four off—but it's a good deal better than nothing. I would really be glad if you would let me talk this matter over with him. He has a very good brain, and he is sound—very sound. A pleasant fellow too. Mrs. Armitage and Lyndall saw quite a lot of him when they were in town just before you came home. Lyndall came in for a few hundred pounds from an Armitage cousin, and he handled the business for her."

"Oh, tell him anything you like." Philip's tone was a weary one. "We shall be lucky if it doesn't have to go farther than that."

Mr. Codrington regarded him with gravity.

"I was about to draw your attention to that aspect of the case. If this affair can be settled inside the family, a great deal of most undesirable publicity will be avoided. Quite apart from everything else, can you at this moment afford to be involved in a *cause célèbre*? You are just taking up a new job. Will that particular kind of limelight be acceptable at the War Office?"

He got an impatient shake of the head. He continued in a manner which had settled into being equable again.

"I think you may put it this way. The family are going to be a great deal more on the spot than any jury when it comes to the kind of thing that has to be looked out for in a case like this. They'll know all the ropes, and if she makes a slip, they won't miss it. If she passes the family, you can be perfectly sure that she would pass with any jury in the world."

Philip walked up and down in silence. Presently he came over to the writing-table, leaned on it, and said,

"I agree to a meeting of the family. Perry's interests are involved—any doubt as to whether I've got a legal wife or not would affect him. He is one of the people who have to be satisfied. He and his wife must come. Then there's Aunt Milly, and Theresa's sister Inez—and why on earth Cousin Maude should have given those two aggravating women Spanish names——"

Mr. Codrington nodded.

"It used to annoy your father."

"Prophetic probably—they've always been a damned nuisance in the family. But I suppose Inez had better come."

"She will probably be a great deal more troublesome if she doesn't."

"Then of course there is Uncle Thomas—and, I suppose, Aunt Emmeline."

Mr. Codrington looked down his nose.

"Mrs. Jocelyn would certainly wish to be present."

Philip gave a short laugh.

"Wild horses wouldn't keep her away! Well, that's about the lot. Archie and Jim are somewhere in Italy, but they're a long way off in the family tree, and in view of the fact that Perry is married, and that Uncle Thomas has four boys all safely under military age, they don't really come into it."

"No, I hardly think we need take them into consideration. And there are no relations of Anne's on her father's side."

"And no Joyces?"

Mr. Codrington shook his head.

"There was only the one son by the Joyce connection. Roger Joyce's wife died when Annie was five years old. There were no other children, and he did not marry again. Your father made Mrs. Joyce an allowance, but refused to continue it to Roger. He was a weak, inoffensive creature, rather fond of drawing the long bow about his grand relations."

"What did he do?"

"We got him a job as a clerk in a shipping office. He was the sort of man who gets into a rut and stays there—no initiative, no ambition."

"And his wife?"

"A teacher in an elementary school—an only child and an orphan. So, you see, there is no one to invite on the Joyce side."

Philip straightened up.

"Well, then, there we are, all set. You'd better get everyone together as soon as you can. But look here, I'm only consenting to this because it's the best chance we've got of tripping her up. If she brings a case, she'll have the next few months to find out anything she doesn't already know—you said that yourself."

"Wait! She won't bring a case against you. She told me to tell you that."

"Bunkum! She wants to get her hands on Anne's money. In the eyes of the law Anne is dead. She'd be bound to do whatever you have to do to get back on the map again. You've told her that already, haven't you?"

"If unopposed, it would be a mere formality."

"And I'd be bound to oppose it."

41

"Unless the proceedings before the family council happened to convince you."

Philip shook his head.

"They won't do that. But if she breaks down, there would be an end to it that way."

"And if she doesn't—what are you going to do then? I told you her terms—six months under the same roof."

"Why?"

"She wants a chance of convincing you. She told me quite frankly that she wanted to try and save the marriage."

"The marriage ended when Anne died."

Mr. Codrington made an impatient movement.

"I am putting her terms to you. If there is no reconciliation by the end of six months, she is willing to divorce you."

Philip laughed.

Mr. Codrington said gravely,

"Think it over. You might find yourself in a very difficult position if she were legally admitted to be Anne Jocelyn and you were neither reconciled nor divorced. Supposing you desire to remarry, she could prevent your doing so——" He paused and added, "indefinitely."

They were alone together, the deep red curtains drawn, a red glow from the wood fire on the hearth, a single overhead light shining down upon the writing-table with its scattered papers. For a moment both men were seeing an unseen third between them—Lyndall, little and slight, with her cloudy dark hair and her cloudy eyes—grey eyes, but quite different from the Jocelyn grey. Lyndall's eyes were smudged with brown and green. They were soft and childish. They had no defences. If she was hurt, they showed it. If she loved anyone, they showed that too. If they grieved, tears rose to brighten them. She was pale because she had been ill. Her colour had been coming back. Now it was all gone again.

Philip walked over to the fire and stood there looking down.

X

THE first headlines appeared next day. The *Daily Wire* splashed them half across the front page, rather crowding the latest Russian victory.

Underneath there was a picture of the white marble cross in Holt churchyard. The lettering stood out clearly:

Anne
Wife of Philip Jocelyn
Aged 21
Killed by enemy action
June 26th 1940.

The letterpress contained an interview with Mrs. Ramage, cook and housekeeper at Jocelyn's Holt.

Mrs. Armitage went down to the kitchen with the paper in her hand.

"Oh, Mrs. Ramage—how could you?"

Mrs. Ramage burst into tears which were a good three parts excitement to one of remorse. Her large pale face glistened and she shook like a blancmange.

"Never said he'd put it in the paper. Got off his bicycle at the back door when the girls were in the dining-room and asked me civil enough if I could direct him to the churchyard, which I said you couldn't miss it if you tried, seeing it runs next the park, and I took and showed him the church tower from the back door step, and you'd have done the same or anyone else. Well, there it is, as large as life and you can't get from it."

"You seem to have said a good deal more than that, Mrs. Ramage."

Mrs. Ramage groped for a pocket handkerchief like a small sheet and applied it to her face.

"He arst me how could he find Lady Jocelyn's grave, and I said——"

"What did you say?"

Mrs. Ramage gulped.

"I said, 'We don't want to think about graves or suchlike, not now her ladyship's come home again.'"

Mrs. Armitage gazed resignedly at the front page of the *Wire*.

"Mrs. Ramage told me she was thunderstruck——" What a pity she wasn't!—" 'I remember Lady Jocelyn coming here as a bride. . . . Such lovely pearls—the same she's wearing in her picture that was in the Royal Academy. And she came back wearing them, and her lovely fur coat too.' . . . Miss Ivy Fossett, parlourmaid at Jocelyn's Holt, says, 'Of course I didn't know who it was when I opened the door, but as soon as I got a good look at her I could see she was dressed the same as the picture in the Parlour.' . . ."

Mrs. Ramage continued to gulp and mop her face. All at once Milly Armitage relaxed. What was the use anyway? She said in her good-tempered voice,

"Oh, do stop crying. It's no use—is it? I don't suppose you had a chance with him really—he was bound to get it all out of you. Only I can't think how they knew there was anything to get."

Mrs. Ramage gave a final gulp. She looked about her. The big kitchen was empty. Ivy and Flo were upstairs making beds, but she dropped her voice to a hoarse whisper.

"It was that Ivy—but girls are so hard to get. I had it out of her last night. She'd an aunt got a guinea from a paper for sending up a piece about a cat bringing up a rabbit along with its kittens, and that put it into her head. She took and wrote a postcard to the *Wire* and said her ladyship had come home after everyone thought she was dead, and a cross in the churchyard and all. And I'm sure I wouldn't have had it happen for the world, not if it was to vex Sir Philip."

"Well, I don't see that it was your fault, Mrs. Ramage. I suppose the papers were bound to get hold of it."

Mrs. Ramage put her handkerchief away in a capacious apron pocket.

"It's a lovely photo of the cross," she said.

Milly Armitage gazed at the paper.

Anne
Wife of Philip Jocelyn
Aged 21

They would have to alter the inscription of course. Philip would have to get it done. Because if it was Anne upstairs in the Parlour with Lyn, then it wasn't Anne's body under the white marble cross. You can't be in two places at once. She wished with all her heart that she could be sure that the inscription on the cross was true. It was probably very wicked

44

of her, but she would much rather be sure that Anne was in the churchyard, and not upstairs in the Parlour. The trouble was that she couldn't be sure. Sometimes Philip shook her, and sometimes Anne shook her. She was as honest as she knew how to be. It didn't really matter whether she wanted Anne to be alive, or whether she wanted her to be dead. What mattered was that they should be sure. It was perfectly frightful to think of Annie Joyce grabbing Anne's money and getting away with Philip and Jocelyn's Holt, but it was even more frightful to think of Anne coming back from the dead and finding out that no one wanted her.

Her eyes remained fixed upon the page.

Annie
Daughter of Roger Joyce

That was what it would have to be if Anne was alive. . . . What a frightful business!

She looked up, met Mrs. Ramage's sympathetic gaze, and said with the frankness which occasionally devastated her family,

"It's a mess—isn't it?"

"A bit of an upset, as you may say——"

Mrs. Armitage nodded. After all, Mrs. Ramage had been twelve years at Jocelyn's Holt. She had seen Philip married. You couldn't keep things from people in your own house, so what was the good of trying—you might just as well make a virtue of necessity. She said,

"Did you recognize her—at once?"

"Meaning her ladyship, ma'am?"

Mrs. Armitage nodded.

"Did you recognize her——" She paused, and once more added, "at once?"

"Didn't you, ma'am?"

"Of course I did. I never thought of anything else."

"No more did I."

They looked at one another. Mrs. Ramage said in an uncertain whisper,

"It's Sir Philip, isn't it? He's not sure——"

"He's so sure that she was dead—it's so difficult for him to believe he could have made a mistake. We didn't see her—he did. It makes it hard for him."

Mrs. Ramage considered, and spoke slowly.

"I've seen a lot of dead people first and last. Some looks like they were alive and just dropped off asleep, but some is that changed you'd hardly know them. And if you was to think of her ladyship with all that bright colour gone and her hair gone straight and wet with the sea water coming over like you told me Sir Philip said—well, that would make a lot of difference, wouldn't it? And if this other lady was so much like her——"

"I didn't say anything about another lady, Mrs. Ramage."

"Didn't you, ma'am? There's been talk about it, as there's bound to be, because it stands to reason if that's her ladyship upstairs, then there's someone else that was buried by mistake for her, and the talk goes it was Miss Annie Joyce that we all see when she come here with Miss Theresa a matter of ten or eleven years ago. Stayed here a week, and anyone could see how she favoured the family."

"Do you remember her—what she looked like?"

Mrs. Ramage nodded.

"Long, thin, poking slip of a girl—looked as if she wanted a deal of feeding up. But she favoured the family all the same —might have passed for Sir Philip's sister, and if she'd plumped out and held herself up and got a bit of a colour, well, it's my opinion she'd have been like enough to her ladyship for Sir Philip to make the mistake he did, seeing the difference there is between a dead person and a live one. And that's the way it was, you may depend upon it."

Milly Armitage opened her lips to speak, shut them again, and then said in a hurry,

"You think it's her ladyship upstairs?"

Mrs. Ramage stared.

"Why, you can't get from it, ma'am. Looks a bit older of course, but don't we all?"

"You're sure?"

"Sure? She come in that door and straight up to me, and she says, 'I do hope you're glad to see me again, Mrs. Ramage.'"

Tears came into Milly Armitage's eyes. Anne coming back, and nobody pleased to see her—— She pulled herself up sharply. Lyn was pleased enough—but she's looking like a ghost now—she isn't sure either——

Mrs. Ramage said,

"A bit hard to come home and find you're not wanted, ma'am."

XI

THE mist which had lain over the churchyard all day had by half past three in the afternoon spread into the park and was creeping up the long slope towards the house. A brief hour of pallid sunshine had failed to disperse the haze overhead. Milly Armitage began to count up bedrooms and rations, because if it was going to be foggy, neither Inez nor Emmeline would want to go back to town, and if they stayed—and of course Thomas —it would really be very much better if Perry and Lilla were to stay too. Three bedrooms. . . . And fish-cakes—the cod went farther that way than when it was boiled or grilled. . . . And if Emmeline thought she could keep to a diet in war-time she would have to go hungry, because the next course would just have to be sausages, and they could have baked apples for a dessert. . . . Mr. Codrington would probably prefer to go back to town unless the fog was very bad indeed. Well, if he stayed he must have the blue room. . . . And Florence must put stone hot-water bottles in all the beds. . . . The question was, if Mr. Codrington stayed, did it mean that his clerk would have to be accommodated too? She supposed it did—and he would have to have the dressing-room at the top of the stairs. A harmless, elderly, confidential person who was to take shorthand notes of everything that was said. Very unpleasant, but of course Mr. Codrington was quite right—it was only fair to everyone that there should be an accurate record.

Her mind swung back to food again. If there were going to be two more, Mrs. Ramage would have to put a lot of rice into the fish-cakes, and they had better have potatoes in their jackets . . . Perhaps it wouldn't be foggy after all. . . . A glance out of the window dismissed this rather optimistic hope.

Mr. and Mrs. Thomas Jocelyn were the first to arrive. Having met them in the hall, Milly led them into the dining-room, where the polished table and its attendant chairs awaited the expected family.

No one could say that the scene was a cheerful one. An aged, dirty, and extremely valuable Chinese paper covered the walls—one of those heirlooms supremely uncomfortable to live with but too costly to discard. Its prevailing tone was that of over-boiled greens. The carpet, which had once possessed a lively Victorian pattern, had now gone away to a murky drab. The furniture, which was in the largest mahogany tradition, reared itself in massive sideboards and serving-tables. If less than twenty-four people dined in the room, it had an under-populated appearance. A large wood fire struggled in vain to mitigate the chill of long disuse.

Mrs. Thomas Jocelyn looked around her, said, "A fine room, I always think," and did up the top button of her fur coat again. Mr. Codrington came in behind her and switched on the light in the chandelier over the table. The shadows retreated to either end of the room, leaving the table and its surround-ings isolated in a warm golden glow. Mr. Codrington's clerk, who had followed him, moved now into this circle of light and proceeded to lay a writing-pad and pencil at one end of the table and set a small attaché case down at the other end, after which he withdrew to the fire and stood there warming himself.

Mr. Codrington nodded in the direction of the case.

"I shall be sitting there. Philip wishes me, as it were, to take the chair. It is all extremely painful for him, but I hope some definite conclusion may be arrived at. If you don't mind, we won't discuss the matter at all beforehand. It is so difficult to remain quite unprejudiced." He shepherded them towards the table. "Now, Philip will be on my right, and the—well, I suppose I had better call her the claimant—on my left. Then Mr. Jocelyn and yourself on her side, and Mr. and Mrs. Perry Jocelyn next to Philip, Miss Inez Jocelyn next to them, and Mrs. Armitage and Lyndall on the other side. My clerk, Mr. Elvery, will sit at the bottom of the table and take a shorthand record of the proceedings." He pulled out the third chair on the left, looked down the table, and said, "Perhaps you will sit down. I think the Perry Jocelyns have just arrived. Miss Jocelyn was to travel with them, so that we shall be able to begin immediately."

Mrs. Jocelyn sat down. As she drew in her chair the light flooded down upon the massive waves of her abundant red hair. At forty it was as lively and burnished as it had been at twenty-two under her wedding veil, but like her figure it was now a good deal more rigidly controlled. Her complexion was still very good, and owed hardly anything to art. If her eyes had been a little more widely set, a little more deeply blue, she would have been a beauty, but no tinting of lashes originally sandy could disguise that shallow milky tint. Every time Milly

48

Armitage saw her she was reminded of the white Persian cat she and Louie had had as children. Louie was gone, and the Persian cat was gone, but here were its eyes in Emmeline's head, for all the world like a couple of saucers of skim milk. For the rest, Mrs. Thomas Jocelyn was a managing woman with everything handsome about her, from the small black fur cap on her careful waves, and the expensive coat that went with it, to her fine silk stockings and well-cut shoes.

Beside her Thomas Jocelyn looked grey and insignificant. He had the family features, but they seemed to have shrunk. He was not much over fifty—five years younger than Philip's father—but he might easily have been taken for sixty-five. Perhaps the confinement of office life, perhaps his wife's exuberant vitality.

The Perry Jocelyns came in. Perry had been laughing, and Lilla was pinching his arm to make him behave. On the brief occasions when they were together it put them both in such high spirits they they found it difficult to be decorous. Perry was fair like all the Jocelyns, but he was not as tall as Philip. He had a squarer face and a more mobile mouth. Lilla was little and plump and rosy, with wide brown eyes, a wide red mouth, and an enchantingly tilted nose. They were so much in love with each other that they brought happiness with them. It flowed from them in warmth and light even in this dreary room.

Behind them, and not too pleased at bringing up the rear, came Miss Inez Jocelyn, talking volubly as was her wont. As she came into view and Milly Armitage turned to greet her after embracing Perry and Lilla, she had to exert considerable self-control in order not to look as startled as she felt.

Even in the midst of these rather wretched pre-occupations Inez Jocelyn's appearance was arresting. Her hair, originally of a mousy fairness, was now quite aggressively platinum. Oblivious of her fifty years, she wore it cascading upon her shoulders from a little black hat of about the size and shape of a jam-pot cover. Everything else was to match—the short flared skirt, the tightly waisted coat, the sheer black stockings, and the stilt-heeled shoes. Against this extreme of youthful fashion there was Inez' unfortunate face, very long, very thin, very elderly in spite of make-up lavishly but not very skilfully applied. Nobody could have taken her for anyone but a Jocelyn, but she was a Jocelyn in caricature.

49

She pecked at Milly's cheek, talking all the time in a piercing voice.

"My dear, I never heard of anything so extraordinary! Incredible, I call it! How do you do, Thomas—how do you do, Emmeline? Where is Philip? Surely he is going to be here! How do you do, Mr. Codrington? Surely Philip is going to be here! Most extraordinary if he isn't—but then the whole thing is most extraordinary. I cannot see how there can possibly be any doubt myself. Either Anne is dead, or she is alive. That is surely beyond dispute."

"Certainly, Miss Jocelyn. Perhaps you would be seated. Philip will be here in a moment. Perry, you and your wife here, please—and Miss Jocelyn beyond you. Now before we go any farther I will just say this. You are here to give your opinion as to the identity of someone who claims to be Anne Jocelyn. She arrived here on Tuesday evening wearing Anne's going-away dress, her fur coat, her pearls, and her wedding and engagement rings, and in possession of Anne's handbag containing her passport and identity card. She was unhesitatingly recognized as Anne by Mrs. Armitage, by Lyndall, and by Mrs. Ramage the cook, who is the only one of the old staff left here. Philip was away in town. When he returned next day he absolutely refused to accept this identification. He asserted then, and he asserts now, that the claimant is Annie Joyce."

"Theresa's Annie Joyce?" Inez Jocelyn's voice was shrill. "Yes."

Emmeline Jocelyn said firmly,

"There surely cannot be any great difficulty about the matter. We all knew Anne—I suppose we should all recognize her. It seems the most extraordinary story."

Mr. Codrington turned to her with some relief.

"Yes, it is—but I think we had better not discuss it now. Ah—here is Philip!"

Philip Jocelyn stood for a moment inside the door. He lifted a hand to the row of switches beside the jamb. All the rest of the lights in the room went on—one over each of the two big sideboards, one on either side of the chimney-breast, one over a serving-table, one over the door itself. The room remained dreary, but it ceased to be dark. Every object in it, every person, every shade of expression, was unsparingly illuminated. The three large windows blanketed with fog receded and lost their importance. The failing light outside could no longer compete. It withdrew and became negligible.

Philip came over to the table and shook hands with his uncle and aunt, with Inez and Lilla. He touched Perry on the shoulder and dropped into the chair between him and Mr. Codrington, who at once turned his head and made a sign to his confidential clerk. Mr. Elvery then left the room.

Milly Armitage thought, "It's exactly like a funeral, only worse. Lyn's stubborn, but I don't know that I want her any different. She's identified herself with Anne, waiting to come in with her like this. It is going to hurt Philip horribly. She's taking sides against him. No, it's not that. She's loyal—she loves Anne, and if there's even a chance that this is Anne, she won't let her down."

Mr. Elvery came back and sat down at the foot of the table, pulling his pad towards him and bending over it, pencil in hand. He left the door open, and almost immediately Lyndall and Anne came in together.

Lyn turned to shut the door, but Anne walked straight on and up to the table. She wore the blue dress in which she had been painted. She wore the pearls. She was well and delicately made up—eyelashes darkened, but no eye-shadow; skin well creamed and powdered, but very little rouge; lips tinted to a coral shade; fingernails enamelled to match. Without hesitation she passed to the right of Mr. Elvery and approached the Thomas Jocelyns, putting out a hand to each.

"Uncle Thomas! Aunt Emmeline!"

It was plain that both were thunderstruck, but without giving them time to speak she went on and took the chair on Mr. Codrington's left. From there she nodded across the table.

"Oh, Perry—how nice to see you! It's such a long time, isn't it? And I haven't met Lilla, but it's nice to see her too." Her eyes went past them. "How do you do, Cousin Inez?"

Philip leaned back in his chair. If this was the first test, she was passing it with honours. But then Annie Joyce would have known enough to pass it. Theresa had all the family history and all the family photographs. She wouldn't have known about Lilla of course, but that, he fancied, was where Lyn came in. He looked at her accusingly. She had taken the chair next to Milly Armitage. She wore a dark green dress with a turn-down collar of some musliny stuff. The colour made her look very pale. Perhaps it wasn't the colour at all. Her skin had the smooth, even pallor of milk. Her queer smudgy eyes were dark behind dark lashes. She wouldn't look at him. He mustn't look at her. He made a frowning effort and turned his eyes away. Lyndall thought, "He's angry—he hates me. It's better that way. What is going to happen to us all? I couldn't let her come in alone."

Mr. Codrington looked down the table and said,

"Has anyone any questions they would like to ask? . . . Yes, Mrs. Jocelyn?"

Emmeline leaned forward.

"You recognized my husband just now—perhaps you will tell us where he comes in the family."

Thomas Jocelyn sat back and looked down his nose. He disliked all this extremely. He wished that Emmeline hadn't come, or that, having come, she would sit quiet and leave the talking to someone else. After nearly twenty years of marriage neither of these two things appeared to him as possibilities. This did not prevent him from dwelling on them.

On his other side Anne made smiling answer.

"But of course—Philip's father had two brothers, Uncle Thomas is the youngest. Perry's father came in between. He was Peregrine too."

Emmeline went on,

"And what children have we?"

"Four boys. I suppose the eldest is about sixteen now. He is Tom—and the others are Ambrose, Roger, and James."

Emmeline said, "We call him Jim," and Anne laughed.

"You know, I don't think this sort of thing gets us anywhere. I mean, if somebody asks me who Cousin Inez is, and I say she's Cousin Theresa's sister and their father was a first cousin of my grandfather's, well, it simply doesn't get us anywhere at all, because Philip seems to think I'm Annie Joyce, and Annie would know all these things just as well as I do."

They all looked at her. Philip looked at her. She seemed frankness personified, her colour a little risen, her lips smiling, her left hand with the big sapphire of Anne's engagement ring overlapping the platinum wedding-ring laid carelessly—or was it carefully?—on the dark shining board. The women's eyes were on the rings. Inez said,

"Perfectly right—that sort of thing is no good at all—sheer waste of time." Her light eyes went maliciously to Emmeline.

"What we want is to be practical. Why does Philip say that she isn't Anne? Why does he think that she is Annie Joyce? That is where we should begin."

Impossible for common sense to take a more irritating form. The voice, the darting glances passing from Emmeline to Lyndall and back to Philip, had a singularly antagonizing quality.

Mr. Codrington looked resigned and said,

"Perhaps Philip will answer that."

Philip looked straight in front of him over the top of Anne's head to the elegant portrait of the Philip Jocelyn who had been a page at the court of William and Mary. Tight white breeches and a lemon-coloured coat, very fair hair tossed carelessly above the brow. Eight years old. At twenty-eight he was dead in a duel over an unfaithful wife. Her portrait hung, banished, in a corner upstairs—all dark love-locks and rose-red fur-belows.

He told his story as he had told it in the Parlour—the fall of France—Dunkirk—the desperate bid to get Anne away—her death in the moment of its success. His voice was throughout extremely quiet and without expression. He was very pale.

When he had finished, Emmeline had a question ready,

"You went over to get Anne, and you saw her and Annie Joyce together. As far as I know, no one else ever saw Annie after she was fifteen—unless Inez did?"

Miss Jocelyn shook the platinum head with its unsuitable fly-away hat.

"I thought Theresa's craze for her ridiculous! I told her so, and she didn't like it. People very seldom like the truth, but I make a point of saying what I think. I said it to Theresa, and she quarrelled with me. Nobody can say that it was my fault. We met at Anne's wedding, but we didn't speak. Theresa had a very resentful nature. As to Annie Joyce, I only saw her once about ten years ago. A most gawky, unattractive child. Nothing to account for Theresa taking such a fancy. But if you ask me, she only did it to annoy the family."

As everyone else round the table shared this opinion, there were no comments.

Emmeline said quickly,

"Please let Philip answer my question, Inez. He saw Anne and Annie Joyce together—you did, didn't you, Philip?"

"Yes."

"Then how much alike were they? That is what we all want to know."

Philip looked at her. Milly Armitage thought, "He's horribly strained. It's worse than any funeral—and it's going to go on for hours."

Then that expressionless voice:

"I wasn't thinking about likenesses, I'm afraid. It was after midnight. I had to break in at the back of the house. Pierre woke up and got the girls. You say I saw them together—we were in the kitchen with a single candle. I hustled them off to get ready. I sent Pierre for the other people. The girls only came back just before we started."

Emmeline persisted.

"But you did see them together—you must have noticed whether there was a likeness."

"Of course there was a likeness."

"Annie's hair was darker than Anne's," said Inez Jocelyn. "Even when she was fifteen I'm sure it was darker."

Emmeline threw her a look.

"Hair doesn't always stay the same colour—does it, Inez?"

Lilla wanted to laugh, and it would be just too dreadful if she did. Those terrible platinum curls! Why couldn't people let their hair go grey when it wanted to? And then all at once she stopped wanting to laugh and thought, "It's horrid—they're not kind."

Philip was speaking to Aunt Emmeline.

"Annie Joyce had a scarf tied round her head. I never saw her hair."

"Then you don't know how much like Anne she might have looked with her hair hanging down on her neck—if that's the way Anne was still wearing hers."

Thomas Jocelyn spoke for the first time. He said,

"This is all very painful, but it will have to be cleared up. You say Anne died in the boat. I take it you identified her afterwards—formally, I mean. Did anyone else?"

"They didn't ask for anyone else."

"And you were quite sure that the girl who died in the boat was Anne?"

"I was quite sure."

"It would have to be a very remarkable likeness to deceive you. But, on the face of it, this likeness must have existed. If this is not Anne who has come back, it is someone so like her

54

that Milly, Lyndall, and Mrs. Ramage accepted her immediately. I must tell you that I myself would have accepted her. We may be mistaken. I am not giving it as my opinion that she is Anne—not yet. But do you not think it at least possible that the mistake is yours, and that it was Annie Joyce who died in the boat?"

"It was Anne."

"You certainly thought it was Anne. It seems to me it would be much easier to make a mistake about a dead person than about a living one. The arrangement of the hair makes a great deal of difference to a likeness. Annie Joyce's head was tied up in a scarf. If that scarf had come off, as I suppose it might very easily have done, may not the family likeness have been intensified sufficiently for you to mistake Annie for Anne—especially after death, when personality and expression are withdrawn and only the features remain?"

The two Jocelyns looked at one another. Philip had always respected his uncle's judgment. He respected it now. He had also a good deal of affection for him. He said in a thoughtful tone,

"I agree that it might happen. I don't agree that it did happen."

XII

ANNE made a quick spontaneous movement. The hand with the ring took hold of Thomas Jocelyn's arm. The other hand went out palm upwards towards Philip.

"Uncle Thomas, I've got to thank you—at once, without waiting—because you've cleared it all up for me. I can see how it could have happened—without Philip knowing. You've shown me not only that it did happen, but just how it happened." Her hand dropped, her eyes went to Philip. "I'm afraid I said some rather horrid things when we talked about it, and I'm sorry. I want to ask you to forgive me. You see, I didn't understand how it could have happened. I couldn't get over the feeling that I had been left——" Her voice died. She looked away from Philip, who had not looked at her. She leaned back in her chair and for a moment closed her eyes.

Without moving, Philip was aware of all she did. Behind

perfect control his thoughts were turbulent and racing. How clever—how damnably clever—the slight gesture, the failing voice. Anne wasn't as clever as that. Anne wasn't clever at all. She had loved life. She had loved her own way, and for a little while she had loved him. Then, like a trickle of cold water— "Suppose she's not being clever—suppose it's real—suppose she is Anne——"

Everyone about the table shared a momentary embarrassment. Lilla sat a little closer to Perry. She slipped her hand inside his arm and squeezed it. She had the air of a small bright bird seeking shelter. Her fur coat, open at the neck, showed glimpses of a rose-coloured jumper, a string of milky pearls, a diamond clip. Everything about her was warm, and soft, and kind. She leaned against Perry, who was the most embarrassed person there. Scenes were the devil, and family scenes were the devil with knobs on. He thought the world of Philip, and he wanted him and everyone else to be as happy as he and Lilla were.

The silence was broken by Emmeline. Her husband's remarks had surprised her very much. It wasn't at all like Thomas to—well, to take charge like that. And he had interrupted her just as she was about to take charge herself, a thing she felt very well qualified to do—much better qualified than Thomas. She said now in her most decided voice,

"There were several things that I was going to say when your uncle interrupted me. We've got to be practical. Handwriting first of all—what about that?"

This time it was Mr. Codrington who replied.

"Certainly, Mrs. Jocelyn. But of course it was a point which suggested itself at once. Neither Philip, nor myself, nor Mrs. Armitage can detect any difference between old signatures of Anne's and signatures which we have seen written in the last few days." As he spoke he opened the attaché case in front of him, took out some folded sheets, and passed them to Thomas Jocelyn. "I think everyone should look at these. Some of them are new, and some of them are old. The new ones have been purposely creased and handled. If anyone can pick them out, he or she is cleverer than I am."

Mr. Jocelyn took his time. Presently he shook his head and let his wife have the papers.

"I might hazard a guess on the colour of the ink, but certainly not on the writing."

Emmeline took her time too. There was one whole letter which began, "Dear Mr. Codrington," and ended, "Yours very sincerely, Anne Jocelyn." In between, a few lines thanking him for the despatch of some papers unspecified.

She took up the next sheet. Three or four lines to conclude another letter. The weather was very damp—she did hope it would clear soon. And once more she was his very sincerely.

There were two more letters, one asking for a copy of her will, and the other thanking him for having sent it.

Emmeline began to say, "I suppose——" then checked herself and passed the letters to Milly Armitage, who had seen them before and pushed them over the table to Inez Jocelyn. She made a great rustling with them, snatching them up, only to discard one, pick it up again, and finally arrange the four sheets like a hand at cards.

"Of course the two about her will must have been written before she went to France. Not a very good choice, if I may say so. She could hardly have been making a will since her return—could she?" That very unpleasant laugh of hers rang out. "I thought of that at once. You can't expect us to think of nothing but the writing, you know. The subject-matter is evidence too, Mr. Codrington." With a toss of the platinum curls she relinquished the letters to Perry, who shook his head over them and said they all looked alike to him.

As Mr. Codrington resumed possession of them he said drily, "The two letters about the will were written a couple of days ago to my dictation."

Mrs. Thomas Jocelyn allowed herself to smile. Then she addressed Philip.

"Well, we had to get that out of the way. What I want to ask you now is about the night you went over to France. I want to know how those two girls were dressed. Because unless their clothes were alike, I don't see how you could have taken one for the other."

"I'm afraid I didn't notice very much. It was dark. They were the sort of things girls wear—the sort of things you don't notice—a tweed skirt and a jumper. Afterwards, I suppose, they had coats on."

"Was Anne wearing her fur coat?"

"I don't know—I didn't notice."

Anne said quick and low, "Yes, I was wearing it. I've got it—I came home in it."

Emmeline said, "Oh——" And then, "It was a very valuable coat—mink, if I remember. Milly would know if it was Anne's coat. Is it, Milly?"

"There isn't any doubt about that," said Milly Armitage.

Emmeline said "Oh——" again. Then she went on with her questions.

"We've got to clear up this business about the clothes, because it's very important. The girl who died in the boat—the one you thought was Anne—how was she dressed? You identified her, so you must have seen her next day."

Perry felt Lilla wince. Thomas Jocelyn was aware of an inarticulate bleak anger. Lyndall looked down at her hands, which were clenched in her lap.

Philip said, "Yes, I saw her. But I'm afraid I don't remember about her clothes, except that they were wet and a good deal stained—the sea kept breaking over us. I'm afraid it's no good, Aunt Emmeline. We've been over this clothes question before, and it doesn't lead anywhere."

"Where was Anne's jewellery—those rings and her pearls? The pearls were real."

Again it was Anne who answered.

"They were all in my handbag. I was carrying it." She hesitated for a moment, and then said, "All except my wedding-ring. I took it off when I quarrelled with Philip about going to France. When I knew he had come over to fetch me, I put it on again."

"Did you know she had taken it off, Philip?"

"Yes."

"If I may ask something——" Inez Jocelyn's tone was edgy. "Of course only if Emmeline has quite finished. I think we ought to know what this quarrel was about. Anne would be able to tell us, but probably Annie Joyce would not."

Anne gave her an unsteady smile.

"Of course I can tell you. It was all very stupid—quarrels generally are. Cousin Theresa wrote and asked me to come over to France. She said she had made a will in my favour when she came over to the wedding, and she wanted to talk to me about personal mementoes for the family. Philip was very angry. He said she had no business to leave the money away from Annie Joyce, and he said I wasn't to go. Of course he was perfectly right about the money, and I wouldn't have taken it—though I didn't tell him that, because I was

58

angry too, and I didn't like being dictated to. So we quarrelled and I took off my wedding-ring and went to France without making it up."

Inez Jocelyn turned her pale eyes on Philip, protruded her pale chin.

"Is that true?"

He said, "Perfectly true," and then looked suddenly at Anne. "Where did we have this quarrel?"

Their eyes met, his very cold, hers very bright. Something in them eluded him.

"*Where?*"

"Yes, where? In what place, and at what time of the day?"

She said very slowly, and as if it pleased her to dwell upon the words,

"In the Parlour—in the afternoon—after lunch."

That cold gaze of his held against the spark of triumph in hers. It was she who looked away.

He said, "Perfectly correct."

There was a silence. Mr. Elvery wrote upon his pad.

"Annie Joyce wouldn't have been very likely to know that!" said Inez Jocelyn. She gave her jarring laugh. "But I suppose Anne might have told her. Not very likely of course, but girls do tattle. Only I suppose there's a limit. Of course, you never know, but—— Why don't you ask her where you proposed to her, and what you said? I shouldn't have expected her and Annie to be such bosom friends that she would have told her that."

Philip glanced across the table and spoke.

"You heard what Cousin Inez said. Do you feel inclined to answer her?"

She looked back at him in a softer way than she had done before.

"We're not to be allowed to have any privacies, are we?"

"Is that what you are going to plead?"

She shook her head.

"Oh, no. It doesn't really matter, does it?" Then, turning towards Inez, "He proposed to me in the rose-garden on the seventh of July, nineteen-thirty-nine. It was a romantic setting, but I'm afraid we were not very romantic about it. We had been talking about all the things Philip would have liked to do to the house if he had had enough money. He said he wanted to pull down the bits my grandfather built on. He called them expensive hideosities, and I said I thought so too. Then I said I'd like to do things to the garden, and he said, 'What kind of things?' So I told him I'd like to make a lily-pool, and get rid of the ramblers out of the rose-garden—things like that. And he said, 'All right, you can if you want to.' I said, 'What do you mean by that?' and he put his arm round me and said, 'I'm asking you to marry me, stupid. What about it?' And I said, 'Oh, what fun!' and he kissed me."

"Is that right?" Inez Jocelyn's voice rang stridently.

Philip said, "Oh, yes."

When he had said these two words his lips closed hard.

Inez leaned right forward, crowding Lilla.

"Well, there must be plenty of other things that you can ask her—things which only you or she can know anything about. After all, you had a honeymoon, didn't you?"

Thomas Jocelyn looked round sharply. Mr. Codrington put up a restraining hand. But before anyone could speak Anne pushed back her chair. Still smiling and without hurry, she passed round the end of the table and laid a hand on Philip's shoulder. When she spoke her voice had a note of tender amusement.

"Cousin Inez wants you to feel quite sure that I went on that honeymoon. Don't you think that the family would be rather *de trop*? I mean—well, even the kindest cousin isn't exactly welcome on a honeymoon. Wouldn't it be a good plan if we went away and had this out together?"

Without waiting for an answer she moved towards the door. After a moment Philip got up and followed her. They went out of the room together. The door fell to behind them.

Everyone except Inez felt a sense of relief. Everyone also felt that Anne had shown a good deal of tact and breeding, qualities in which Miss Jocelyn was painfully deficient.

Emmeline raised her fine eyebrows and said,

"*Really!*"

"Really what, Emmeline? You know as well as I do that the only definite proof would be something that was absolutely private between them. What's the good of saying '*Really!*' at me just because you haven't got as much courage as I have? After all, we're here to find out the truth, aren't we? And I'd like to know how else you think we're going to do it. What is the good of being mealy-mouthed? If she can tell Philip things which only his wife could have known, why, then she is Anne. But if she can't, why, then she isn't."

It was while Inez was still speaking that Lilla got up and came round the table to sit by Lyndall. She put a small warm hand over the clenched fingers in Lyndall's lap and found them icy cold.

"Lyn—I do so want you to come up and stay with me. Perry goes off again tomorrow. Couldn't you come back with us?"

Without looking at her Lyndall said,

"Your last evening? Oh, no."

"Tomorrow then? Do be an angel and help me out! Cousin Inez has her eye on our spare room. She doesn't like being evacuated to Little Claybury. She thinks there isn't going to be any more bombing and she wants to get back to town, and I don't really think I can bear it."

They spoke behind a barrage of voices. Everyone except Perry and Mr. Elvery was talking now. Lyndall said quick and low,

"Yes, I'll come."

"I shall *love* to have you."

The family was still talking when the door opened and Anne came in with Philip behind her. Anne was smiling, and Philip deadly pale. She went back to her place and sat down, but he remained standing. As everyone turned and looked at him, he said,

"I made a mistake. I must have made one three years ago. I have to beg her pardon. She is Anne."

XIII

AFTER all nobody stayed the night. The only person who showed any disposition to do so was Inez, but receiving no encouragement, she departed as she had come, with Perry and Lilla.

A fleeting qualm of conscience prompted Milly Armitage to draw Lilla aside.

"Look here, I don't want her—we've got enough on our hands without Inez. But if it means that she's going to land herself on you and spoil the last evening of Perry's leave, well,

I'll have her. I suppose if it comes to that, it isn't really for me to say. If Anne's back, it's her house and I'm only a visitor."

Lilla looked at her with affection.

"Anyone would love to have you as a visitor. And it's quite all right about Cousin Inez, because she's staying with her friend Roberta Loam, and they haven't quarrelled yet, though I think they're on the brink. Lyn says she'll come to me tomorrow, so that's all quite safe and fixed. What are you going to do?"

Milly Armitage made a face.

"Philip wants me to stay on here. Of course I can't—at least I don't see how I can—unless Anne wants me too. She says she does, so I suppose I'll have to try it for a bit. None of it's easy, is it?"

Lilla said "No." Then she squeezed her hands and kissed her very warmly indeed.

Philip came back from seeing them off, with the remark that his cousin Inez was without exception the most disagreeable woman he had ever met. She had been arch with him on the doorstep, had shaken those dreadful curls at him, and screamed parting jocosities about a second honeymoon from the window of the moving taxi.

"Theresa was bad enough. She bounced, and quarrelled, and interfered, but she had an awful sort of *joie-de-vivre*. And she wasn't vindictive, and she didn't dye her hair—at least she hadn't dyed it last time I saw her, because I remember its looking like a large grey bird's nest."

"At our wedding," said Anne. She used a light, pleased voice and spoke as if there had never been a cloud between them since that wedding-day.

Then, before Philip's silence could become noticeable, she was making herself charming to the Thomas Jocelyns and Mr. Codrington. She was no longer "the claimant" on her probation, but very much Anne Jocelyn speeding the parting guests from Jocelyn's Holt.

It was some hours later, in the empty time before the evening meal, that Philip found Lyndall in the Parlour alone. She had changed into a dark red house-gown which caught the firelight and reflected it back from warm velvet folds. Only one lamp was on, the shaded one by the far window. It showed Lyndall in her red dress crouched forward over the fire with both hands stretched to the blaze. He took a moment watching her. Then he came up to the hearth and stood there.

"I want to talk to you."

She did not move, but her hands shook a little. She said, "Yes."

He looked, not at her, but down into the fire.

"Everything in my mind says that she is Anne—reason, logic, evidence. And everything else keeps shouting, 'She's a stranger.' What does one do?"

Lyndall said in a small voice like a tired child,

"I can't tell you that—can I?"

"No. I suppose the fact of the matter is that we are strangers. The point at which we touched is a long way behind us both. We have gone off in different directions. I can't see any meeting-point ahead. She thinks there might be one, and that we owe it to each other to try and come together again. I have told her that she owes me nothing. I can't tell her that I don't owe her anything either. From her point of view I owe her a good deal. However it came about, I did fail her—she was left in danger whilst I went back to safety."

"Philip!" She turned round, her eyes imploring him.

"Lyn, don't you see how it must have looked to her—how it might be made to look to anyone? I came away without her—I identified another woman's body as hers—and I came in for every penny of her money. When she comes home again, you recognize her, Aunt Milly recognizes her—Mrs. Ramage, Mr. Codrington, the whole family recognize her. But I stick out, I go on saying she isn't Anne, until the weight of the evidence overbears me by main force. I don't need to dot the i's or cross the t's, do I? You see what it looks like—I deserted her, I lied about it, I denied her."

"Philip—please——"

The rapid, bitter flow of words was broken, but only for a moment. He stared down at her as if he saw, not her, but some fantastic abyss whose unsteady edge might yet give way and launch him headlong.

"Don't you see? If you don't, Mr. Codrington does. He told me in so many words how grateful I ought to be for the way in which she is taking it. If she had chosen to bring a case, if she had shown resentment, if she hadn't displayed the most extraordinary forbearance, my name would be mud. She wants to make it up, she wants to be friends, she wants us to give each other a chance. She doesn't suggest our living together now. She only asks that we should to a normal and reasonable extent live under the same roof—show ourselves together in public—until all the talk and gossip has died down. What can I do? I can't refuse her that, can I?"

Lyndall said, "No." She stood up, moving slowly and a little stiffly, because if she let them her knees would tremble. She controlled them very carefully, but the effort made her feel like one of those stiff, jointed dolls.

When she was on her feet, she said gently,

"You must do what she wants. You did love her. It will come back again."

"Will it? *On revient toujours à ses premiers amours.* I have always thought that a particularly crass sort of lie. I told you we had gone in opposite directions. Lyn, even now, with evidence that I am bound to accept, I tell you she isn't Anne to me."

"Who is she?"

"A stranger. I can't feel that we have ever shared a single experience—not even when she tells me things which only Anne could know." He moved abruptly. "You are going away?"

"Yes."

"When?"

"Tomorrow."

There was a long, heavy silence. It weighed on the room, it weighed upon their hearts. Tomorrow she would be gone. They had nothing more to say to one another, because that said everything. If he put out his hand it would touch her. But he couldn't put it out. They were already divided, and with every moment of that silence each could see the other receding, whilst between them thought and feeling wrenched and broke.

When Milly Armitage came in, neither had moved from where they stood, yet each had travelled a long way.

XIV

THE nine days' wonder died down in the Press. On the whole it had been discreet. Annie Joyce's connection with the family, the likeness which had made the mistake in identity possible, was handled tactfully, and presently the affair receded. A week after Anne's return the telephone bell had ceased to ring, or reporters to clamour for interview.

Anne received a ration-book, which also contained clothes coupons, and went up to town to shop with a cheque-book in her handbag and the knowledge that there was a comfortable sum in her account at the bank. She had a very full day mapped out. Clothes were going to be a problem. Twenty coupons of her own—very aggravating to find that she couldn't spend more than that before the end of January. Fifty produced by Mrs. Ramage, who preferred saving her money to buying what she called "those utilities." And the prospect of a further allowance from the Board of Trade when her case had been considered, which would certainly take time. Eighteen coupons for a coat, the same for a coat and skirt, eleven for a dress, seven for shoes, and then underclothes—the coupons were just going to trickle away like water through a sieve. Impossible to blame Aunt Milly for giving away a dead Anne Jocelyn's wardrobe to the blitzed, but enraging to the last degree.

Then she must have her hair waved and set again, and a facial treatment, and a manicure. It was going to be a very full day indeed, but she would have looked forward to it if it hadn't been for the letter in her bag. She kept telling herself that it was tiresome but no more.

The matter could be dealt with easily enough. She could have dealt with it herself as far as that went. Easy enough to write, perhaps in the third person, something on the lines of "Lady Jocelyn is afraid that there really is not anything she could add to what has appeared in the papers with regard to the death of Annie Joyce. She does not think——" No, that wouldn't do—too stiff, too much *de haut en bas*. It was no good hurting people's feelings. Quite a simple letter would be best. "Dear Miss Collins, I don't think I can tell you anything that you do not know already about the death of poor Annie Joyce. The cutting you enclose has all the information that I have myself. I would meet you if I felt that it would serve any useful purpose, but I really think it would only be distressing for us both." Yes, that would do.

She had a fleeting regret that she had not written and posted just such a letter. After all, who was to know that Nellie Collins had ever written to her, or she to Nellie Collins? And even as the thought was in her mind, she knew that she couldn't hide this or anything else, and that the answer she wrote, or whether she wrote an answer at all, was part of a pattern which was none of her designing—a very strict pattern to which she would be most strictly kept. Just for a moment she had something like a black-out. It was a very strange sensation—between one second and the next a shock like the shock of concussion, leaving her numb, dazed, and reluctant. It passed, and afterwards she would have been frightened if she had let herself think about it.

Fortunately, she had a great many other things to think about. There were still excellent clothes to be got, but you had to look for them, and they were a shocking price. She gave twenty-five pounds for a coat and skirt in a good Scotch tweed, sandy beige with a brown line and a brown fleck—very becoming. Eighteen coupons gone. A pair of brown outdoor shoes, and a pair for the house—fourteen. Six pairs of stockings—another eighteen. She found herself thinking less of the price of a garment than of the number of coupons that had to be given up.

It was three in the afternoon before she really had time to remember that she had been afraid. She stood hesitating imperceptibly between the rather narrow windows which displayed on the one side a smiling wax model with an elaborately dressed head of golden hair, and on the other a snowy hand with tinted nails lying on a velvet cushion. The back of both windows was curtained in the very bright shade called *bleu de roi*. The cushion under the hand and the golden-haired lady's draperies were of an equally bright rose colour. A gold scroll over the door bore the name *Félise*. Anne Jocelyn pushed down the handle and went on.

If she had hesitated a little longer, or if she had not hesitated at all, some things might have happened differently, and some might not have happened. If she had gone straight in, Lyndall would not have seen her. If she had waited a little longer, Lyndall would have caught her up before she entered the shop, in which case she probably would not have kept her appointment with Mr. Felix, and she might, just possibly she might, have answered Nellie Collins' letter herself.

As it was, Lyn's moment of startled recognition brought her to a standstill on the opposite pavement just too late for her to be sure that it was Anne whom she had seen. And if that

66

was all, it wouldn't have mattered, but she wasn't sure whether she herself had been seen by Anne, because the upper half of that door between the two windows was made of looking-glass. The question was, how much did it reflect, and how much could Anne have seen before she pushed open the door and went in? If it was Anne, and she had seen Lyndall looking at her, she would think—well, what would she think? That Lyn wouldn't cross the road to speak to her? That she had some reason for avoiding her? It would be quite dreadful if she were to think anything like that. There mustn't be anything of that sort, ever. There wouldn't be if she could prevent it.

She had to wait whilst what seemed like an endless stream of traffic went by. By the time she managed to cross over, her courage had gone cold, but it held. She was not yet sure that it was Anne whom she had seen, but she was going to make sure. She had seen a fur coat and a glimpse of blue go into the shop. If there was a fur coat and a blue dress on the other side of that looking-glass door, it wouldn't take a moment to find out whether Anne was inside them.

She went in, and saw two women waiting by the counter, and a buxom assistant reaching something off an upper shelf with her back turned to the shop. Neither of the two women was Anne Jocelyn, but neither of them was wearing a fur coat, and quite definitely Lyndall had seen a fur coat go in at the looking-glass door.

She stood there waiting for the assistant to turn round. But she didn't turn round. One of the women was explaining just what sort of setting-lotion she wanted, and every time it was possible to get in a word edgeways the buxom girl said they hadn't got it, but that something else would do just as well, in fact very much better. Lyndall could see that it was likely to go on for ages. On the spur of the moment she walked across the shop and through the curtained archway on the other side of which the cubicles for hairdressing and manicure would be found. If Anne was having her hair done, that was where she would be. It wouldn't take a moment to find out. She could always say she was looking for a friend.

As soon as she was through the archway she could hear the swish of running water. The cubicles had curtains, not doors. It was quite easy to look through the curtains. A fat woman with a red neck—a thin one with her head over the basin—a

67

little dark girl having a manicure—a permanent wave—another manicure. Not a sign of Anne, not a sign of the fur coat. After all, it had got to be somewhere.

At the end of the passage between the cubicles was another of those looking-glass doors. She saw her own reflection coming to meet her like a *doppelgänger*—Lyn Armitage in a grey tweed coat and skirt and a dark red hat, looking scared. It was frightfully stupid to put yourself in the wrong by looking scared. If you were doing something which made you feel not quite so sure of yourself as you would like to be, that was the time to put your chin in the air and look as if you had bought the earth and paid cash down for it.

She pushed the door as she had pushed the other one, and came into a small square space with a wooden stair running steeply up on the left, a door on the right, and another straight ahead. It was dark after the brightly lighted shop, and it was cold after the warm, steamy heat of the passage between the cubicles. There was a damp, mouldy smell. Quite evidently these were back premises with no allurements for customers. Anne wouldn't be here. And as the thought went through her mind, she heard Anne Jocelyn's voice.

It frightened her, she couldn't think why. It was only the voice, no words, but she wasn't sure—no, she wasn't sure about it being Anne's voice. If she hadn't been thinking about Anne just at that moment, perhaps she would never have thought of its being her voice. She took a hesitating step forward. Now that her eyes were getting accustomed to the changed light, she could see that the door in front of her was not quite shut. It wasn't open, but it hadn't latched when it was closed. Some doors are very tiresome like that—they latch and spring open again, or they close and do not latch.

Lyndall put her hand on the panel of the door. She had no design in doing this; it was neither thought nor planned. She saw her hand come up and move the door. It moved quite easily. There was a line of light all down the edge of it like a thin gold wire. She heard the voice which was like Anne's voice say, "You might just as well let me write to Nellie Collins. She's quite harmless." A man's voice said in a carrying whisper, "That is not for you to say."

Lyndall took her hand away from the door and turned round. Her heart had begun to beat with suffocating violence. She felt ashamed and inexplicably frightened. If she let herself

68

move quickly, panic might take gold of her. She must get away. She must move quickly, but she mustn't make any noise. She was very near to feeling that she couldn't move at all.

Warmth and scented steam met her between the cubicles. She passed the curtained archway, and found the scene in the shop unchanged—the two women by the counter, the babble of voices, the assistant, with her back still turned, shifting bottles. She passed out into the street and shut the door behind her. No one had seen her come or go.

XV

PELHAM TRENT was, as Mr. Codrington had called him, a very pleasant fellow. Lyndall Armitage certainly found him so. He dropped in as often as he could at Lilla Jocelyn's flat, and Lilla was delighted to see him come. As she said to Milly Armitage, "They are just friends. At least, that's all it is with her—I'm not so sure about him. But it's exactly what she wants just now—someone to take her out and make her feel she matters."

Lyn went out with Pelham Trent. She found him a most agreeable companion and the best of hosts. It was better than sitting at home and feeling as if your world had come to an end. When you felt like that, the thing to do was to get into somebody else's world as quickly as you could. It was her world which had crashed—hers and Philip's. Perhaps Anne's too. But Pelham Trent's world kept its steady orbit. It was a safe, cheerful world in which you could laugh and have a good time—dance, see a film, a play, or a cabaret, and put off for as long as possible the return to the cold, shattered place where your own warm world had been.

They did not always go out. Sometimes they stayed in Lilla's charming drawing-room and talked. Sometimes he played to them. Those rather square hands of his with the strong, blunt fingers were quite extraordinarily agile on the keys of the Steinway baby grand. He would sit there playing one thing after another whilst the two girls listened. When the time came to say goodnight he would hold Lyndall's hand for a moment and say, "Did you like it?" Sometimes she would say, "Yes," and sometimes she would only look, because when she felt deeply she never found it at all easy to translate her feelings into words. Except with Philip who nearly always knew what she was thinking, and so because no words were needed they came quite easily.

Music let her into a world which was neither hers nor Pelham Trent's, though his playing was the gate through which she entered it. It was a world where feeling and emotion were sublimated until they possessed nothing except beauty, where sorrow spent itself in music and loss was solaced. She came back from this world rested and refreshed.

After all, Milly Armitage did not stay on at Jocelyn's Holt. It was not in her to refuse what Philip asked, but she had never responded to any of her sister-in-law Cotty Armitage's not infrequent appeals with more alacrity. Cotty enjoyed poor health. For twenty-five years or so she had had recurring attacks to which no doctor had ever been able to give a name. They involved the maximum of trouble to her family with the minimum of discomfort to herself. She had worn a husband into his grave, two daughters into matrimony, and the third to the brink of a breakdown. It was when Olive appeared likely to go over this brink that Cotty took up pen and paper and invited her dearest Milly to visit them. And Milly, incurably soft-hearted, invariably went.

"Of course what she really wants is for someone to pour a hogshead of cold water over her."

"Then why don't you?" said Lilla, with whom she was lunching on her way through London.

"Couldn't lift it, my dear. But someone ought to. Every time I go there I make up my mind to tell her she's a selfish slave-driver, and that Olive is simply going down the drain, but I don't do it."

"Why don't you?"

"Olive wouldn't thank me, for one thing. That's the awful part of that kind of slave-driving—in the worst cases the victim doesn't even want to be free. Olive's like that. You known, Lyndall only just got away in time. She was two years with Cotty after her father and mother died. They were killed together in a motor accident when she was nine and it nearly did her in. She's sensitive, you know—no armour-plating. Things aren't awfully easy for people like that. You're an angel to have her, Lilla."

"I love having her, Aunt Milly."

Milly Armitage crumbled her bread in a wasteful manner.

Lord Woolton would not have approved, nor would Milly herself if she had noticed what she was doing, but she did not. She wanted to say something to Lilla, but she didn't know how to set about it. She could be warm, generous, and endlessly kind, but she couldn't be tactful. She sat there in her baggy mustard tweeds with her hair rather wild and her hat at a rollicking angle and crumbled her bread.

Lilla, in a yellow jumper and a short brown skirt, had that air of having just come out of a bandbox which seems to be the birthright of American women. Her dark curls shone. Everything about her was just right both for herself and the occasion. There was a perfect ordered elegance which appeared as natural as it is in a hummingbird or a flower. Through it all, like the scent of the flower and the song of the bird, there came that friendly warmth which was all her own. She laughed a little now.

"Why don't you just say it, Aunt Milly, without bothering how?"

Milly Armitage's frown relaxed. A wide rueful smile showed her excellent teeth.

"I might as well, mightn't I? I can't see any good in beating about the bush myself, but people seem to expect it somehow. My mother always said I just blurted things out, and so I do. If they're pleasant, what's the good of wrapping them up? And if they're not, well, it's a good thing to get them off your chest and out of the way. So there it is—Philip and Anne are coming up to town. It's too much for him going up and down every day. He said so at dinner one evening, and Anne went up next day and took a flat. If you ask me, that wasn't at all what he meant, but he couldn't very well say anything. She did it in the most tactful way of course. Not being built that way myself, I don't awfully admire people being tactful—there's something soapy about it. You know—voice well kept down—gentle—hesitating. She hoped he'd be pleased. She'd been thinking what a bore that going up and down would be in the winter, and when she heard of this flat it seemed too good a chance to lose. They wouldn't hold it open—someone else was after it—all that kind of thing." She screwed up her face in an apologetic way. "There—I've no business to talk about her like that, have I? But I never did like her, and I never shall."

Lilla sat with her chin in her hand looking across the table, her puzzled brown eyes just touched with a smile.

"Why don't you like her, Aunt Milly?"

"I don't know—I just don't. She's a disaster for Philip—she always was—but they might have shaken down together if there hadn't been this break. But when a man has just begun to realize that he's made the wrong marriage, and then for three and a half years he thinks he's got free of it, what do you imagine he's going to feel like when he finds he's up to his neck in it again? Even without his having got so fond of Lyn."

"Is he fond of Lyn?" The brown eyes were very deeply troubled.

Milly Armitage nodded.

"I suppose that's one of the things I oughtn't to say. But it's true. And there wasn't anything wrong about it until Anne turned up. Lyn is just right for him, and he is just right for her. What do you suppose he is feeling like? I tell you I'm glad to be getting away to Cotty, and I can't put it stronger than that. You see, the worst part of it is that they're both trying quite desperately hard—I've never seen people trying harder. Anne is trying to get him back by being all the things she was never meant to be. It gives me pins and needles all over to watch her being gentle, and considerate, and tactful, and Philip being controlled and polite. He feels he's got to make up for not having recognized her at first, but it's all against the grain. If they'd snap at each other, or have a good red-hot, tearing row, it would be a relief—but they just go on trying."

"It sounds horrid," said Lilla in a distressed voice.

Milly Armitage made the face which she had been forbidden to make when she was ten years old. It made her look quite extraordinarily like a frog, and conveyed better than any number of words the discomfort of the Jocelyn *ménage*. Then she said,

"It's going to be very hard on Lyn having them in town. She is devoted to Anne—at least she was. I don't know how much of it's left now, but she'll think she ought to be, and it will tear her to pieces. They're bound to meet. I don't think Anne knows anything—I don't think it would occur to her. She thinks about Lyn as she was before the war—just a little schoolgirl who had a crush on her. And Lyn won't give anything away. She'll make herself go and see Anne and be friends with her because she'll think that's the right thing to do, and if she feels a thing is right she'll do it. She's got no armour—

she'll get horribly hurt. And I can't bear her to be hurt—that's why I'm saying all this."

"Yes?"

Milly Armitage put out her hand impulsively.

"That's why I'm so glad about Pelham Trent. I don't mean that I want anything serious to come of it—he's a bit old for her."

"He doesn't seem old."

"About thirty-seven, I should say. But that doesn't matter. It's a perfect godsend to have someone to admire her, to take her about, to take up her time. I don't suppose anything will come of it, but she likes him, and he'll help to tide her over a bit of bad going."

The conversation ended, as it had begun, with Pelham Trent.

XVI

MISS NELLIE COLLINS settled herself in the corner of an empty third-class carriage. She hoped someone else would get in—someone nice. She never really cared about travelling in an empty carriage, because of course there was always the chance of someone getting in who was *not* really nice. When she was a little girl she had heard a story about a lunatic who got into a train with a friend of her Aunt Chrissie's and made her eat carrots and turnips all the way from Swindon to Bristol. Her Aunt Chrissie's friend had a very severe nervous breakdown after this experience, and though it had happened at least fifty years ago, and this local train from Blackheath to Waterloo stopped much too frequently to give a lunatic any real scope, Miss Nellie preferred to be on the safe side. She sat up very straight in her best coat and skirt, her Sunday hat, and the fur necktie which she kept for great occasions because it was beginning to shed a little, and you couldn't tell how long it would have to last with fur the dreadful price it was now. The coat and skirt was of rather a bright shade of blue, because when Nellie Collins was young someone had told her that she ought to dress to match her eyes. He had married somebody else, but she remained perseveringly attached to the colour. Her hat, it was true, was black. She had been brought up to consider a black hat ladylike, but it boasted a blue ribbon which didn't quite match the coat and skirt, and a little bunch of flowers which did. Under the rather wide brim her hair stuck out in a faded frizz which had once been the colour of corn, but was now as old and dusty-looking as August stubble. When she was a girl she had had one of those apple-blossom complexions, but there was nothing left of it now. Only her eyes were still astonishingly blue.

Just as she was beginning to think that no one was going to get in, some half dozen people came past the porter who was inspecting tickets. Two of them were men. They walked straight across the platform and into the nearest compartment. Miss Collins heaved a sigh of relief. She thought they had a jovial appearance, and that one of them was not quite steady upon his feet. There remained a heavily built woman with two children, and a small upright figure in a black cloth jacket with a fur collar which had seen better days.

The family party followed the two men into the train, but the little woman in the dowdy coat came on. Miss Collins hoped very much that she would get in with her. She even loosened the catch of the door and allowed something that was almost a smile to relax her features. And all at once there was the door opening, and just as the train began to move, the lady in black got in and settled herself in the opposite corner. As she did so she met Miss Collins' sympathetic gaze and heard her say, "Oh dear, you very nearly missed it!"

The lady who had got in was Miss Maud Silver. Her original occupation had been that of governess, and she still looked the part, but for a good many years now her neat professional card had carried in one corner the words *Private Investigations*. It was part of her business to be a good mixer. She owed no small measure of her success to the fact that people found her astonishingly easy to talk to. She neither repelled by stiffness nor alarmed by gush. If there is a middle way between these two extremes, it could be said that she pursued it equably. She now produced a mild but friendly response and remarked that it was always very annoying to miss a train— "but my watch is out of order, and I had to depend upon my niece's dining-room clock, which is not, I am afraid, quite as reliable as she gave me to understand."

This was exactly the kind of opening which Miss Collins could be trusted not to neglect.

"You have been staying with a niece? How very pleasant."

Miss Silver shook her head. She was wearing a pre-war black felt hat, but the ribbon had been renewed, and the bunch of pansies had only done one winter.

"Not visiting," she said. " I came down to lunch and I should have been very sorry to miss this train, as I have a tea engagement in London."

Miss Collins gazed at her with envy. Lunch with a niece, and then a tea engagement—how gay it sounded!

"How very pleasant," she repeated. "I have often thought how nice it would be to have nieces to go and see, but there was only my sister and myself in our family, and neither of us married."

Miss Silver coughed.

"Marriage can be a very happy state, but it can also be a very unhappy one."

"But it must be very nice to have nieces. Not such a responsibility as children, if you know what I mean, but near enough to make you feel you've got something of your own."

Miss Silver's smile was restrained. If it had been her niece Ethel Burkett whom she had been visiting, she would have responded rather more warmly, but she had always inclined to the belief that Gladys was spoiled, and her visit today had done nothing to alter this opinion. Younger than Ethel and a good deal prettier, she was also considerably better off, having married a widower twice her age with an excellent practice as a solicitor. She could not, of course, say so to a stranger, but in the privacy of her own thoughts Miss Silver did not consider Gladys a great deal more dependable than her dining-room clock. And she had allowed herself to be patronizing about Ethel and Ethel's husband, who was a bank manager, and Ethel's children, to whom Miss Silver was deeply attached. She opened her handbag now and took out the sensible grey stocking she was knitting for Johnny Burkett.

"Of course," said Miss Collins, "in a way it's a responsibility bringing up children, whether they're your own relations or not. There was a little girl my sister and I brought up, and if she was alive I might be going up to see her—very much as if she was my niece, as you might say."

Miss Silver looked discreetly sympathetic.

"She died ?"

"I suppose she did." Miss Collins' tone was a hesitant one. A little flush came up on to her cheek-bones. "You see, my sister and I had a very refined little business. I have it still—fancy work, with a few toys and calendars at Christmas. We had the whole house, and when my mother died we let off the first floor—very nice quiet people with a little girl between three and four—no trouble at all. And we got fond of the child—you know how it is. And when Mrs. Joyce died—well, what could we do? We couldn't turn poor Mr. Joyce out—really quite crushed he was. And it came, as you may say, to our bringing Annie up. I suppose people talked, but Carrie was a good bit older than me, and after all—well, you've got to be human, haven't you? And there weren't any of his grand relations came bothering about him when he was left like that."

Miss Silver's needles clicked, the stocking revolved at a great rate. Her eyes had an attentive expression. When Miss Collins paused she was encouraged to proceed by a sympathetic " Dear me!"

"Never came near him," said Nellie Collins with emphasis. "Always talking about them, he was, because, you see, if his father had done the right thing by his mother, he'd have been a baronet with a fine estate instead of a clerk in a shipping-office, and you'd have thought those that came in for it instead of him would have taken a bit of interest—but not they. Twelve years he had our first floor, and believe it or not, no one ever came near him—not in the way of a relation, if you know what I mean, and not until the breath was out of his body."

"Someone came down after his death?"

Miss Collins tossed her head.

"A cousin, she said she was."

Miss Silver gave her slight cough.

"Miss Theresa Jocelyn, I presume."

"Oh!" said Miss Collins with a kind of gasp. "Oh! I never said—— I'm sure I never dreamed——"

Miss Silver smiled.

"You mentioned the name of Joyce, and you called the little girl Annie. You must forgive me if I could not help putting two and two together. The papers have been full of Lady Jocelyn's return after being mourned as dead for three and a half years, and of the fact that the person buried in her name was an illegitimate connection of the family who had been adopted by Miss Theresa Jocelyn, and whose name was Annie Joyce."

Miss Collins was very much taken aback.

"I'm sure I would never have said a word if I'd thought—the name must have just slipped out. I wouldn't have had it happen for the world—after I'd passed my word and all!"

"After you had passed your word?"

Miss Collins nodded.

"To the gentleman that rang me up and made the appointment for Lady Jocelyn. He didn't say who he was, and I've been wondering if it was Sir Philip—because of course you read about baronets, but I've never spoken to one that I know of, unless it was him."

Miss Silver was giving her the most flattering attention.

"Pray, what did he say?"

"Well, you see, I wrote to Lady Jocelyn—I hope you don't think it was pushing of me——"

"I am sure you would never be pushing."

Miss Collins nodded in a gratified manner.

"Well, I thought I had a right to, after bringing Annie up."

"What did you say?"

"I wrote and told her who I was, and I said I'd like to come and see her if she'd let me, because of hearing anything there was to hear about poor Annie, and of course I was looking for an answer and wondering what she would say. And then there was this gentleman ringing up. I had the telephone put in when my sister was ill, and the lady who has the first floor now pays half of it, so it isn't such a great expense, and ever since Carrie died I won't say it hasn't been company, knowing you can ring a friend up if you want to. So I put the telephone number on the top of my letter, and he rang up like I told you. But he didn't give any name—only said Lady Jocelyn would see me, and would I be under the clock at Waterloo Station at a quarter to four and hold a newspaper in my left hand so that she would recognize me."

The newspaper was folded neatly beside her. Miss Silver's eyes went to it for a moment and then returned to Miss Collins' face. She was really showing the most gratifying attention.

"And of course, as I told him, that wasn't necessary at all, because if Lady Jocelyn is anything nearly as like poor Annie as she must be for Sir Philip to have made a mistake between them, why, I should recognize her the very first minute she came in sight. And he said, 'Oh, would you?' and I said,

77

'Indeed I would, because one of the papers had a picture of Lady Jocelyn, and I'd have known it anywhere.' From the likeness to Annie, you know—the very same identical features, and that's a thing that doesn't change. Right from the time I took her over when she was five years old Annie had those features. You know, some little girls, they change a lot—fat one year and thin the next, so that you'd hardly know them. But not Annie—features, that's what she'd got, and features don't change. And Lady Jocelyn's got them too. So I said to the gentleman, "Well, I'll carry that paper, though it isn't necessary, because I'd know her anywhere.'"

Miss Silver continued to gaze in that interested manner.

"What did he say to that?"

Nellie Collins leaned forward. She was enjoying herself. Her life was a lonely one. She missed Carrie very much. Mrs. Smithers who occupied her first-floor rooms had always got plenty to say, but she never wanted to listen. She had eight children, all married and in different parts of the world, so that the steady stream of family news never ran dry—births, illnesses, engagements, accidents, promotions, fatalities, christenings, funerals, fortunate and unfortunate occurrences, prizes won at school, the total wreck of a business, a son-in-law's disastrous pre-occupation with a strip-tease artist—there was never any end to it, and Nellie sometimes found it a little daunting. It was balm to pour out her own tale to this quiet, interested lady who seemed to desire nothing better than to listen.

The train had already stopped more than once, but no one had entered the compartment. She leaned forward in a confidential manner and said,

"Well, he asked me whether the picture was a lot like Annie, and I said yes it was. And he said did I think I'd have known the two of them apart—that is, Lady Jocelyn and Annie, you know—and I said not in a picture I mightn't, but if I was to see either of them I'd know fast enough. He said, 'How?' and I said, 'Well, that's telling!' So he laughed and said, 'Well, you can tell Lady Jocelyn when you see her.' A very pleasant gentleman he sounded, and I wondered if it was Sir Philip. Do you think it could have been?"

Miss Silver coughed.

"I really could not say."

It would have pleased Nellie Collins to be encouraged in the idea that she had spoken to a baronet. She felt a little disappointed, and went on talking to make up for it.

"I thought it might have been. Perhaps I could ask Lady Jocelyn when I see her. Do you think I could do that?"

"Oh, yes."

"I think it must have been really, because of his asking me whether I had told anyone I had written, and asking me not to tell anyone I was coming up to meet her. He said they had had a dreadful time with reporters. That sounds as if it might have been Sir Philip—doesn't it?"

The grey stocking revolved briskly. Miss Silver said, "Yes."

"So of course I promised I wouldn't say a word to anyone, and I haven't—not even to Mrs. Smithers. That's the lady I've got in my first-floor rooms now—the same the Joyces used to have. She's all right, but you can't get from it she's a talker, and things do get round."

"They do indeed. I think you were very wise not to talk about it." Miss Silver coughed. "You said just now that you were quite sure you could always have told Annie Joyce from Lady Jocelyn. Did you mean, I wonder, that there was some distinguishing mark—something that would identify Miss Joyce beyond a doubt?"

Nellie Collins moved her head in a way that might have been meant for a nod if it had ever got so far. Whatever it was, she checked it, pursed up her lips, and sat back. After a moment she said,

"I didn't say anything about that."

"Oh, no—of course not. I was only thinking how difficult a positive identification might be. The papers have been very discreet, but it seems to me that the family were not immediately convinced that it was Lady Jocelyn who had returned to them. In that case any special knowledge which you possessed might be very important."

For the first time for many years Nellie Collins found herself considered as a person of importance. It went to her head a little. There was quite a bright colour in her cheeks as she said,

"And that's what I as good as told him. 'You couldn't take me in,' I said—'not if it was ever so.' He laughed very pleasantly, I must say, and said, 'You're very positive, Miss Collins'—that's my name, Nellie Collins. And I said 'Of course I am,' but I didn't tell him why. Only it stands to reason when you've had a child from five years old, and washed it and dressed it and done everything, well, if there's anything to know about it you'd know it—wouldn't you!"

Miss Silver was in the act of saying "Yes, indeed," when the train once more drew up. But this time the platform was crowded. Almost before it was really safe the door had been wrenched open and a number of people poured into the compartment, not only filling the seats, but taking up all the standing room.

Miss Silver put away her knitting, and Nellie Collins picked up her newspaper. Further conversation was impossible.

But when they arrived at Waterloo Miss Collins turned back upon the platform to bid Miss Silver a polite good-bye.

"It's always so pleasant to have company on a journey. Perhaps we shall meet again if you are coming down to see your niece."

Miss Silver's small, neat features expressed a polite response. It was exceedingly improbable that she would repeat her visit to Gladys—at least not for a considerable time—but she did not think it necessary to say so.

"I am quite near the station. Anyone would direct you— The Lady's Workbox—lavender and blue curtains. And my name is Collins—Nellie Collins."

Miss Silver could do no less than reciprocate, and at once Nellie Collins was opening her bag and finding pencil and paper.

"Do please write it down for me. I am so bad at remembering names."

Miss Silver wrote her name in a clear, legible hand. After a moment's thought she added the address—15 Montague Mansions, West Leaham St.

Miss Collins tucked the slip of paper away behind the little mirror which fitted a pocket in the side of her bag. Then she shook hands rather effusively.

"I do hope we shall meet again!"

Miss Silver said nothing. She was frowning a little as she walked down the platform to give up her ticket. Some way ahead of her amongst the crowd she could see the bunch of bright blue flowers in Nellie Collins' hat. It appeared, disappeared, and reappeared like something bobbing up and down in a choppy sea. Presently she lost sight of it. Really the platform was very crowded—very crowded indeed. So many of those nice American soldiers. Canadians too. French sailors in their very becoming caps—only really more like tam o' shanters, with the red bobble on the top. And Poles—curious to see their skins, not fair at all against that very fair hair. All most interesting, and quite cosmopolitan. She glanced up at the clock and saw that it was already ten minutes to four. As she dropped her eyes she caught a last glimpse of blue in the crowd. It might have been the bunch of flowers on Nellie Collins' hat, or it might not. She could never be sure.

XVII

Miss Silver continued on her way. Her pleasure in the anticipation of an agreeable tea-party was very slightly tinged by something to which she could hardly have given a name. Miss Nellie Collins had interested her—she had interested her very much. She would have liked to have witnessed her meeting with Lady Jocelyn. That was the worst of not being tall—one's outlook in a crowd was limited, sadly limited. To no one but herself would Miss Silver have admitted that her lack of inches might be a handicap. In point of fact, a crowd was the only place in which she had ever felt it to be one. In all other circumstances she stood firmly on her dignity and found it a perfectly adequate support.

She entered a room in which three or four people were talking, and was very warmly received by her hostess, Janice Albany, who had not so very long ago been Janice Meade.

"Garth is hopeless for tea, but he asked to be remembered, and he is so sorry to miss you. . . . Mr. and Mrs. Murgatroyd. . . . And this is Lyndall Armitage—she's a sort of cousin."

The Murgatroyds were both immense. Mr. Murgatroyd was jovial. He laughed and said,

"What sort of cousin, Mrs. Albany?"

Janice laughed too. Her hair with its close crop of curls caught the light. Her eyes matched the curls exactly.

"The sort you say is a very near relation, if you like them. Lyn is a very near relation."

Miss Silver shook hands, and began to make polite enquiries about Colonel Albany, about the six months' old baby who had been christened Michael after the inventor of harschite, and about Colonel Albany's aunt, Miss Sophy Fell. It appeared that Garth was well, and very busy at the War Office—"Of course he doesn't get home till all hours"—and that Michael was down at Bourne with Miss Sophy. "Better for him than being in London. And I go up and down. I've been lucky enough to get my own old Nanny, so I do a part-time job up here and keep an eye on Garth."

Two or three more people dropped in. Miss Silver found herself sitting next to Lyndall, and in the most natural way in the world was very soon in possession of the facts that Miss Armitage was in the Wrens, that she had been ill and was at present on sick leave—"but I do so want to get back to work."

Miss Silver had a penchant for girls. She looked kindly at Lyndall and said,

"But you must make the most of your leave. Time which is being spent pleasantly passes surprisingly fast, does it not?"

"Oh, yes."

Miss Silver became aware that time was passing neither pleasantly nor quickly for Lyndall Armitage. She was pale, there were shadows under her eyes. Of course she had been ill, but no passing illness gives a young girl's eyes that patient look. Miss Silver was sorry to see it there. She said,

"You are staying with friends?"

"With a cousin. At least I suppose she isn't really my cousin, but the aunt who brought me up is her aunt too, because Lilla married her nephew, Perry Jocelyn." When she had got as far as that she broke off, smiled a little shyly, and said,

"It sounds dreadfully complicated, doesn't it?"

Miss Silver said in a bright voice,

"Family relationships are always difficult to explain to a stranger. Did you say that your cousin's name was Jocelyn!"

"Yes."

"Dear me! Do you know that is quite a coincidence. I happened to travel back to town today with a Miss Collins who was going up to meet Lady Jocelyn."

Lyndall undoubtedly looked surprised and just a little startled.

"*Lady Jocelyn?*"

Miss Silver gave her slight deprecating cough.

"Is she, perhaps, a relative also?"

"Yes—she is my cousin Philip's wife."

It was said with the extreme of simplicity, and not until the words were there floating in the air between her and MissSilver did it occur to Lyndall that they were not true. Philip was no more her cousin than Perry was, but whereas it was quite simple to explain Perry, she found it impossible to explain Philip. There was no cousinship between them, but take that tie away, and it left too many others. She could not speak his name without feeling them pull at her heart.

Miss Silver, watching her with attention, was aware of something that was hurt and winced away. No one less experienced in observation, less sensitive to atmosphere, would have noticed it at all. It was the slightest, the most momentary thing—not, she thought, because it was evanescent in character, but because there was a strong habit of control.

Almost without any pause at all Lyndall was saying,

"But Anne wouldn't be meeting anyone today—at least I don't see how she could. They are just moving into a flat in Tenterden Gardens. She was only coming up from Jocelyn's Holt this afternoon, after seeing things off from there. Lilla Jocelyn, the cousin I'm staying with, has gone round to help her unpack. I don't see how she can have been meeting Miss Collins."

"Miss Collins was certainly expecting to meet Lady Jocelyn——" Miss Silver paused and added, "under the clock at Waterloo."

Lyndall looked at her rather blankly. She was feeling as if she had missed a step in the dark. Jarred, surprised, not quite knowing where she was—it was just like that. In her mind she was looking at a thin line of light along the edge of a door. The door wasn't quite shut. The light ran along the edge of it like a fine gold wire. She heard a voice say, "You might just as well let me write to Nellie Collins." It might have been Anne's voice, but she wasn't sure—she couldn't get nearer to it than that. And a man said, "That is not for you to say." The inexplicable feeling of fear and shame which had come on her in the passage behind the hairdresser's shop touched her again. She gave a little quick shiver and said,

"Won't you have some more tea? Please let me take your cup."

After that someone else came in. She didn't have to sit down by Miss Silver again. Mrs. Murgatroyd caught hold of her as she passed. And all Mrs. Murgatroyd ever wanted was someone who would listen whilst she talked about her daughter Edith, and Edith's truly remarkable baby.

It was to be supposed that Edith also had a husband somewhere, but he never emerged. The endless theme was Edith, and Edith's complexion, her features, talents, and activities—her marvellous baby, and its features, talents, and activities—what Sir Ponsonby Canning had said about Edith at her first ball—what Captain Wilmot had said when he proposed to her within half an hour of being introduced—what Amory had said when he asked if he might paint her portrait. It went on, and on, and on a gentle unending flow, and all you had to do was to look appreciative and say "How marvellous!" every now and then. Lyndall had had plenty of practice. She couldn't, in fact, remember a time when she hadn't known the Murgatroyds, and Mrs. Murgatroyd had always talked about Edith. The only difference was that as Mr. and Mrs. Murgatroyd became steadily fatter year by year even in war-time, so did Edith's perfections continually increase.

Lyndall sat with her eyes fixed attentively upon Mrs. Murgatroyd's face, which was large and round and pale, and sometimes reminded her too much of a crumpet.

Mrs. Murgatroyd thought her a very good listener. She felt affectionately towards Lyndall, and patted her hand in the kindest manner when Pelham Trent presently appeared to take her on to see *The Dancing Years*.

XVIII

THE flat which the Jocelyns had taken was a furnished one. They settled into it almost as easily as if it had been their own and they were returning to it after a brief absence. Philip, profoundly unhappy and holding his mind relentlessly to a new and exacting job, yet found himself unable to bar out the thought that three and a half years in a French village had developed in Anne a talent for organization which he certainly hadn't supposed her to possess. The girl who had dropped her hat, her coat, her scarf just where she found it convenient to discard them had changed into the woman who with the minimum of household help kept their flat orderly and shining—the girl who probably had boiled a kettle and possibly an egg or a potato into the woman who produced delightful meals from war-time ingredients. When he proposed bringing Mrs. Ramage up to town she wouldn't hear of it—"She'd be quite dreadfully unhappy. And there's no need—I can cook."

"Since when?" said Philip, and got a limpid look from steady grey eyes.

"Since I was in France, darling. Quite a good place to learn, don't you think?"

The little scene left a flavour behind it—the kind of flavour which is hardly there but lingers on the palate. For the rest, things would go more easily than at Jocelyn's Holt. They would not have to sit alone together in a horrid travesty of the *solitude à deux*. There was nearly always work to be finished at home. He could bring a man back with him. Anne could see her friends. She was busy ringing people up, asking one to lunch, another to tea—picking up the threads which had been dropped nearly four years ago. These activities were a great relief to Philip. The fuller Anne's life was, the less strain was placed on their relationship. The last thing he desired was the concentration of thought and interest upon himself or upon his work. That the latter was highly confidential and could not afford a meeting-ground hardly affected the position, since he would in any case have kept the door locked upon his private affairs.

Unfortunately Anne did not appear to see this. He could imagine her having been brought up on the simple axiom, "Always talk to men about their work—they like it." From what he had ever heard of her mother, she was just the sort of woman to say just that sort of thing. He was forced at last into a blunt,

"I can't talk about my job—and anyhow it would bore you stiff."

She looked a shade reproachful.

"It wouldn't—really. But—do you mean—it's—secret?"

She saw him frown. He controlled his voice to say,

"Most staff work is confidential. Anyhow I'm at it all day. I wouldn't want to talk about it if it was as public as Hyde Park."

"I thought men liked to talk about their work."

He turned a sheet of the *Times* and made no answer.

That was the first evening in the flat. It was also the evening on which Nellie Collins did not come home.

Mrs. Smithers rang up the police in the morning.

"My landlady, Miss Collins—she hasn't come home. I really don't know what to make of it at all."

In the police station Sergeant Brown, a family man, employed a soothing manner.

"How long has she been gone?"

"Since yesterday afternoon!" said Mrs. Smithers in an angry voice. "Most inconsiderate and uncalled for—leaving me alone in the house like this! And her shop not opened, and not my business to open it of course, *nor* yet to take in the milk, only, being war-time, I couldn't be expected to let it go to waste!"

Sergeant Brown said, "No." And then, "Just when did you say Miss Collins left?"

"Early yesterday afternoon. Went off in her best coat and skirt, and told me she was going up to meet a friend. Nothing about not coming back, or hoping it wouldn't put me out if she stayed in town—nothing like that! And here it's ten o'clock, and not a word to say where she is or when she's coming back, and I don't consider it's treating me right!"

Mrs. Smithers sounded so much annoyed that Sergeant Brown found himself saying the word "accident."

"She may have met with an accident."

"Then why can't she say so?" said Mrs. Smithers in a tearing temper.

By the time that Sergeant Brown hung up the receiver he was feeling a little sorry for Miss Collins. She was going to need something very substantial in the way of an accident if she wished to placate Mrs. Smithers. He began to ring up the London hospitals. When none of them knew anything about a middle-aged lady in a bright blue coat and skirt and a black hat with a bunch of blue flowers on it, he rang up Scotland Yard.

XIX

MISS SILVER was accustomed to feel very piously and sincerely grateful, not only for the success which attended her professional activities, but for the modest comfort which this success had brought her. Part of her gratitude arose from the fact that she regarded it as a privilege to thwart the designs of the evil-doer and to serve the ends of justice, which she would certainly have spelt with a capital letter. Her experience provided many occasions on which through her agency the innocent had been protected and restored. She found a benevolent pleasure in remembering these cases. Garth and Janice Albany had figured in one of them.*

On the day after her expedition to Blackheath Miss Silver was sitting by a neat bright fire in her flat in Montague Mansions. She had almost finished the stocking for Johnny Burkett which she had been knitting in the train on the previous day. As soon as this pair was completed she would begin another, since she had promised her niece Ethel three pairs before Christmas. So extremely fortunate that she had laid in a good stock of this useful wool before the coupon system came in. Not that she had expected anything of the sort—oh, dear me, no—but she remembered only too well the alarming price of knitting-wool during and immediately after the last war, and had accordingly taken precautions. She could therefore make herself responsible for Johnny's stockings without feeling that she was robbing his brothers, Derek and little Roger, who would also be requiring foot-wear for the winter.

As she knitted she regarded her room with satisfaction. Very comfortable, very tasteful, very cosy. The prevailing colour was that shade of blue known to the period of Miss Silver's youth as peacock. The plush curtains, which had cleaned so well and which she had not yet drawn; the carpet which had been turned round so as to bring the worn piece under the book-case; the upholstery upon the Victorian chairs with their curly walnut legs—all partook of this shade. The big workmanlike desk with its two rows of drawers was of the same shiny yellow wood as the chairs, the colour being again repeated in the maple frames of the engravings which decorated the walls—*Bubbles, The Soul's Awakening, The Black Brunswicker, The Monarch of the Glen*. A further selection of these Victorian favourites adorned her bedroom, monotony being avoided by an occasional interchange between the two rooms. Upon the mantelpiece, upon the top of the book-case, and upon a table between the two windows, stood innumerable photographs, most of them framed either in silver or in silver filigree upon plush. There were a great many babies, a good

* *The Key.*

many young mothers, a great many little boys and girls, with here and there a tall young man in uniform—some of them relations, but many of them the people she had helped in her service of Justice, and the children who might never have been born if it had not been for that service. It was not only a portrait gallery; it was a record of achievement.

Miss Silver herself, in indoor dress, was seen to possess a good deal of mouse-coloured hair, very neatly plaited at the back and arranged in front in the high curled fringe coming down in a point between the eyebrows popularized by the late Queen Alexandra. After more than thirty years of obsolescence it had some ten years previously enjoyed a fleeting return, but whether it was in the fashion or out of the fashion Miss Silver continued to do her hair that way, the whole being very competently controlled by an invisible net. For the rest, she wore a dress of olive-green wool made high at the neck by a little vest of tucked net, with a collar supported at the sides by slips of whalebone. The skirt was of a decorous length, but it disclosed that Miss Silver's quite neat ankles and feet were encased in black woollen stockings and slippers with beaded toes, how and whence procured only she herself could have said. The olive-green dress was fastened in front by a brooch of bog oak representing a rose, with a pearl in the middle of it. A fine gold chain supported the pince-nez in occasional use for very fine print, but because the use was only occasional, the glasses themselves were looped upon the left-hand side and secured by an old-fashioned bar brooch set with pearls.

At the sound of the telephone bell she balanced Johnny's stocking on the arm of her chair and went over to the writing-table. As she lifted the receiver, a familiar voice pronounced her name.

"Miss Silver—is that you? Sergeant Abbott speaking from Scotland Yard. I would like to come round and see you if I may."

"By all means." Miss Silver's tone was cordial.

"What about now—would that suit you?"

"Perfectly."

She had added about three-quarters of an inch to the stocking by the time Detective Sergeant Abbott was ushered in, to be received very much as if he had been a well-regarded young relative. That his feelings for Miss Silver were those of respect and affection was evident. For her, as for very few people, his cool, superior manner thawed into admiration. The ice-blue eyes took on a tinge of warmth. For the rest he was a tall, elegant young man, product of the public school and new Police College. His earliest friends still addressed him as Fug, a nickname prompted by a lavish use of hair-oil at school. He still wore the hair rather long and immaculately slicked back. His dark suit was admirably tailored, his shoes admirably cut and polished. In a public place Miss Silver would have addressed him as Sergeant Abbott, but in the privacy of her flat he was greeted as "My dear Frank." If the rising young man of Scotland Yard looked up to her in veneration touched with humour, she in her turn considered him to be a very promising pupil.

Compliments passed. They seated themselves. Miss Silver resumed her knitting and enquired,

"What can I do for you, Frank?"

Frank Abbott said, "I don't know." And then, "Something, I hope—perhaps a good deal—perhaps not." He produced a pocket-book, took out a scrap of paper, and leaned forward to lay it on her knee. "Do you happen to recognize this?"

Miss Silver laid down her knitting and picked up the scrap of paper. It was roughly triangular in shape, the base not quite two inches across with an uneven edge, the other two sides quite regular. Obviously the corner torn from a sheet of writing-paper. The side she was looking at was blank. She turned it over, and coming away from the base line were, one below the other, the following syllables—ver; -nsions; -ham St. She contemplated them with gravity. The second of these two words, or fragments, was heavily smudged.

Frank Abbott said, "Well?"

Miss Silver coughed.

"It is my name, my address, and my handwriting. If you had not recognized all three you would scarcely be here."

He nodded.

"You wrote them down for someone. Can you remember who it was?"

She had taken up her knitting again. The fragment of paper lay on her knee. Her eyes remained upon it whilst the needles clicked.

"Oh, yes."

"You can be quite sure?"

Her cough had a trace of rebuke.

"I should not tell you that I remembered if I were not sure."

"No, I know you wouldn't. But it's important. Will you tell me to whom you gave this address, and when, and in what circumstances?"

Miss Silver transferred her attention from the paper triangle to his face.

"I went down to Blackheath yesterday. On my return journey I was alone in a compartment with a Miss Collins—Miss Nellie Collins. She told me she kept a small fancy-work shop not far from Blackheath station, and that she was going up to town to meet someone who she hoped would be able to give her news of a young woman whom she had looked after as a child and whom she now believed to be dead. She had an appointment to meet the person at Waterloo at a quarter to four. When we separated she invited me to come and see her if I should visit Blackheath again. I responded by giving her my own name. She asked me to write it down for her, and I did so. Pray, what has happened to her, Frank?"

He said, "You added your address. Why did you do that? Was it for a personal reason, or—for a professional one?"

"Why do you ask me that?"

There was a glint in the pale blue eyes.

"Because I should like to know whether you wrote down your name and address for a stranger because you felt drawn to her and wanted to see her again, or because you had an idea that she might be wanting your help professionally."

Miss Silver coughed.

"It was not, I think, quite so definite as that. Pray tell me, is the poor thing dead?"

"I think it likely that she is. At the moment the body has not been identified. I am afraid I may have to ask you——"

Miss Silver inclined her head.

"You had better consider whether that would be the wisest course. She gave me her address, and mentioned that she had a lodger—a Mrs. Smithers. It might be better if formal identification came from her. I would, of course, be willing to identify my fellow traveller, but it might be wiser if that were done privately, and just for the benefit of the police. I think that this may prove to be a very serious matter, Frank. I would like you to tell me a little more. Where was the body found, and where was this scrap of paper found?"

"You gave her your name and address written down on a piece of notepaper. Did you see where she put it?"

"Certainly. She opened her bag and folded it away in a pocket behind a small fitting mirror. Pray, where was it found?"

Sergeant Abbott still delayed to answer this question.

"Your Mrs. Smithers rang up the local police this morning. They notified us, with a description of Miss Collins and her clothes. None of the London hospitals had her. It might have been the merest moonshine. Mrs. Smithers, who had worked up an alarm, said that Miss Collins went up to meet a nameless friend. She might have gone off on the spur of the moment to stay with this friend. It wasn't really Mrs. Smithers' business whether she did or whether she didn't. She had her own latchkey and did for herself. The Blackheath people obviously thought that Miss Collins had gone off on a jaunt. People do that sort of thing every day and can't imagine why anyone should get hot and bothered about it. Well, late this afternoon we got a report from Ruislip."

Miss Silver repeated the name in an enquiring tone.

"Ruislip?"

"On the Harrow line."

"I am aware of that, Frank. Pray, what sort of report?"

"Road accident. Body found in a lane—elderly woman in a blue coat and skirt—battered black hat with a bunch of blue flowers. Wheels had been over it—wheels had been over the woman. As there was a hard frost, no identifiable tyre-prints. Police surgeon says she had been dead at least twelve hours. Lane very lonely and unfrequented. Quite possible for the body to have been there all that time. It was found by a boy who delivers papers. He was bicycling in to collect them. He says he didn't touch anything, just tumbled off his bike and had a look-see, and made tracks for the police station, where he fetched up at half past seven." He paused.

Miss Silver had stopped knitting. She said,

"Go on."

"The body was a little on the left of the middle of the lane, on a diagonal slant. It was on its face, hands flung out— very natural attitude. The hat had come off and was lying about a yard away to the right. Handbag quite close to the body on the left. Inside the handbag a plain handkerchief, a fancy pencil, and a purse containing a pound note, eleven and

91

sixpence in silver, some coppers, and the return half of a third-class ticket to Ruislip——"

Miss Silver interrupted.

"In which direction did she appear to have been proceeding—towards Ruislip station or away from it?"

"Away from the station. The lane where she was found is a good mile away from it. To return to the handbag. In a side pocket there was a broken mirror and apparently nothing else, but the constable who was handling it cut his finger on the glass and thought he'd better empty the bits out. He found that scrap of paper amongst them."

There was a moment's silence. Miss Silver took up her knitting again.

Frank Abbott went on. If she wanted to say anything she would say it. If she didn't want to say anything, it was no use waiting. He knew his Miss Silver.

"The bits of words on the paper suggested you, even before I saw the handwriting. Lamb told me to come round and see you."

Miss Silver inclined her head.

"I hope that Chief Detective Inspector Lamb is well?"

Frank had a momentary picture of his superior officer looking at him in an exasperated manner, his eyes quite extraordinarily like bulls-eyes, and saying in an even more exasperated voice, "Hang that woman! Can't they so much as have a road accident in Middlesex without her cropping up in the middle of it? Oh, yes, go and see her if you like—and come back with a mare's nest full of eggs, as likely as not!" He dismissed the pleasing vision, and assured Miss Silver that the Chief was in excellent health.

"A most worthy man," said Miss Silver, knitting rapidly. Then she asked a question. "How do you suppose the corner was torn from the piece of paper upon which I wrote my address?"

"How big was the original piece?"

"It was a half sheet of small notepaper which she took out of her bag."

"You saw her put it away in the pocket behind the mirror. Did you notice whether the glass was broken then?"

"I cannot say. The upper edge was intact, but these small mirrors are very easily broken—they seldom survive for very long. And the bag was not a new one, not by any means. It

92

had certainly been in use since before the war. That class of bag is not obtainable now. I think it very unlikely indeed that the mirror was unbroken."

"In which case the corner might have been caught and torn off when the half sheet was removed. But wouldn't it have been noticed?"

Miss Silver's needles clicked.

"By whom, Frank?"

"By the person who thought it worth while to remove that paper. He couldn't have helped seeing that there was a corner missing—could he?"

"Unless it was done in the dark.'"

Frank Abbott whistled.

"After the accident, you mean?"

"After the murder," said Miss Silver.

This time he did not whistle. The ice-blue eyes narrowed a little. Then he said,

"Murder?"

"Certainly."

"What makes you think so?"

Miss Silver coughed.

"Did you not think so yourself?"

"There was nothing to make me think so."

She smiled.

"Are you in the habit of discussing an ordinary road accident at so much length?"

"Perhaps not. It was your handwriting that brought me here, and as soon as we began to talk I felt tolerably certain that you had something up your sleeve."

With the slightest possible change of expression Miss Silver managed to convey the fact that she was not altogether pleased with this figure of speech.

Frank Abbott produced an ingratiating smile.

"You have—haven't you?"

Johnny's stockings revolved briskly. Miss Silver said,

"Miss Collins talked a good deal in the train. We had the carriage to ourselves. She told me the name of the person she was going to meet. She also told me that she had promised not to disclose this information to anyone. You may think it strange that she should have confided in someone she did not know, but having inadvertently let slip another name—one which she had no reason to suppose I should recognize——"

"You did recognize it?"

"I did. And when she realized this she felt, I think, that it no longer mattered whether she told me the rest."

"What name did she mention?"

Miss Silver spoke slowly and carefully.

"She told me that she had had the charge of a little girl for some years. When the child was fifteen the father died and she was taken away by a member of a family with whom she was illegitimately connected. That would be ten or eleven years ago. It was while she was telling me this that the name of Joyce slipped out and she alluded to the child as Annie."

Frank Abbott's face changed.

Miss Silver coughed.

"I see that the name conveys to you what it did to me—Annie Joyce. Miss Collins did not put the two names together. She spoke at one time of Mr. Joyce, and at another of the child as Annie. She lives alone and was obviously in a very excited state and wanting to talk—quite full of her connection with a case which had been in the newspapers and eagerly looking forward to the appointment she was about to keep. As soon as she found that I recognized the name of Joyce she told me all about it."

"What did she tell you?"

Miss Silver took a moment. Then she said,

"Like everyone else, she had read the papers. Of course she realized that the return of Lady Jocelyn implied the death three and a half years ago of Annie Joyce. I think she may have been upset, but she had not seen the girl for ten years, and there was a good deal of excitement mixed up with it. She had led a very humdrum life. The sister who had shared her home and, I gather, dominated her was dead, her lodger full of her own family affairs. Miss Collins took the step of writing to Lady Jocelyn to ask for an interview, ostensibly for the purpose of hearing all that there was to hear about Annie's death, but actually, I think, because she saw a chance of being associated with a case which was attracting a good deal of attention." She paused, and added, "I am sure that the idea of blackmail had never entered her mind."

Frank Abbott exclaimed.

"Blackmail—Miss Silver!"

"I told you it might be a very serious case."

He ran his hand back over his hair, already mirror-smooth.

94

"Serious?" he said. "Good lord—go on!"

Miss Silver frowned slightly upon this form of address. She was indulgent towards the young, but early experience as a governess had left her with a feeling that she was responsible for their manners.

"I have already stated my conviction that poor Miss Collins had no such design, but I fear that she may have conveyed a quite erroneous impression to the person who rang her up."

"What person?"

"No name was given. Miss Collins told me that she wrote to Lady Jocelyn, I presume at Jocelyn's Holt, but received no reply from her. Instead a gentleman rang up. He gave no name, but stated that he was speaking for Lady Jocelyn. Miss Collins was, I think, under the impression that she was talking to Sir Philip. She was a good deal fluttered and pleased at the idea, as she had never, so she said, conversed with a baronet before. I tell you this in order that you may realize her state of mind—very simple, fluttered, and excited."

"Philip Jocelyn—I wonder——" His expression was dubious. Miss Silver's needles clicked.

"Quite so, my dear Frank. But on the other hand. . . . We should, I feel, withhold our judgment."

He nodded.

"Well, someone rang Miss Collins up. What did he say?"

"He asked her whether she had told anyone that she had written about Annie Joyce. She said she had not done so. He made an appointment for her to meet Lady Jocelyn under the clock at Waterloo at a quarter to four yesterday afternoon. She was to hold a newspaper in her left hand so that she might be easily recognized. It was at this point that Miss Collins made what, I fear, was a very sad mistake. She told the man she was talking to that she would recognize Lady Jocelyn anywhere if she was so like Annie, and from that she went on to explain that though the likeness would help her in this way, she would never have been taken in by it. I am not giving you her words, as she was very diffuse, but merely the gist of them. After she had spoken of seeing Lady Jocelyn's picture in the papers the man asked whether she would have known her from Annie, and she said no, not in the picture, but if she were to see either of them she would know. He said 'How?' and she said, 'Well, that's telling!' It was when she told me this that I became a little uneasy. It was not my business, but I could not help thinking that Miss Collins was unwise to have taken such a tone. Even in repeating what she had said, her intention to hint at special knowledge was quite unmistakable. I asked her how she could be sure that she would always know Annie Joyce from Lady Jocelyn—whether there was, for instance, any distinguishing mark which would certainly identify Miss Joyce. I said it seemed to me that the family was not immediately convinced that it was Lady Jocelyn who had returned to them, in which case any special knowledge possessed by Miss Collins might be very important.''

"You said that?"

"Yes, Frank. When I had done so, she began to talk in quite an excited manner. I am afraid, poor thing, that she was gratified and flattered at the idea that she was the repository of an important secret.''

"What did she say?"

"I will give you her own words as accurately as I can. She said, 'That's as good as what I told him. You couldn't take me in, I said, not if it was ever so.' Then she said the gentleman laughed very pleasantly and told her she was very positive, and she said of course she was, but she didn't tell him why. But she said to me that when you had had a child from five years old, and washed it and dressed it and done everything, well, it stood to reason you would know anything there was to know. I do not know how much more she would have said, because just then the train stopped and a crowd of people got in. We had no further conversation of a private nature, but she turned back on the platform and asked me to come and see her next time I was in Blackheath, and I gave her my name and address.''

Frank Abbott was watching her keenly.

"Yes—why did you do that?"

Miss Silver rested her hands upon her knitting.

"I thought that she had been indiscreet. I feared she might have conveyed a false impression. I considered it possible that she might find herself in a difficulty. I did not think that she knew anyone of whom she would willingly seek counsel—— I thought it possible that she might be in need of it. Something like that, Frank, but perhaps not quite so definite. It is difficult to avoid being wise when the event has declared itself.''

He was silent for quite a time. Then he said,

"It comes to this—Nellie Collins had, or pretended to have, some special information about Annie Joyce. If Annie Joyce is dead, this information wouldn't be of the slightest interest to anyone—unless the Jocelyns had any lingering doubts as to whether it really was Lady Jocelyn who survived, in which case they would be very glad of corroborative evidence, and grateful to Nellie. There's no possible motive for murder there. On the other hand, if it was Annie Joyce who survived, and Lady Jocelyn had been dead for three and a half years as her tombstone says, then the woman who took her place would have been playing for a pretty big stake—she would think that she had brought it off. And then up bobs Nellie Collins with her 'I washed her and I dressed her, and if there was anything to know about her, I'd know it, wouldn't I?' You don't want a much stronger motive than that."

Miss Silver said, "No."

"But it was a man who telephoned to make the appointment——"

"Yes—for Lady Jocelyn."

"You are quite sure Nellie Collins said that?"

"Quite sure, Frank."

He pushed back his chair and got up.

"Then it's a million to one that Lady Jocelyn has a completely unbreakable alibi!"

XX

ANNE JOCELYN opened the door of her flat. She looked with surprise at the two men who had been waiting for her to do so. She saw a ponderous middle-aged man who might have been a chapel pillar, and an elegant young one who might have been more at home in a drawing-room.

Introducing himself as Chief Detective Inspector Lamb, the older man crossed the threshold, briefly indicated his companion as Detective Sergeant Abbott, and remarked in a voice which had not quite lost its original country accent,

"Perhaps you would let us have a word with you, Lady Jocelyn."

There was a moment before she moved. The landing from which they came was almost dark, the hall of the flat lighted only from the half open sitting-room door. If she turned round, she would have to face the light. But she must turn round, or they would know that she was frightened. Frightened—how did any word express that sensation of everything having come to an end? She wrenched at her will, setting it to command her body, and it obeyed. There was really only the least possible pause before she led the way towards that half open door.

They came into a pleasant room. Light shining from the ceiling through a Lalique bowl. Another, in very heavy glass with a design of birds pecking at fruit, held a sheaf of tawny chrysanthemums. The drawn curtains were of honey-coloured brocade. They gave the light in the room a faintly golden tinge. All the colouring was in the range of shades between honey and russet.

Lady Jocelyn wore a blue dress and two rows of noticeable pearls. She said,

"You want to see me——" then broke off.

It was no good pretending. Anyone who wasn't a complete fool could see that she was frightened, and neither of these men were fools, not even the old one, with his heavy policeman's figure and his stolid, florid face. She made a disarming little gesture which old Lamb stigmatized as foreign.

"You will think me very stupid—but you frightened me so much. You know, I have been in France for more than three years under the Occupation, and when for three years the police have meant the Gestapo, it's not always easy——" She broke off again, and said with a smile, "My nerves played me a trick. What can I do for you? Won't you sit down?"

They sat. The light shone down on them. Frank Abbott's eye ran over her. Pretty woman—strung up—very quick off the mark with a cover-up, but might be quite genuine. *Ars est celare artem*—but if it was art, he took off his hat to it. There might, of course, be nothing to conceal. That the Gestapo could get on a girl's nerves in an occupied country needed no stressing.

Lamb had allowed the silence to settle. Now he said,

"I am sorry we startled you. I have reason to believe that you may be able to give us some assistance with regard to a case which we are investigating."

"A case? I—of course anything I can—but I don't know——"

Chief Inspector Detective Lamb proceeded as if she had not spoken. His eyes, which reminded his irreverent Sergeant so forcibly of bulls-eyes, were fixed upon her very much as if she had been a chair or a sofa. They showed no appreciation of the fact that she was young, charming, pretty, and Lady Jocelyn. He just looked at her. She might have been an old scrubwoman, a door-post, or a cat. He said in that robust country voice,

"The case was reported to us as a road death. The deceased has been identified by her lodger as Miss Nellie Collins of the Lady's Workbox, Blackheath Vale. Did you know her?"

Frank Abbott saw the natural colour sink away from the surface skin of Lady Jocelyn's face. It left two islands of rouge and the scarlet shape of a mouth painted on in lipstick. Before this happened the tinting had been so skilfully done that it was hard to say where nature ended and art began. Now not even art was left. The remaining colour stood up on the blanched skin like crude daubs upon a linen mask. With this evidence of shock before his eyes, he saw the throat muscles tighten. They held her voice steady for the single word she needed.

"No."

"You did not know Miss Collins?"

"No."

"Never heard of her?"

Frank Abbott looked quickly down at the hands in Anne Jocelyn's lap. Hands were the biggest give-away of the lot. He had seen so many women's hands tell what the face withheld. But Anne Jocelyn's hands told nothing at all. They neither clung the one to the other, nor were clenched each upon itself. They lay at ease in her lap—at ease, or under perfect control. They did not move at all till she said,

"Yes—she wrote to me."

Chief Inspector Lamb sat there like an image, with a hand on either knee. He had put down his bowler hat on a chest in the hall, but had merely unbuttoned his overcoat without removing it. His eyes never left her face, but remained expressionless. He might have been having his photograph taken—one of those stolid photographs in which the father of the family stares at the camera with a blank eye and a vacant mind. He said,

"Will you tell me why she did that?"

"She wanted to see me."

"What reason did she give for wanting to see you, Lady Jocelyn?"

She drew in a long, full breath. If she had had a shock, it was passing. Her colour was coming back. She said,

"I'm sorry—I'm being stupid—you did frighten me. It's all very simple really. I expect you will have seen in the papers that my family thought I was dead. Someone else was buried in my name—a woman called Annie Joyce. She was an illegitimate connection—as a matter of fact a first cousin—and we were very much alike. Miss Collins knew Annie when she was a little girl. She wrote and told me she had been fond of her, and asked if she could come and see me. She wanted to know all about her."

"I see. What reply did you make?"

"Well, I'm afraid I didn't answer the letter."

"You didn't answer it?"

"No. It really only came a few days ago, and I've been very busy over the move. We have only just got into this flat."

"When did you move, Lady Jocelyn?"

"Yesterday."

"Yesterday? And you were moving from——"

"Jocelyn's Holt—in Surrey. My husband is at the War Office. He found it took too much time going up and down."

"Yesterday——" Lamb dwelt on the word. "Then where were you during the afternoon?"

"I saw our things off from Jocelyn's Holt in the morning, and travelled up myself after an early lunch. I got to the flat about three, and spent the rest of the afternoon and evening getting things straight."

"Anyone with you?"

"I brought one of my maids up from Jocelyn's Holt. I'm not keeping her here because she's a young country girl, but she helped me yesterday and stayed the night. I sent her back this afternoon."

"Will you kindly give me her name and address?"

"Ivy Fossett. She's down at Jocelyn's Holt."

Frank Abbott had been writing down these questions and answers. He wrote down Ivy's name.

Lamb went on,

"Did you leave the flat at all after you arrived at—what time did you say?"

"It was ten minutes to three. No, I didn't go out again."

"You didn't go to Waterloo station to keep an appointment with Miss Collins?"

"No, of course I didn't—I hadn't any appointment with her. I didn't go out at all."

"Can anyone beside Ivy Fossett corroborate that?"

Anne Jocelyn's colour had risen. She had a puzzled look.

"I don't know what you mean. My cousin, Mrs. Perry Jocelyn, came in just before three. She stayed to tea and helped me to unpack."

"How long did she stay?"

"Till just before seven."

"May I have her address please?"

Abbott wrote it down.

Anne Jocelyn threw out her hands in a sudden gesture.

"Why are you asking me all these questions? What does it matter whether I went out or not? I hadn't any appointment with Miss Collins, but why should it have mattered if I had?"

Lamb just went on looking at her.

"Miss Collins was under the impression that she had an appointment with you under the clock at Waterloo at a quarter to four yesterday afternoon."

"But that's nonsense——"

"She came up from Blackheath to keep that appointment, Lady Jocelyn."

"But she couldn't—I wasn't there. I was here, in this flat, unpacking. I never even wrote to her. How could she have an appointment with me?"

"There are other ways of making an appointment except through the post. There is the telephone, Lady Jocelyn. Miss Collins put her telephone number at the head of the letter she wrote you, didn't she?"

"I don't know—she may have done—I really didn't notice."

"May I see that letter?"

"Well—I'm afraid I didn't keep it."

Still no expression on his face.

"You didn't keep it. But you hadn't answered it—had you?"

There was another of those gestures, slight, graceful, just a little foreign.

"Well, she had a shop, you know. I remembered the name —I could have written later. To tell you the truth, I wasn't at all sure that I wanted to write. There really was nothing that I could tell her about Annie. The whole Joyce connection was —distasteful. And I thought Miss Collins was perhaps—well, a sensation-hunter. If you knew the letters we have had from people who didn't know us at all!"

"So you destroyed the letter. Can you remember the contents?"

"I think so. It was rather a rigmarole—all about how fond she had been of Annie, and could she come and see me, because she wanted to hear all about her sad death—that sort of thing."

"Did the letter suggest any special knowledge about Annie Joyce?"

"I don't know what you mean."

"Did it suggest that the writer would be able to identify Annie Joyce?"

She let her eyes meet his for a moment, cold under the raised brows.

"No—of course not. What an extraordinary thing to say! How could she identify Annie Joyce? She is dead."

Lamb said, "Do you mean that Annie Joyce is dead? Or do you mean that Nellie Collins, who might have identified her, is dead?"

She caught her breath.

"Why do you say that?"

"Because I would like to know, Lady Jocelyn."

She said, her voice lower than it had been at all,

"Annie Joyce is dead."

Lamb said gravely,

"And so is Nellie Collins."

XXI

"I TOLD you she would have a cast-iron alibi."

Frank Abbott sat back in his chair and waited for Miss Silver's reaction. It was hardly noticeable. She had begun Johnny's second stocking and almost finished the ribbing at the top. Her needles did not check, nor did her expression change as she replied,

"You are naturally in a hurry to let me know that you were perfectly right."

He spread out his hands with a laughing gesture.

"Revered preceptress!"

Miss Silver permitted a very faint smile to relax her lips.

"When you have finished talking nonsense, Frank, perhaps you will go on telling me about Lady Jocelyn. It is all very interesting."

"Well, when we came away from the flat the Chief asked me what I made of her. He has a way of doing that, and when you've told him he doesn't utter. He may think it's tripe, or he may think it's the cat's whiskers, but he won't let on—just sticks it away behind that poker face and takes the next opportunity of snubbing you good and hard. I've got an idea that the snub is in inverse ratio to the value he sets on your opinion—in fact the bigger the snub, the bigger the compliment. I got Remarks from a Superior Officer to a Subordinate on the Dangers of Swollen Head, all the way down the stairs."

Miss Silver coughed.

"And pray, what did you make of Lady Jocelyn?"

"Ah—now that is very interesting. I think the Chief thought so too—hence the homily. She opened the door to us herself, and if we'd been Gestapo with death-warrants spilling out of all our pockets, she couldn't have been more taken aback."

Miss Silver coughed again.

"She has, after all, been living under the Gestapo for more than three years."

"So she took occasion to remind us. Grasped the nettle with great firmness and presence of mind, said we'd frightened her dreadfully, and led the way to the drawing-room, where she very nearly passed out when the Chief mentioned that we'd come to ask questions about Miss Nellie Collins, who was dead. I don't think I've ever seen anyone come so near fainting and not do it. And the only reason she didn't do it was because she wouldn't. She made the sort of effort that is painful to watch—it was like seeing a steel spring being coiled up. And she pulled it off. But the really extraordinary thing was the isolation and concentration of the effort—the throat muscles were perfectly tense, but the hands lying in her lap remained quite lax. Odd, you know, and pointing to great powers of control. Only what was it all about? She was horribly frightened when she first saw us, but she was pulling out of that. Then the Chief told her Nellie Collins was dead, and it very nearly knocked her out. I'll swear she didn't know it till he told her, and it came as a quite terrific shock. Why? She was frightened before she knew that Nellie Collins was dead—horribly frightened. She hears of the death and nearly faints. I want to know why. If she hadn't any guilty knowledge, why the initial fright? If she had, why the subsequent shock? What does it matter to her that Nellie Collins should be a road casualty? What's Hecuba to her, or she to Hecuba?"

Miss Silver gazed at him silently.

"Annie Joyce might have two excellent reasons for shock. Relief, the effects of which are often quite overwhelming, or affection—she may have been really fond of Nellie Collins."

He said, "Annie Joyce——"

The needles clocked.

"Certainly, my dear Frank. Abnormal interest in Nellie Collins suggests very strongly that it was Annie Joyce who survived, and not Anne Jocelyn. Lady Jocelyn would have no reason to be afraid of any special knowledge which Miss Collins might possess. Annie Joyce impersonating Lady Jocelyn would have every reason to fear it. I can think of no possible reason why Nellie Collins' death on the road should inflict any shock upon Lady Jocelyn. The news of it would be no more to her than the death of a person just heard of but never encountered. Such things happen every day, and are dismissed with a casual expression of sympathy. We say, 'How sad!' and do not think of the incident again. If the death of Nellie Collins inflicted so severe a shock as you have described, I am forced to the conclusion that this shock was inflicted upon Annie Joyce."

He looked at her keenly. The basis of their relation was the fact that each admired and stimulated the other. In her presence all the mental processes were quickened and intensified, thoughts stood out sharply. He said,

"If that is so, your second reason doesn't apply, I'm afraid. She certainly wasn't shocked at Nellie Collins' death because she was fond of her. That stuck out about a mile—it's the sort of thing you can't miss. The Chief went on talking about her, and there wasn't a trace of affection in Lady Jocelyn's replies. Of course if she is Annie Joyce, she wouldn't be wanting to show any particular feeling, but if there had been anything there, I think I'd have got it. All I did get was—well, it isn't easy to put it into words, but indifference comes near—genuine indifference to Nellie Collins as a person, combined with knock-out shock on hearing of her death. Now just how do those two things combine? They were there—I'll swear to that."

Miss Silver nodded gently.

"Yes—that is very interesting,"she said. "Assuming that Lady Jocelyn is Annie Joyce, the logical deduction would be that she considered herself to be threatened by Nellie Collins. I told you that I feared the poor thing might have laid herself open to misconstruction. Certainly her conversation on the telephone with the unknown man who represented himself as acting for Lady Jocelyn may have given him reason to fear an attempt at blackmail. There is nothing more dangerous than the attempt of an amateur to blackmail an experienced criminal. I am quite sure that Miss Collins had no such intention, but I fear she gave the impression—the very strong impression— that her continued existence would be dangerous. I must direct your attention to this unknown man. It is clear that he knew of Miss Collins' letter to Lady Jocelyn—she probably handed it on to him. This would explain the behaviour which puzzles you. Still assuming that she is Annie Joyce, the appearance of the police would naturally be very alarming. When to this general alarm there is added the sudden intelligence that Nellie Collins has been murdered—and in the circumstances there could be no doubt that it was murder—the shock would naturally be very great. It is quite possible, in fact extremely probable, that she did not know what was intended. She may have thought that Nellie Collins was to be dealt with in some other way—dissuaded from coming to see her, convinced that she had nothing to gain, discouraged in any attempt to pursue an unprofitable connection. The shock of finding herself involved in a murder might well produce the effect which you described so vividly."

He nodded.

"Yes—it might be like that. I think it's clear that she wasn't in at the death, so to speak."

Miss Silver primmed her mouth.

"A distasteful metaphor, Frank."

"Apologies—you know what I mean. The girl at Jocelyn's Holt, Ivy What's-her-name, says she came up to town with Lady Jocelyn and was never out of sight or sound of her for more than a minute or two until they all went to bed just short of eleven. All the doors of the flat were open, and they were going to and fro from one room to the other, unpacking and arranging things. Mrs. Perry Jocelyn arrived just before three, and they all three carried on. She stayed till seven o'clock, when Lady Jocelyn went into the kitchen and began to prepare the evening meal. Ivy says she's a lovely cook, but I think she considered it a bit *infra dig*. Sir Philip got in at half-past seven. After dinner he was working in the study, and Ivy and Lady Jocelyn went on clearing up. Mrs. Perry Jocelyn corroborates—says she was there from just before four until just after seven. She and Ivy both say that Lady Jocelyn never left the flat. Well, as far as active participation in the crime is concerned that washes her out. She is accounted for right through the afternoon and evening and up to just before eleven at night, when the three people in the flat went to bed. The medical evidence comes down heavily on Nellie Collins having been dead well before then. As First Murderer, Lady Jocelyn, or if you prefer it Annie Joyce, is out of it. But of course it's too easy—the First Murderer is undoubtedly the agreeable gentleman who Miss Collins hoped was a baronet. We have only to find him."

Miss Silver's small nondescript eyes met his with an unexpected spark of humour.

"Are you by any chance thinking about a needle and a bundle of hay?"

He laughed.

"Make it a whole hay-harvest and have done with it! The Chief has put me on to follow up anything I can find. So far all we've got to go on is, first, Miss Collins' description of a very pleasant gentleman, and her supposition that he might be Philip Jocelyn, which of course he wasn't. Now you talked to her, and I didn't. Would it be safe to assume that this means the fellow was what is called a gentleman? I mean, do you think she would know?"

"I should be inclined to think so."

"Because, you see, that would be a clue—cultured murderer with an agreeable telephone manner. Secondly—and here we are on firmer ground—he is someone who knows Ruislip and its surroundings pretty well. You know, I don't think she was killed there. I think she was taken there afterwards, and I'll tell you why. The lane where she was found is just about the most likely place for a body to lie undiscovered for the whole black-out period. And then take another look at this."

He produced the triangular scrap of paper torn from the half sheet upon which Miss Silver had written her name and address for Nellie Collins. One below the other, coming in from the jagged edge, stood the syllables -ver; -sions; -ham St., the second of these being so badly smudged as to be almost illegible.

Miss Silver looked at the smudge.

"That has been worrying me," she said. "How did it happen!"

"I think it was done on purpose. Smeared probably with a damp handkerchief. There weren't any finger-prints. You know, we both thought this corner had got caught on the broken glass and left behind that way. But now I don't think so—I think that's what we were meant to think. Actually, I'm pretty sure it was deliberate. Because there's a Cunningham Street in Ruislip, and a Miss Oliver who lives there in a house called Soissons. Now do you see why somebody smudged the torn-off part of your *Mansions*? The local police were feeling very clever, and quite sure they had linked up the torn address with poor Miss Oliver, who is an eminently respectable spinster and so much upset at the idea that she might have to identify a body or attend an inquest that she probably presented a most convincing picture of guilt. The poor lady assured me in a quavering voice that she had never heard of Nellie Collins in her life. I quite believe her, but if I hadn't recognized your writing, and you hadn't recognized this scrap of paper, we should have had a very nice red herring trailed across the path. And poor Miss Oliver might have had to face that inquest."

Miss Silver coughed and said, "Just so. There is a clever mind behind all this, Frank."

He nodded.

"Well, our cultured gentleman knows Ruislip pretty well. Of course he may have sat down with a directory and just gone on looking till he found something to fit in with your scrap of paper, but I don't somehow think so. It would have taken too long, it wouldn't have been worth while. I think he just had a brain-wave, remembered Miss Oliver, and chucked her in to keep things humming. It's got a spur-of-the-moment smell about it."

Miss Silver agreed. He went on.

"Well, culture and Ruislip—neither of them very hot scent.

And then there's Lady Jocelyn. There must be a connection there if we can find it."

Miss Silver coughed.

"The connection would be, I think, with Annie Joyce."

Frank ran a hand over his shining hair.

"Who left England more than ten years ago, and whose associations and dossier since then are submerged in occupied France. What a hope!"

XXII

It was next day that Lyndall went round to see Anne Jocelyn. Impossible to stay away. Impossible to remain aloof when Lilla, who hadn't even known Anne before, had spent hours helping her to unpack and get things straight. Even if there wasn't anything left to do, she who had been Anne's bridesmaid must at least go round and see her. Her feet carried her reluctantly. If it hadn't been that she was expected, she might even then have been tempted to turn back. No, that was nonsense. She wouldn't listen to thoughts like that, she certainly wouldn't let them influence her. But her feet dragged, and her heart dragged too.

It was very cold in the street. Low clouds looked as if they might come down in snow at any moment. A freakish wind lay in wait at every corner, stinging her face, her knees, her legs in their thin silk stockings, trying to twist the hat from her head. She had no distance to go, but she was tired before she reached Tenterden Gardens.

It ought to have been pleasant to pass into the warmth and golden light of Anne's drawing-room, but something in her looked back to the icy street. Anne came to meet her, smiling, and they kissed. That is, Anne offered a cool cheek, and Lyndall touched it with cold lips. As she did so, an aching shudder went through her. Up to that moment her love for Anne had been in her heart as something real and treasured, even if there was pain there too. Now quite suddenly, with that faint touch of her lips, the place was empty—there was nothing there any more. She did not know how pale she was as she drew back, or how wide and startled a look met Anne's enquiring one.

"What's the matter, Lyn? You look frozen. Come to the fire and get warm. Tea is all ready. I'll just get the kettle."

When she came back, Lyndall had taken off her gloves. She was bending over the fire, her hands held to the blaze. An extraordinary feeling of unreality filled her consciousness. The pleasant room, the warmth, the flowers in their Lalique bowl, the familiar tea-things—Queen Anne silver and bright flowered cups bordered with gold and apple-green—Anne in her blue dress and her pearls with Philip's sapphire on her hand—all were apart from her in some bright vacuum. Nothing came to her from them, nothing passed to them from her.

She turned round slowly from the fire, drank the tea which Anne gave her, and crumbled a piece of cake. And then quite suddenly the feeling passed. She was warm again, and she was right here in the room, with the firelight reaching her and Anne pouring her out a second cup of tea. It was like waking up out of a nightmare, but she could hardly trust her own relief. She sipped the tea and listened to Anne telling her how quickly they had settled down.

Presently she said what she had come to say. She hadn't been sure that she would be able to say it, but she knew that it must be said. Because if it wasn't, she would never be able to get it out of her mind again, and that sort of thing poisoned you if you kept it shut up amongst your thoughts—it poisoned everything.

She put down her cup on the edge of the silver tray and said simply and directly,

"Where do you have your hair done, Anne?"

Anne Jocelyn looked just a little surprised.

"I had a permanent wave at Westhaven after I landed. I thought I told you. They didn't do it at all badly. Of course I really ought not to have it waved, because it spoils the natural curl, and my hair used to curl naturally, but it's been terribly neglected, and I don't like going about looking a complete mess whilst I'm waiting for it to come back."

Lyndall had let go of her cup, but she kept her hand on the edge of the silver tray. A finger moved there, tracing the pattern.

"But where do you go in town?"

"Why? Have you got someone to recommend?"

"No—I just wondered. Do you know a shop called Félise?"

There—she had got it said! Nothing is so difficult as the

109

first step. When you have taken that the others follow. But she couldn't look at Anne. She looked down at the edge of the silver tray. A drop of tea had fallen there and dried. There had been time for it to fall, and time for it to dry. It wasn't true that everything was standing still. The drop of tea had dried. It made a small brown stain on the bright surface of the silver.

Anne said, "I don't know—I seem to have seen the name. Why?"

"I happened to pass it. I thought I saw you go in. It was the Wednesday of last week."

"Well, I may have done—I don't know. I go into all those shops. I haven't got a powder I like yet, or the right lipstick or anything. It's all so difficult—isn't it?"

Lyndall lifted her eyes. They didn't really see very much, because there was a mist in front of them, but to Anne Jocelyn their grieving look accused her.

"Anne, I must tell you—I think I must——"

Anne's delicately arched eyebrows rose. She said sweetly, "What is all this about, darling?"

The sweetness was like saccharine, it cloyed and left a bitter taste. Anne was angry. But Lyndall couldn't look away, and she couldn't stop now. Something drove her on. She said,

"I thought I saw you go into the shop, and I went in after you. I didn't want you to think I had seen you and just gone on, so I came into the shop——"

Anne looked at her with the bright eyes of anger.

"And I suppose we met and had a long conversation—in this dream of yours!"

"No—you weren't there."

"How very surprising!"

"I went right through the shop. There were two women there. The assistant was looking for something on a shelf behind the counter. No one took any notice of me. I thought you might be in one of the cubicles, so I went through. There was another door at the end. I opened it, I don't know why. There was a bit of dark passage with a stair going up, and more doors. One of them had a little light at the edge—it wasn't quite shut. I heard you say, 'You might as well let me write to Nellie Collins. She's quite harmless.' And a man said, 'That isn't for you to say.' And I turned round and ran back through the shop."

110

Anne's face was bleak. Lyndall would have liked to look away, but she couldn't. Anne's eyes held hers—scornful, rejecting not only what she had said, but herself—putting her amongst foolish, negligible things.

"Really, Lyn! What a story! Do you expect me to believe it?"

Lyndall said nothing. Her eyes were steadfast as well as grieving.

Anne laughed and said, "Go on! I'm sure there must be something more. Another thrilling instalment in our next! What happened after that?"

"I went home."

"Rather an anti-climax."

"I wasn't sure about its being you. I hadn't ever heard about Nellie Collins—then."

"Nellie Collins?"

"Yes. I didn't know the name when I heard it in the shop, but it's in the paper today, because she is dead. Did you know that she was dead? "

"Lyndall—what do you mean?"

"It says in the paper that she was coming up to meet some-one under the clock at Waterloo station at a quarter to four on Monday. They give a description, and they say the police would like to hear from anyone who saw her or noticed who she met. She was found dead in a lane near Ruislip early next morning, and they want to know how she got there, because it was right out of her way. She had come up from Blackheath. She was expecting to meet you—wasn't she?"

Anne's face was as tight and hard as a bolted door. She said, "You made that up—it wasn't in the paper. How could I have met her? I was here with Lilla."

"Yes, you were here with Lilla. But she was expecting to meet you. You see, I met someone who travelled up in the train with her. She talked to her, and told her she was going to meet you. It was a friend of Janice Albany. I met her there at tea that afternoon. She asked me where I was staying, and as soon as I mentioned Lilla's name she said that was curious, because she had just come up from Blackheath in the train with a Miss Collins who was meeting Lady Jocelyn, and would she be any relation? So I said yes, but I thought there must be some mistake, because you were moving into your flat and Lilla was helping you, so I didn't see how you could be meeting anyone at Waterloo. And she said, 'Miss Collins was certainly expecting to meet Lady Jocelyn—under the clock at Waterloo, at a quarter to four'."

Anne's face remained locked, but the lips smiled. They were bright with lipstick that might have been the very colour of anger. They made Lyndall feel herself despised. They said,

"What a rigmarole! What is it all supposed to mean?"

"I don't know."

She had said what she had come to say. It horrified her. Things were worse when you had said them—they took shape. She had thought she would be able to get rid of them. No, not thought—that was too definite. She had had a frightened, clinging hope that Anne would say or do something that would make everything all right again. She did not know what Anne was to say or do. The little trembling hope let go and faded out.

Anne pushed back her chair and got up. She went quietly over to the fire and kneeled down in front of it, putting on one or two pieces of coal in a careful, deliberate way. Then without getting up she turned and spoke to Lyndall.

"You say you don't know what you mean. I am sure I don't. So it's rather difficult—isn't it? I don't quite know what to say about it. We have had a good deal of publicity lately—I shouldn't have thought you'd have wanted to bring any more of it down on us. You used to say that you were fond of me, and"—she gave a little laugh—"anyone can see you are fond of Philip. May I ask you why you want to spread a damaging story about us? I should really like to know."

Lyndall had turned too. The fire leapt brightly behind Anne's shoulder. Something in Anne's eyes burned like the fire, bright, and hot, and hurting. She said,

"I haven't spread any story. I haven't spoken of it to anyone but you."

"Well, that's something. Because, you see, you really might do a great deal of harm—to Philip. To put it frankly, we can't afford to be in the papers any more at present. Philip is ambitious—I expect you know that. He's got the sort of job they only give to a rising man, and the wrong sort of publicity would be very damaging for him. Now I'm going to tell you all there is to tell, and trust to your friendship and common sense not to go on making mountains out of molehills. Nellie Collins knew the Joyces—I believe they lodged with her.

About a week or ten days ago I had a letter from her. She had been reading all the stuff in the papers, and she said now that she realized Annie was dead, could she come up and see me, because she would like to hear all about her last moments. I thought it was all very tiresome and morbid, and I had my hands full with the move, so I didn't answer the letter. I don't even know what happened to it. The police wanted to see it, but I couldn't find it for them."

"The police——"

The anger was gone from Anne. She looked frankly at Lyndall.

"Yes. Miss Collins seems to have talked about coming up to see me. Wishful thinking, I should say. I certainly never invited her. But she seems to have talked, and there it is. Why she went to Ruislip and how she got herself run over, I've naturally no idea. As for your story of overhearing a conversation about her in a hairdresser's shop—well really, darling, if you don't mind my saying so, it sounds completely mad. Of course Collins is a very common name. You might have heard it anywhere—I suppose you might have heard it at your hairdresser's. But why you should fasten this crazy conversation on to me—come, Lyn, are you prepared to swear you saw me?"

"No—I thought it was you——"

"And you thought you heard me speak. Is that a thing you would swear to—a voice through a shut door? Are you sure it was my voice, Lyn?"

Lyndall said steadily,

"No, I'm not sure. I thought it was your voice."

Anne said, "Because you thought you had seen me go in?"

"Perhaps."

Anne laughed quite good-humouredly.

"Well, darling, there doesn't seem to be much left of your story, does there? I think I'd keep quiet about it if I were you. If you'll forgive my saying so, you don't come out of it any too well. I'm sure you didn't mean it that way, but there's a sort of spying sound about it——" She put out a hand. "No, that's horrid of me. I didn't mean it. But—honestly, Lyn, I *don't* want Philip to have any more bothers just now."

Lyndall said nothing at all. When Anne spoke of Philip like that, the very quick of her heart was bruised. She had nothing to say in words. Her eyes spoke for her.

It appeared that Anne was answered. She got up with one of her graceful movements and stood there smiling.

"Well, we'll leave it at that. I think we've been getting a little intense. It's just that Philip and I do hate all this publicity, and it would be too tiresome to have it starting all over again just when we hoped it was dying down. So you won't mind my asking you not to go round telling people that you thought you heard me talking about poor Miss Collins in the back of a hairdresser's shop."

"I haven't told anyone but you. I think it was silly of me to tell you. I won't tell anyone else."

As she spoke she felt again the cold breath of fear which had sent her running away from the little dark passage behind the mirror door. She had promised never to speak about that. She must try never to remember it. She did not know that she was to break her promise, and to try with all her might to remember every detail of what had happened in Félise's shop. She did not know what circumstances would compel her to this. But if she had known, she would hardly have been more afraid than she was.

Anne came past her and sat down behind the tray with its pale gleaming silver and its flowery cups. Her cheeks were pink, and she was smiling. She said,

"Have another cup of tea, darling."

XXIII

PHILIP JOCELYN came home early that evening. As he let himself in with his key he could hear Anne at the telephone. He stood for a moment, listening not so much to what she was saying as to her voice, wondering as he always did when he allowed himself to think, why it should be Anne's voice as he remembered it and yet a stranger's, just as Anne was herself a stranger. He had no thought of overhearing a private conversation. She appeared to be making an appointment to have her hair done. He heard her say, "Is that Félise?" . . . "This is Lady Jocelyn speaking. I want an appointment with Mr. Felix. He isn't there, I suppose? . . . No? Well, will you tell him I don't think the treatment he prescribed is suiting my hair at all. I am very upset about it—will you tell him that? I want to see him as soon as possible. Tell him I can't go on with the treatment and he must change it. I can come tomorrow afternoon—that's one of his days, isn't it? Will you get into touch with him and find out what time he can see me, and then ring me up and let me know? I shall be in all the evening."

She hung up the receiver and turned from the study table to see Philip in the doorway.

"I didn't hear you come in."

He said, "You had your head in the telephone."

"I was just making an appointment about my hair."

She had gone over to the window and was straightening the curtains there.

"So I heard. What endless time women spend having their hair done."

She came back to the table, half smiling.

"Mine has got into such a bad way—I do want to get it right again. This man is said to be very good, but the stuff he gave me to rub in isn't suiting me at all."

"Then I shouldn't use it."

"I've just been making an appointment to tell him he must give me something else. Why are you home so early?"

He had come up to the table and set an attaché case on it.

"I've got something I can work on here. I shall probably be late."

"What time would you like dinner?"

"Oh, the usual. I'd like some coffee in here afterwards if it wouldn't be a trouble."

"Of course it wouldn't." She smiled at him again and went out of the room.

He found himself thinking, "Domestic scene between any husband and wife—any charming, affectionate wife." She didn't let it become obtrusive, but he was constantly aware that Anne was presenting herself in this light. The flat was beautifully run, water always hot, meals punctual to the moment and beautifully cooked. A smile and a pleasant word for him whenever a smile and a word were called for. He hadn't seen her out of temper or out of humour yet. The girl he had married had none of this efficiency and tact. If she didn't like anything she said so. If he had wanted to work late into the night, leaving her to sit alone, it would have been, "Oh, Philip, what a bore!" He opened his despatch-case and began to get out his papers. On every possible count Anne had gained, and so had he. Only it didn't feel like it. Most ungratefully, he didn't feel like it. He felt rather like Ben Jonson when he wrote:

> "Still to be neat, still to be drest,
> As you were going to a feast;
> Still to be powdered, still perfumed:
> Lady, it is to be presumed,
> Though art's hid causes are not found,
> All is not sweet, all is not sound."

His lip twisted as he sat down to the table.

The telephone bell rang whilst they were having dinner. Anne went to it, leaving the door open. He heard her from across the passage say, "Yes, that will be all right."

She came back and shut the door.

"Just to confirm my appointment. He's a specialist—he doesn't live in."

His mind on the work which he had left, he hardly noticed what she said.

It was later in the meal that he remembered he had something to tell her.

"I ran into a friend of yours at lunch-time."

"Oh, did you? Who was it?"

"Girl who was your bridesmaid—the lumpy one—Joan Tallent. She's in the A.T.S. Very buxom, but better looking than she used to be. She wants to come and see you."

"When?"

He laughed.

"You don't seem over-joyed."

"Well, I'm not. She was rather a tiresome girl."

"Why did you have her for a bridesmaid?"

"Oh, I don't know. I used to see a lot of her when I was with Aunt Jane—she was some sort of fiftieth cousin of the Kendals. I'm sure she'll bore me horribly now."

"Well, you'll have to bear it. She's as keen as mustard."

Anne looked resigned.

"When is she coming?"

"She did say something about tonight, and I'm afraid I rather encouraged her. I thought you could have coffee and a heart-to-heart whilst I was working. It's very dull for you."

She shook her head, smiling.

"Oh, no—after the last three years it's heaven. I don't feel dull—I feel safe."

For the first time, something she said touched him. He had been sorry for her before, but at a distance, like hearing about a famine in China. Now all at once something in her voice when she said " safe" brought her much nearer. He thought, "She's had a hell of a time." He said aloud,

"You'd better wait and see if she turns up. I don't mind when I have my coffee."

The front door bell buzzed just as Anne finished washing up. Rather to her surprise, Philip had not vanished into the study. He did not vanish now. Before she could reach the door herself he was opening it and ushering in the guest.

Joan Tallent was certainly buxom. She filled her khaki uniform to capacity. Under the peaked cap her cheeks were as hard and red as apples. She said in a hearty, ringing voice,

"Well, Anne, it's a long time since we met. I expect I've changed more than you have. It's the uniform. Of course I'm lucky—I've got a good colour. Girls who haven't look grim in khaki. Don't you think I'm thinner? Of course one doesn't want to get too thin, but I've still got some way to go." She laughed a hearty laugh. Then, as they came into the lighted drawing-room, she fixed a round blue stare on Anne. "I say, you're not slimming or anything, are you? You've got much thinner."

"I've been in occupied France. One doesn't have to slim there."

The blue stare was turned on Philip.

"You ought to make her drink cocoa—that's the stuff for putting on. I adore it, but I simply daren't. We've got a corporal who drinks it all the time. She's had her uniform let out three times, and now there's no more stuff. We're having bets on whether they'll put a bit in next time or give her a new uniform."

Philip had draped himself against the mantelpiece. He showed no sign of going to the study. As Anne went to fetch the coffee she heard him say in a languid voice,

"She might sign the pledge and go off cocoa for the duration."

When she came back Joan was still talking about food. "You simply can't eat it all," she said with the earnest expression of one who has tried.

When she saw Anne she sprang up brightly and very nearly upset the coffee-tray in an effort to be helpful. And whether she was stumbling over a footstool, dragging a chair forward which jerked and rucked the carpet, or balancing a coffee-cup on a precarious knee, she never stopped talking. The old days—the wedding—"You looked marvellous, Anne." The bridesmaids' dresses—"Mine was too tight—I couldn't eat any lunch. Wouldn't it have been awful if it had unzipped in church? And of course white is frightfully enlarging. I don't know that it really suited any of us. You know Diana's in the Middle East. And Sylvia's married—two babies, and she can't get any household help. And that little thing—what was her name—Lyn Something or other—I believe she's in the Wrens. She had a frightful crush on you, hadn't she? Wasn't she frightfully pleased when you turned up again?"

Still in that languid voice, Philip said,

"She was."

With all her heart Anne wished that he would go, but he remained just where he was, incredibly tall, fair, and aloof, his coffee-cup at his elbow only occasionally sipped from, a cigarette between his fingers which he hardly smoked.

Joan Tallent had a cigarette too. She smoked, as she talked, in hearty jerks. She went on talking about Lyndall until Anne could have boxed her ears. But she had learned to conceal her thoughts. She sat there smiling and pleasant. Philip could change the subject if he wished to. She wouldn't do it for him, or let him see she cared who spoke of Lyndall, or what was said.

"She wasn't exactly pretty, but there was something about her, don't you think?"

This time Philip had nothing to say. He came over and filled his cup with black coffee. As he stood there, Joan swung round in her chair to face them both, grabbed at her cup just in time to save it, and said,

"I'll have some more too. Do you still keep your diary, Anne?"

Reaching for the cup, Anne smiled and shook her head. Joan craned up at Philip with the coffee-pot in his hand.

"Does she show it to you?" She giggled. "It was the most marvellous diary. We used to rag her about it. She used to put down simply everything." She turned to Anne. "Did you stop doing it when you married?"

Another smiling shake of the head.

"I stopped when I got to France. It would have been too dangerous there. Imagine what would have happened if one had said what one really thought about the Germans!"

She took the coffee-pot from Philip and began to fill Joan's cup. He picked up his own and went back to the fire. He said,

"Does one put that sort of thing in a diary? I keep one, but it doesn't run to anything more compromising than 'Lunch—Smith—1.30.'"

Joan gave a loud giggle.

"Anne's wasn't a bit like that. I read a piece once, and she nearly killed me. She put down simply everything—I mean, the sort of things you wouldn't think anyone would—like that old what's-his-name Pepys, only of course I don't mean to say the same sort of things, because his was all about having affairs with women. Anne's wasn't like that, only she just put down everything, the same as he did."

Anne was still smiling. She said smoothly,

"Rather taking my character away, aren't you, Joan?"

And with that her look crossed Philip's. The two pairs of grey eyes, so much alike, glanced together, and glanced away. There was just a moment, then Philip drained his cup and came over to set it down on the tray.

"Well, I must go and work," he said.

XXIV

GARTH ALBANY came into Philip's room at the War Office next morning. He raised an eyebrow at the girl clerk, and Philip sent her away. Garth, having been somewhat against his will absorbed into Military Intelligence, might very easily wish to dispense with even the most confidential clerk.

But when they were alone Garth still stood there on the far side of the desk. He had picked up a piece of red sealing-wax and was looking down at it with frowning intensity.

Philip sat back in his chair.

"Anything wrong with my sealing-wax?"

Garth put it down in a hurry.

"No. Look here, Philip, I've come on a damned awkward errand, and I don't know where to begin—that's the truth of it."

Philip's eyebrows rose slightly.

"First rules of composition," he murmured—"you begin at the beginning, proceed to the middle, and continue to the end. Don't you think you'd better begin?"

Garth looked darkly at him.

"It's damned awkward," he said. He pulled up a chair and sat down, leaning forward with his elbows on the table. "The fact is they've sent me along because of the family connection, and our being friends and all that."

Without any change of expression Philip said,

"I suppose it's something about Anne."

Garth registered relief. Once you got the ice broken you could say anything. He hadn't relished the job of breaking it. He knew Philip's obstinate pride. What neither he nor anyone else would ever know for certain was just how much of it stirred and stood on guard under that easy, languid manner. He would have liked to know, but he didn't.

Philip said, "Well?" and he had to start out in the dark. He said abruptly.

"They're not satisfied. It's this business of your having thought she was dead, and then her turning up after all this time. The D.M.I. wants to see you about it. I'm just an advance delegation, so to speak. The fact is, it's a beastly job and they've shoved it on to me."

"Go on."

"Well, as you know, there's a certain amount of coming and going across the Channel. Someone was told off to make enquiries, and we've had a report."

"Yes?"

"It says what you know already, that Theresa Jocelyn was living at the Château de Mornac with her adopted daughter, Miss Joyce. Anne came to stay in April '40, and in June you ran over in a motor-launch and tried to get her away. You did get someone away, but she died in the boat. She was buried as Anne. That's not in the report, it's just common knowledge. Now we get back to the report again. It says Theresa Jocelyn had been buried about a week when you came over and took Anne away. Annie Joyce remained at the Château. She was said to be ill. The two old servants, Pierre and Marie, looked after her. The Germans were in the village. They sent a doctor up to see her."

"Yes, I knew all that. I suppose you've heard Anne's story.

She says she went back to the Château and called herself Annie Joyce. She says she had pneumonia. Afterwards, when she was well again, she was sent to a concentration camp."

Garth looked unhappy.

"I'm afraid there's more to it than that—according to the report. It says Annie Joyce got well very quickly. The German doctor continued to visit the Château, and so did Captain Reichenau. They seemed to be on very friendly terms with Annie Joyce. Presently the doctor was transferred. Captain Reichenau continued his visits. There was naturally a good deal of talk in the village. A few months later Reichenau disappeared from the scene. Some time after that Annie Joyce was sent to a concentration camp, but a couple of months later she was back at the Chateau. She said they had let her out because she was ill. She was certainly thin, but she did not seem like a person who has been ill, and she was in very good spirits. She told Pierre and Marie that she wouldn't be with them for very much longer—she was going to England. There was some delay, but in the end she got off."

"Is that all?"

"There's one thing more. After her return from the concentration camp the Germans left her alone. There were no visits, no contacts."

Philip said very coolly, "You'd have damned her if there had been contacts. Are you going to damn her because there weren't any?"

"No—no, of course not. Philip, are you absolutely sure she is Anne? No, wait a minute—you weren't sure, were you? Things get round the family, you know. Inez Jocelyn talked. You weren't sure—were you?"

Garth appeared to be incapable of speech. He stared. Philip went on.

"I was as sure of it as you can be of anything. She was utterly strange to me. I couldn't believe that she had ever been my wife. She looked like Anne, she spoke like Anne, she wrote like Anne, and still I didn't believe that she was Anne. And then it was forced on me—against the grain, against my instincts, against my feelings—because she knew things which I thought only Anne and I could know." He got up and walked away across the room. There was a slight pause, then he turned round and said, "That's what I thought—until last night."

"What happened last night?"

"A girl came in. She'd been one of Anne's bridesmaids. She giggled and she prattled, and in the course of the giggling and prattling she came out with some very illuminating remarks about a diary. It appears that Anne kept one after the model of the late Mr. Pepys, in which, as Joan had it, she put down 'every single thing, even the sort you wouldn't think anyone would,' with a lot more to the same effect. Anne was not at all keen on discussing the diary. No reason why she should be, of course, but she wasn't. In fact abnormally restrained. I'd like to have a look at that diary, Garth. I'd like to see whether Anne wrote down in it the things which I found so convincing—the things that only Anne and I could know. Because if she did, and if Annie Joyce got her hands on the book, then my instinct was right, and all my reasons for accepting this woman as Anne, well, they go by the board."

Garth had turned round in his chair. He looked seriously at Philip and wondered what he should say. Before he could make up his mind Philip spoke again.

"We're living under the same roof, but we're not living together. There's nothing between us. She's a stranger."

"Am I to tell the D.M.I. that?"

"I don't know. I shall have to tell him myself, if it comes to that, because behind all this business of your fellow's report there's the suggestion that Annie Joyce was sent over here to impersonate Anne for a definite reason, and the reason isn't far to seek." He came back to his chair and dropped down into it. "Garth—it might be. And I'll tell you why. This girl Annie Joyce—you know about her, don't you? Daughter of an illegitimate son of my great-uncle Ambrose—brought up to believe very intensively that her father ought to have been Sir Roger instead of a tuppenny-ha'penny clerk—brought up to see Anne and myself as supplanters. Then Theresa adopts her —not legally, but that's what it amounted to—quarrels with the family about her, takes her out to France, and after ten years disinherits her because she's taken a sudden fancy to Anne. It would rather pile up, wouldn't it? It isn't very hard to imagine that a girl with that sort of thing on her mind might be—shall we say, approachable. Your report suggests that she was approached by this Captain Reichenau. It's possible. If it happened, then they chose their time to send her over. I suppose information about the where and when of the second front would be what they'd just about give their eyes for. They might very well think they'd got a first-class opportunity of planting an enemy agent on me. That's one side of the picture. Here's the other. If she is Anne, she has changed very much—not in appearance but in herself. But she has had enough to change her—no one can reasonably deny that. If she is Anne, she could believe that I had deserted her. She was ill. She had to hide under another name—keep the Boche guessing. She was sent to a concentration camp and got ill again. Finally she gets over here, to find that she has been dead for three and a half years. There's a tombstone with her name on it, and—she isn't wanted. I don't recognize her—or I say I don't. If she is Anne, she has every reason to resent my attitude. When I am finally convinced, it is quite obviously against my will. She has every right to be cut to the heart."

"And is she?"

"No, she isn't—or if she is she doesn't show it. She has the most admirable self-control. She is easy, charming, and extremely efficient. Anne wasn't either easy or efficient. She said what she thought quite bluntly, and if she didn't get her own way she let you know all about it. How much can a girl change in three and a half years? She's much cleverer than Anne. She's adroit, she's tactful, she's damned clever. Anne wasn't any of those things. She was just young and full of life. She said what she thought and did what she chose. We were not going to hit it off—I knew that before we'd been married six months. But if this is Anne, she's had an appallingly raw deal, and I've got to try and make it up to her. And if she's Anne, you can wash out that report, or at any rate its implication. No conceivable circumstances would have laid Anne open to an approach from the Boche, nor would it have occurred to him to approach her. I can't think of anyone more completely unsuited to the part of a secret agent—it just wouldn't have occurred to anyone, least of all to Anne herself. Do you accept that?"

"If she is Anne, I accept it. I didn't know her so very well, but I should put her down as just what you say—quite a simple character—no frills—healthy, lively girl, quite pleased with everything as long as she got her own way—very pretty and charming and all that—definitely no subtleties, if you don't mind my speaking frankly."

"We're all going to say worse things than that," said Philip with an odd intonation. "As a matter of fact you've only said what I did. Well, all that's gone. She can look like Anne and talk like Anne, but she can't think like Anne, because a subtle mind can't think like a simple one, and when you live with a woman you get on to the quality of her thinking. And that's what has been at the back of my resistance all along. I've lived with Anne, and I've lived with this woman who calls herself Anne, and they don't think the same way. I could more easily get over a change of face than such a change of mind."

Garth lifted a frowning gaze to Philip's face and said, "Then you don't believe she is Anne?"

Philip said, "Last night I'd have said, 'I don't know.'"

"And to-day?"

"At the moment I'm inclined to think I've been planted with Annie Joyce."

XXV

On the same afternoon Anne rang up Janice Albany.

"It's Anne Jocelyn speaking. Look here, I wonder if you can help me."

Janice said, "What is it? What can I do?"

"Well, Lyn was here yesterday. You had her to tea last week. She was talking about someone she met then, and I stupidly forgot to ask her the name. I've been wondering whether this woman was related to some people I met in France. Lyn's out, and it's teasing me—you know the way things do."

"Would it have been Miss Silver? She was talking to Lyn, and I think I caught your name."

"Does she live at Blackheath?"

"Oh, no, she lives in Montague Mansions—15 Montague Mansions." Then, after a little pause, "She has a niece at Blackheath."

"Who is she?"

"She's a pet—straight out of the last century. She wears beaded slippers and a boxed-up fringe, but she's a marvel at her job."

"What is her job?"

"She's a private detective."

Anne took a long breath and leaned forward over the study table. The room was full of a throbbing mist. Through it she heard Janice telling her things about the murder of Michael Harsch. They came to her in snatches, with a continual burden—"Miss Silver was really too marvellous." Presently she managed to say,

"No, she isn't the person I thought of. I don't know why I got it into my head she might be—it was just one of those things. . . . By the way, don't tell her I asked—she might think it odd."

"Oh no, I won't."

Anne rang off, but she did not get up for a long time after that.

Later on she kept her appointment. When she came to the shop with the bright blue curtains and the name of Félise over the door she walked straight in. With a murmured "I have an appointment with Mr. Felix," she passed the girl at the counter, went down the passage between the cubicles and opened the looking-glass door. She stood for a moment in the dark as Lyndall had stood, and then moved towards the line of light which showed at the edge of the door that faced her. She pushed it open and went in, putting up her hand to shield her eyes.

The light came from a reading-lamp with a dark opaque shade tilted so as to leave the farther side of the room in a shadow and to direct a dazzling cone of light upon the door and upon anyone coming in that way. As she turned to get it out of her eyes and to make sure that the latch had caught, she thought, "What a stupid trick! That's what happened last time—I was dazzled, and I didn't make sure the door was shut. I'd like to tell him that."

She turned back to the room, her hand up again, and said in an exasperated voice,

"Turn the light off me, can't you!"

The room was sparsely furnished—a square of carpet on the floor, a writing-table roughly cutting the space in half, a plain upright chair on the far side, a plain upright chair on the near side, and the electric lamp standing on the table. In the farther chair, and in the deepest shadow, Mr. Felix. He lifted a gloved hand and turned the lamp a little. The beam now lay between them. If anyone with a fancy for metaphor had been present, it might have been compared to a fiery sword.

From the nearer chair Anne looked across it and saw very little—no more in fact than she had seen at two previous interviews, a man in a chair, looking bulky in a big loose coat. Nothing else would give just that density and shape to shadow. Gloved hands—she had seen that when he turned the lamp; thick hair, and as he leaned forward, a suggestion that the hair might be red; large round glasses—she thought tinted from the way in which they occasionally picked up a reflection from the place where the beam struck on the whited wall. She had never seen more than that, and she knew better than to try. In this game nothing was so dangerous, *nothing*, as to know too much.

She leaned back from the beam and heard him say,

"Why did you come? I did not send for you."

The voice was a husky whisper. There was nothing that could be called an accent, only every now and then an intonation which suggested familiarity with some language other than English. She had her own ideas about this, but she was perfectly well aware that it was wise not to formulate them, even for her own private consideration. Better to accept what you were given, do what you were told, and ask no questions. Only there were some things. . . . She said,

"Why did you do it? I told you she was harmless."

"Is that why you have come here—to ask questions about what is not your business?"

She ought to have stopped there and let it go. Something boiled up in her. For a moment she didn't care. She had been hating him hard for nearly forty-eight hours—hating him because the police had come down on her, because Joan Tallent had dropped out of the blue to tattle in front of Philip, because of Nellie Collins who had never done anyone any harm. The middle reason was of course quite illogical, because he didn't know that Joan existed. But logic has very little to do with the primitive instincts. The hating stuff boiled over, and she said,

"I suppose it isn't my business if you've brought the police down on me!"

The toneless voice came back.

"You will explain what you mean by that."

"She talked about coming up to see me."

"She promised——"

Anne laughed angrily.

"She talked to a woman in the train! Told her all about bringing up Annie Joyce and asking if she could come up and see me!"

"How do you know?"

She said in a hesitating way,

"The police told me."

"There is something more than that. You will tell me. Who is this woman?"

She had not made up her mind whether she would tell him or not. He had been too quick for her—she would have to tell him now. But she wouldn't tell him any more than she need. Let him find out the rest for himself. She said with an appearance of frankness,

"She is a Miss Silver."

"Did the police tell you that?"

"No—Lyndall Armitage told me."

After a slight pause he said,

"How does she come into it? Does she know this Miss Silver?"

"She met her out at tea."

"How do you know?"

"Lyndall told me."

"Tell me every word she said. You will be accurate."

She repeated as nearly as possible word for word what Lyndall had said.

"So you see, Nellie Collins did talk, and the woman she talked to is in touch with the police. She told them Nellie Collins said she was coming up to meet me under the clock at Waterloo at a quarter to four that Monday afternoon, and they naturally wanted to know what about it. Fortunately, I wasn't ever really alone all day or up to eleven o'clock at night."

Mr. Felix said gently,

"That is because you followed your instructions, which provided you with a series of very good alibis. This will perhaps convince you of how wise it is to obey orders and ask no questions."

She sat there with the beam between them and digested this. It was most convincingly true. She had been told to bring Ivy Fossett with her up to town and keep her overnight. She had been told to ask Lilla Jocelyn, or failing her some other friend or relation, to be at the flat not later than three o'clock, and to keep her there until seven. It was also true that she had asked no questions. She had not even asked them of herself. She had obeyed, and Nellie Collins had died. Impatience rose in her. What did it matter whether one little chattering woman died or not? The world was soaked with blood and sodden with grief. You couldn't live other people's lives—you could only fight for your own hand and struggle to survive.

Mr. Felix said, "What did you say to the police? Every word of it!"

When she stopped speaking he nodded.

"You did very well, I think. It is unlikely that they will trouble you again. But there is a point I do not understand. This girl Lyndall—what made her speak to you about Nellie Collins? Why did it seem sufficiently important to her? That is the point—did it seem important? You have told me her words, but what I want is the manner in which those words were said. You have given me the conversation, but I want the setting. How did it all come up? Was it amongst other things in the course of conversation—first this and then that, and then what you have repeated to me? Or did this girl, this Lyndall, make a visit to you in order that she might tell you what she did tell you?"

Anne moistened her lips.

"She came to tell me."

"She came with the purpose to tell you that she had met someone who talked about Nellie Collins—who said that Nellie Collins had come to London to meet you?"

Anne said, "Yes."

She heard him say, "That might be serious. Will you stop speaking as if your words were rationed, and tell me what I want to know—not what she said, but the manner in which she said it. The words are nothing, the manner is everything. In what manner was it said? Was it narrated as a coincidence, or as if she had some suspicion in her mind?"

He lifted that gloved hand, and suddenly the light was on her face again. She said sharply, "Don't do that!" and he laughed and shifted it.

"Then you will stop playing with me and tell me what I want to know!"

She felt a burning anger, and behind it fear. She had the same thought about Lyndall as she had had about Nellie Collins—what did one girl matter? If she had pushed into this business she must take the consequences. If you could keep your own feet you were lucky. You couldn't afford to bother about anyone else. She said in a smooth voice,

"You don't give me time to tell you. I'm not holding anything back. But I don't want you to think it is more important than it really is."

"I will be the judge of that. You will find it safer not to keep anything back."

She said, "I was going to tell you. It is just that—well—Lyndall saw me come in here last week."

"That was very careless of you. Go on!"

"I didn't see her—she was on the other side of the road. She followed me into the shop. She wasn't sure about its being me—she hadn't seen my face. So she came through the shop to see if I was in one of the cubicles. She opened the door at the end and got as far as the other side of this door. It wasn't latched—you may thank this glaring light of yours for that. If you hadn't blinded me as I came in, I should have made sure it was properly shut. She heard me say, 'Why don't you let me write to Nellie Collins? She's quite harmless.' And she heard you answer, 'That is not for you to say.' Then she panicked and ran away."

The gloved hand fell to the table's edge, gripping it hard. He said,

"She recognized your voice? For certain?"

"No. She just thought it was my voice—she wasn't sure. I could have made her think it was all a mistake if she hadn't met this damned woman at the Albanys' and heard about Nellie Collins saying she was coming up to meet me."

"To how many people will she have told this story?"

"She hadn't told it to anyone—yesterday."

"How do you know?"

"She said she hadn't." Her shoulders moved in the slightest possible shrug. "Actually she's one of those people who tell the truth. I don't think she could get away with a lie even if she tried to, and I don't think she would try."

"What did you say to her?"

"I reeled off my alibi to prove that I couldn't have anything to do with Nellie Collins' unfortunate accident. I said the whole thing was nonsense—she'd mistaken someone else for me. And I pitched it hot and strong about the unpleasant publicity we had already had, and just how damaging it would be for Philip if she started any gossip about Nellie Collins. She promised she wouldn't say a word, and I really don't think she will."

"Why?"

"Because she's in love with Philip."

He took his hand off the table.

"Is he in love with her?"

"I believe so."

"And you say that she is safe—that she will not talk?"

"She won't do anything to hurt Philip."

He leaned forward.

"Are you as stupid as you sound? If she tells no one else she will tell him."

She laughed.

"Oh, no, she won't! They don't see each other, for one thing, except in the bosom of the family. It was all *pour le bon motif*, you know. Philip was on the point of proposing to her —hence his joy at my return. They suffer in silence, and hope that no one notices. *Also*, Lyndall was one of my bridesmaids and very devoted. It is surprising, but I believe she was the only person who was genuinely glad to see me. She ran right across the room and flung her arms round my neck. At the moment, she thought about me, not Philip. Which I consider a triumph—don't you?"

He said abruptly, "How old is she?"

"Twenty, or twenty-one—younger than that in herself."

There was a silence. He rested his head upon his hands as if he were thinking. When he did not speak, she said,

"I think it's safe so far. She won't tell Philip because she used to be fond of me. And she won't tell anyone else because she is fond of Philip. But it's gone far enough—I won't come here any more."

He said, "No, it would not be safe. There must be another arrangement. You will have your instructions."

"I said it had gone far enough. It's too dangerous. I won't go on with it."

"You won't?" The voice was the same monotone, only just above the level of a whisper, but it sent a shiver over her.

On the other side of the beam he had looked up. For a moment the lenses which screened his eyes threw back a faint menacing gleam.

She said, "It's too dangerous."

"That is not your business! You are to obey your orders,

not to think whether they bring you into danger! In any army in the world the man who thinks like that will find himself before a firing-squad."

She controlled herself to say, "This is England."

The faintly foreign intonation was accentuated in his answer.

"And you think that makes a difference?"

She didn't answer that. When the silence had lasted just long enough he said, very softly indeed,

"It did not make so much difference to Nellie Collins—did it?"

No one would have known that she was frightened. For a moment she felt quite sick with fright, but it didn't show. She had had a lot of practice in not letting her feelings show. Years of practice—years of making herself agreeable when she was tired, when she was angry, when with all her heart she hated her necessity. The bitter apprenticeship served her now. She could say without a temor,

"Are you threatening me?" Then, with the slightest of laughs, "There is really no need. And—it would be stupid too."

"You are confident that I should not be stupid? Thank you, Lady Jocelyn! But you would be wiser not to say such things again. They are liable to be misunderstood, and misunderstandings are always dangerous. I am willing to believe that you mean nothing when you say that you cannot go on——"

She interrupted him, putting her hand up and leaning forward.

"Wait—I want you to listen. You did misunderstand what I said. I would like you to listen while I explain. I told you I couldn't go on because it was too dangerous. I didn't mean that I was afraid—I meant there's no chance of success. I don't know what Philip brings home, but he keeps his case locked and his keys on a chain in his pocket. If he found me meddling with his papers, it would be all up. Don't you see, I'm on my probation. In a way he believes in me because I told him things that convinced him, but underneath he holds back —he doesn't really believe. If I gave him the slightest reason, he would break with me. I want to play for safety—let him get used to me, make him comfortable, make him need me, give him time to get over his fancy for Lyndall. After all, I'm what he fell in love with once, and why shouldn't he do it again? And then—I'd be some use to you. If a man's in love, there isn't much you can't get out of him."

She was aware of scrutiny, deep and prolonged. At last he said,

"Six months' delay, shall we say?"

"Yes—yes!"

"Six months whilst you dig yourself in—whilst you make Philip Jocelyn so comfortable that he falls in love with you!"

"Yes!"

"And during this six months everything stands still and waits for you?" He made a gesture with that clumsy gloved hand, moving it from left to right upon the table as if rubbing something out, and said "*Quatch!*"

The single vulgar German word was like a blow in the face. It has perhaps no equal in its gross finality. What she said was rubbish, but no other language has so rude a term for it. She knew then that she had made her throw and lost, but instead of being frightened she began to be angry. He had better not threaten her. There were things that she could do if she was put to it.

He was watching her across the table. He said,

"Let us talk sense. You will do what you are told, and you will go on doing it. The first thing you will do is this." He pushed a little packet over to her. "You will take an impression of that key. You will be careful not to leave any of the wax sticking in the wards like the clumsy criminal of a detective story. You will do that tonight."

"I can't—he has the key on him."

"He sleeps, doesn't he? There are some tablets in that packet, as well as the wax. If you put two of them in his coffee, he will sleep very well tonight. Whilst you have the key you will open the case and photograph the papers. You have the camera. You need not be afraid—he won't wake. Next morning you will go out shopping as soon as Jocelyn has left the flat. Half-way down the stairs you will meet a man coming up. Just before he reaches you he will stumble, missing the step and coming down on his knees. You will move to help him, and he will thank you and say, 'It's nothing. I've been hurt twice as much as that in the old 78th.' Then you will drop your parcel with the films and the impressions and he will pick it up. You will go on and do your shopping."

Her anger had passed into determination. He was asking

132

her to throw everything away. Because it wouldn't come off—she had a clear conviction that it wouldn't come off. She said so.

"I can't do it. It would just be throwing everything away. You don't know Philip—I do. Under that manner he's on a hair trigger. You can't cover up from him. He sees things, and what he doesn't see he feels. It isn't enough to be careful of how you look and what you say—I have to be careful what I think. I can tell you it's not easy when we're there alone. If I were to go back and have all this on my mind, he'd know."

The tinted glasses caught the light again—just a gleam. He said,

"I wonder if you convince me. I begin to wonder too why you know so much about Philip Jocelyn. And I wonder—yes, I wonder very much whether you have been foolish enough to fall in love with him."

"Of course not!"

As soon as the words were out she knew that she had spoken too quickly. She heard her own voice, and the tone of it was wrong. It wouldn't convince him—it wouldn't convince anyone.

He said, "So that is it? But you will go through with it all the same."

"No, it isn't that. You're wrong, I'm telling you the truth. It won't do you any good if I try—and fail. If he finds me out, there will be no second chance—you know that. What good is it going to do you?"

"Why should he find you out? What have you been doing—saying? What are you keeping back? If he is suspicious, what has given him these suspicions? Answer me at once!"

She was sitting up straight now, her head a little drawn back as if to put a distance between them. He had taken her by surprise. Her thoughts ran all ways at once. "Why did I say that? . . . I didn't say anything. . . . What did I say? . . . If he thinks that Philip suspects, he won't risk it—he'll let me alone. . . . I don't know—perhaps he won't—perhaps—I can't think——"

The voice which was just above a whisper came again, bleak as a crawling wind.

"He suspects you?"

Out of the turmoil of her thoughts she said,

"I don't know."

"Quite useless to lie to me. Something has made him suspect you."

"I don't know——"

The words seemed to come of themselves. She could find no others.

"I said it was useless to lie. Something has happened. You will tell me what it is!"

She thought, "If I let him beat me down now, it's all up."

It was a thought, not words—an instinct which dragged courage from some deep place and put a smile on her lips and a different tone in her voice.

"Please—please—you know, you are frightening me! But you are right—there has been something, and I don't quite know. That is why I don't want to do anything just now."

"What has happened?"

She had herself in hand again. She went on easily.

"Nothing really—one of those little things, but—well, you can judge for yourself. A girl came in to see me last night—one of my bridesmaids—the world's fool. She began talking about the diary."

"What did she say?"

She told him.

"Said I put everything down in it—even the sort of things nobody would—like Pepys." She laughed again. "She explained she didn't mean anything against my moral character—giggled and asked Philip if I showed him what I wrote!"

"And he?"

"He looked at me——" Her voice went thin on the words.

"How?"

"I don't know——"

"He looked as if he suspected you?"

Anger came up in her again.

"I tell you I don't know! If you go on asking me for ever, still I don't know! But I say this is not a good time to make any move. That girl did something. I don't know just what she did, but I could feel that she had done something to Philip's mind. I can feel it focused on me again like it was at the beginning. There—you wanted the truth, and you've got it! Is this the time to start anything? I leave it to you."

He said, "No—perhaps not. Why did you not tell me this at first? You wait until I drag it out of you. You say it is one of those little things"—he repeated the words—"*one of those little things*. You really think that, I suppose? You expect me to believe that to you it is a little thing? You hold it back for as long as you can, and then you only say it because you think it will turn me from what I have told you to do. And now I will tell you why you are using everything you have got to turn me. You find yourself very comfortable as Lady Jocelyn —you have a position, you have a great deal of money, and you have a husband who is a very rising young man. You have, in fact, got all you want. You have, in fact, no further incentive—you would like to sit back and enjoy these things. I would ask you to remember that you have not finished earning them. Those who provided you with these good things can also take them away. There is no more to be said. Now you will listen to me. You will hear no more from the police. They are now convinced that Nellie Collins met, as you have said, with an unfortunate accident. A woman who lives at Ruislip has come forward to say that she has known her for years, and that she has often invited her to come and see her. This is very satisfactory as you will agree. The police will now be satisfied that anything Nellie Collins may have said in the train was just the result of a desire to be in the limelight, and that she was really going to see this friend of hers at Ruislip."

She looked at him, and saw no more than a dark bulky shape, a shock of hair, the just discernible gleam from the tinted glasses. Her voice slowed down as she said,

"Do you think so?" And then, "You arranged it, I suppose."

He said, as he had said before,

"That is not your business. Here are your orders. You will take the impression of the key as I told you. But you will not risk taking photographs unless you find the code. That must be copied or photographed—but if he has any suspicions, you will not find it. Where have you put the diary?"

"It's safely hidden."

"You had better put it in your bank."

"No—I must have it."

He did not press the point. Instead he said curtly,

"You have your orders. See you carry them out!"

There was a pause before she said,

"I can't do it."

XXVI

SHE came out of the heated shop into cold, bright air. The dropping sun looked between two black clouds and washed the whole length of the street with gold. As she walked quickly away, it seemed to her that the path before her was all lit up. Her spirits were strangely high. She had held her own, and now that it was done it seemed an easy thing to do. She wondered that she had been so much afraid—that she had submitted to so much. After all, what could he do? To expose her would be to expose himself. Threats were a game that two could play. She had let him see that, and he had been quick to moderate his tone. She had come away without any orders on his side or any undertaking on hers. She had fought her battle and won it. She had shown them that she was not to be used just as a tool. What she did she would do in her own time and in her own way—if she did anything at all. That would depend on Philip. Why, they must think her a fool to risk throwing away all that had been gained. She wasn't that kind of fool, or any other. When you got what you had wanted all your life you didn't risk it, you held it close. What she could do safely she would do. If there were a very good chance tonight, she might even get Mr. Felix his wax impression, but if she did it, it would be because she chose, and not under any orders of his.

At the corner she turned. She lost the sun, but not her lighted mood. A half-formed thought emerged and took the light. Contemplating this thought, the outline of a plan began to form. Her pace slackened. She walked slowly, her attention all turned inwards. The darkening street, the cold, thin wind which slanted across it, were no longer there. She looked at the plan, and coveted it as she might have coveted a diamond necklace or a high-powered car. Like these, it was beyond her reach. But was it—was it? If she was a tool, it wouldn't be the first time a tool had turned in the hand that used it. She began to consider very carefully whether the plan could be used. There would be some risk of course, but she stood in danger all the time. It would be worth some risk to get free and be safe. For a moment her heart sickened. Safety seemed so desperately far away.

Then she went on. In the end she temporized. Leaham

Street was not so far away. She had looked it up on the tape-map before she came out. She would go and have a look at Montague Mansions. No need to make up her mind whether she would go in or not. There was, perhaps, at the back of her thought some undefined idea that something might come along to point the way. She began to walk briskly in the direction of Leaham Street.

Miss Silver sat knitting by the fire. She had finished Johnny's second stocking and had begun a pair of socks for little Roger. Johnny's other two pairs of stockings could wait until she had knitted up this very nice wool. There was not enough of it for stockings, but it would come in very well indeed for little Roger's socks and be a great help to Ethel, who really had not time to knit for her family. Three boys and a husband to cook, and clean, and wash, and mend for—three afternoons at a canteen—were enough and to spare for one pair of hands.

As she knitted she went over in her mind her last conversation with Frank Abbott. Recollection of it made her shake her head. Chief Inspector Lamb was no doubt an experienced officer and a very estimable man, but that was not to say that she could always agree with his conclusions. By no means— oh dear me, no. In this particular instance she did not agree with them at all. She had told Frank Abbott so. But of course it was not her business—she was not professionally engaged upon the case. If the Chief Inspector was satisfied, there was no more to be said. He was, of course, a Man. Miss Silver had no dislike for the male sex. In their proper place they could be very useful indeed. She admired all their good qualities, and regarded their failings with indulgence. But occasionally she reflected, as she was doing now, that they were too much inclined to believe in their own opinions, and too much convinced that these opinions must be right. If Chief Inspector Lamb could believe that poor Miss Collins had merely met with a very sad accident whilst on her way to visit her old friend Mrs. Williams of Ruislip—if he could believe that she had missed her way and wandered into the dark lane where she was found, it was more than she herself could do. She did not care how respectable a person Mrs. Williams seemed to be, she did not for a moment believe that Miss Collins had had any intention of going to see her. She might have known Mrs. Williams, or she might not—upon this point Miss Silver kept an open mind. But on that Monday afternoon she had been going up to town with the intention of meeting Lady Jocelyn under the clock at Waterloo at a quarter to four. If it was not Lady Jocelyn whom she met there, it was someone who knew of the appointment and kept it in Lady Jocelyn's place. Lady Jocelyn, it seemed, could not have kept it herself—the Chief Inspector expressed himself quite satisfied as to that. Miss Silver primmed her lips. She considered that he was too easily satisfied.

It was at this point in her meditations that her attention was attracted by a sudden change in the light. It had been a singularly dark and cheerless day, but now quite suddenly the air outside was bright. With a slight regretful sigh Miss Silver put down her knitting and went over to the window. It was cheering to see the sun after so many gloomy days. The light came slanting down the turning opposite, a level beam of sunshine from where the sun was caught between two threatening clouds. No real sign of clearing up, she feared. Merely a transitory gleam, but pleasant—very pleasant.

She remained at the window until it faded. Just as it did so, she saw a woman stop on the opposite pavement and look up. She wore a small fur-trimmed cap and a very handsome fur coat. Her hair was bright under the cap. Miss Silver looked at her, and immediately recognized Lady Jocelyn. Every paper had carried its print of Amory's portrait. It was like her—very like her indeed.

She stood there looking up as Miss Silver looked down, her smoothly tinted face without expression, her fine grey eyes steady under arched brows. She might have been looking at a view, or watching a chess problem. Then all at once she turned and went back along the way that she had come, walking easily and without hurry. Miss Silver watched her go.

Anne Jocelyn went home and let herself into her flat. She felt gay and confident. The plan gave her a feeling of power. It was there to her hand to use or not to use. She might use it, or she might not—she hadn't made up her mind. Meanwhile it gave her that sense of power.

Some time after tea the telephone bell rang. As she lifted the receiver she heard a slight cough. A woman's voice said, "Lady Jocelyn?" She wondered who was ringing her up and said, "Yes."

"I think you will know my name. It is Silver—Miss Maud Silver."

"Why do you think I should know it?"

There was that slight hortatory cough.

"I think you came to see me this afternoon, or at least to see where I live. You did not come in. If you intended to do so, you changed your mind and went away. It was just as well."

"I really don't know what you are talking about."

"I think you do. I have rung you up because there is something you ought to know. You were being followed."

Anne made no sound. She stood holding the receiver in a rigid hand until she could command her voice. Even then she kept it low. The low voice said,

"I really don't know what you mean."

Miss Silver coughed.

"Lady Jocelyn, you would do well to listen to me. You came along Leaham Street this afternoon just before four o'clock. You stood on the pavement and looked across at Montague Mansions. I happened to be looking out of my sitting-room window and I recognized you at once. Your resemblance to the Amory portrait is—remarkable."

Something in Anne said, "She knows——" and then, "How does she know?"

Quietly and precisely Miss Silver continued. She might have been answering that unspoken thought.

"I beg that you will listen to me, because I know great care was taken to prevent that unfortunate Miss Collins from reaching you. Has it not occurred to you that the same care might be taken to prevent you from reaching me?"

"I really don't know what you are talking about." The repetition was by now a mechanical one. The voice was lifeless, the words without meaning.

Miss Silver said, "I think you had the intention of coming to see me, but you could not make up your mind. In the end you decided against it. The person who was following you was a woman in a shabby brown coat with a brown and purple scarf tied over her head. Whilst you were waiting on the pavement she stood under the porch of one of the houses higher up. When you went back she turned with her face to the door as if she were waiting for someone to answer the bell. But when you had gone past she came down the steps again and followed you."

Anne said nothing. Miss Silver went on.

"I believe that the police are not interested in your movements. I have reason to believe this. It follows that someone else is interested. It is for this reason that I am ringing you up. You will know better than I who this someone may be, and to what extent you are in danger. I felt bound to warn you. If you would care to consult me, I am at your disposal. It would not, I think, be safe for you to come to me, but I would come to you."

Anne's head came up with a jerk. What was she doing, allowing herself to be talked to like this? She must have gone crazy. Quite crazy, because something in her wanted to say, "Yes, come, come, *come*!" She controlled it, as she had controlled her voice, and murmured,

"I am sure you mean to be very, very kind, but I still don't know what you are talking about. Goodbye."

XXVII

ANNE hung up the receiver. She had a sense of relief, a sense of having escaped. She had almost said "Come." It seemed incredible now, but she had wanted to say it. She thought it was the strangest conversation she had ever had—strange in what had been said, and strange in the way in which it had affected her. This woman, this Miss Silver—she spoke as if she knew. Nellie had talked to her in the train. What had Nellie said to her? How much of what Nellie said to her had been repeated to the police? Even through her sense of relief at having got away from the telephone she could feel the urge to see Miss Silver and find out. Then all at once it was what Miss Silver has said that possessed her mind—the hard, unshaded fact that Felix had put someone on to shadow her. She hadn't the slightest doubt that it was Felix, and that meant . . . She knew very well what it meant. She hadn't really won her battle, she had only made him suspect her. He had ceased to press his orders, not because she had convinced him that they were inexpedient but because he no longer trusted her to carry them out. And when he knew that she had been to Leaham Street, and had stood there looking at Montague Mansions with the name stuck up over the door, he wasn't going to be exactly reassured. She hadn't gone in that time, but she might the next.

Well, she would have to make up her mind. She could throw in her hand, call Miss Silver up now at this moment, and give Felix away. . . . Could she? . . . She didn't know who he was. What had she to give away? He knew how to cover his tracks, and every word she said would accuse herself. The plan began to look shaky and shoddy when you got it out in the light of common sense. If Miss Silver hadn't recognized her, she could have rung up from a call-box and told what she knew about Felix and his appointments behind the hairdresser's shop which called itself Félise. But what was the good of saying "If"? Nellie Collins used to say, "If if's and ans were pots and pans, what would the tinkers do?" Miss Silver had recognized her. It was too late—she couldn't get out that way. She must play for safety—she must get Felix the impression of the key. That would placate him. If by some marvellous piece of luck she could get the code too, she would be in the clear. He couldn't go on suspecting her after that.

Of the two dangers she was in, that from Philip had suddenly become negligible. It was Felix who must be placated and reassured at any cost. She knew very well what happened to the useless or untrustworthy tool—it went on the scrap-heap with as little compunction as if it had really been a question of rusty iron or broken steel. The confidence of her mood did not vanish; it took a change of direction. She felt astonishingly easy and certain of herself. She even planned the words in which she would tell Felix that she had walked round by Leaham Street to have a look at Montague Mansions, and if he said "Why?" she would laugh and say, "Oh, I don't know—it amused me—like looking through the bars at something that would bite if it got the chance."

When Philip came home he found her with just that touch of gaiety lighting her up. There was still some time before supper, and he sat down and talked. When she went to prepare the meal he followed her into the kitchen, propped his long figure against the dresser, and went on talking. Without quite noticing how, she found that they were talking about France, and that he was asking her questions, not in any suspicious way but as if the subject interested him, as if it was a meeting-ground. While she flaked fish for a pie and prepared a cheese sauce she realized that for the first time they were conversing,

141

and that Philip, interested and laying himself out to please, could be very attractive indeed.

Over the meal he began to talk about his work. What was said was nothing, but the fact that he could talk about it at all lifted her up. She was very careful, showing only a friendly interest, asking no questions, except that when he mentioned that he would have to finish some writing after supper she said,

"Will it take you long?"

"Not very. I ought to have waited to finish it in the office—I don't really like bringing the code-book away. However——No, I shan't be long."

As the meal went on, her confidence grew. She was on the crest of her wave. When she went to fetch the coffee she put two of the tablets which Felix had given her into Philip's cup. The tray stood on the dresser. Lifting her head, she saw her own reflection in a small cheap mirror propped on the dresser shelf. For a moment it startled her. Natural colour glowed in her cheeks, her eyes shone, her lips had a new curve. She thought, "I look as if I was in love with him." And then, "Well, why not? I could be if he wanted me to. Why not?"

She picked up the tray and went through with it to the living-room. Philip had got out of his chair. He was standing by the hearth looking down into the fire. As she set down the tray, he said,

"I'll take my coffee through and finish what I brought home. It won't take long. If I sit down now I shan't want to get up again. I'll come back for a bit when I've finished, and then go early to bed. I could sleep the clock round."

She had the feeling that everything was playing into her hands. In any other mood she might have wondered why. Tonight it never crossed her mind that things might be going too easily.

An hour later, when he came back, she was sitting under the lamp sewing delicately at a piece of fine underwear. The light fell softly on peach-coloured satin and écru lace, on the bright steel needle, along a skein of embroidery silk laid out on the arm of the chair. She looked up as he came in, and saw him put up a hand to hide a yawn. From his other hand there swung a length of chain with a key-ring at the end of it. She lifted her eyebrows and said, "Tired, Philip?" and he gathered up the chain into his palm and said, "Dead. It's no good trying to sit up any longer. I'll go off." As he turned he looked

142

back to say good-night. Then he went out and shut the door behind him.

Anne went back to whipping the lace on to her peach satin petticoat. There was a little clock on the mantel-piece, a bright modern trifle all chromium and crystal. It struck ten with a tinkling chime. It struck eleven. Anne went on sewing for another half hour. Then she got up, folding her work, and went to put it away in her bedroom, not hurrying herself. To anyone watching her she would have been any pretty woman going about the business of tidying up before she went to bed.

When she had put her sewing away she came back to the sitting-room to straighten the chairs and plump up the cushions, going to and fro without haste and without noise. Then she went back to her room and took off her shoes. In her stocking feet she went along to Philip's door and tried the handle. It turned easily, as she had known that it would. She stood there with the door a handsbreadth open, listening to Philip's breathing and thinking that she hadn't left anything to chance. She had tested the door very carefully and could be sure that it wouldn't give her away. Not that the creak of a hinge or the click of a lock would wake him now. She thought he would have been safe enough even without the tablets, and with them it would take an air raid to shift him. Yet as she stood there, a very faint compunction stirred at the ege of her mood. It had no strength either to change or to deflect it. It was just there, a quite vague feeling about the defencelessness of sleep. In a moment it was gone, caught up with that sense of everything going right for her. Tonight, if ever in her life, she had power in her hand. Other people were there to be used—Philip, Felix, Lundall, Miss Silver——

She pushed the door wide open and went in. At the dressing-table she switched on a pocket-torch, screening it from the bed. The key-ring lay flung down on the right with a note-case, a handful of coins, a folded handkerchief. It was all quite easy. She picked it up without making a sound and went out of the room, drawing the door to behind her.

In the study she put on the overhead light and sat down to the table. The locked despatch-case was on her left. She pulled it down across the blotting-pad, fitted the smallest of the keys, and threw back the lid. Right on the top was her piece of unbelievable luck—the code-book. She took a long breath, savouring her triumph, full of that sense of power.

XXVIII

PHILIP JOCELYN did not go directly to his own room at the War Office next morning. With the case he had taken home the night before, he made his way along a number of corridors. In the room he entered Garth Albany sat writing. He looked up, and received a slight shock. Philip never had much colour, but this morning he looked ghastly—skin bloodless, face drawn, every line deepened and emphasized.

He said, "Well?" and was rather horrified when Philip laughed.

"Is it? Perhaps it is. We'll see—unless she's been too clever for us. I was doped last night."

"What!"

Philip gave a casual nod.

"Undoubtedly. Slept like the dead. I'm not really out of it yet, in spite of cold water and the very excellent breakfast coffee which was provided. It's a pity Miss Annie Joyce is an enemy agent, because she's a very good cook. Anyhow she drugged me last night, and what she did after that I am not in a position to say. You'd better get your fingerprint people on to the contents of my case and my keys. I've taken care not to touch them, or anything inside or outside the case except the handle. Of course she may have worn gloves, in which case she's done us down, but I hardly think she'd do that—not in the domestic circle." He set the case down and dropped a knotted handkerchief on Garth's blotting-pad The shape of the keys showed through the linen, the key-chain clinked. With a brief "See you later", he turned and went out of the room.

Garth Albany felt relief. A beastly business, and Philip was taking it hard.

At a little after one o'clock Lyndall Armitage was in the drawing-room of Lilla Jocelyn's flat. It was a charming room, L-shaped, with windows looking east and west so that it caught both the morning and the evening sun. The two west windows faced you as you came in at the door, but the one east window was out of sight round the corner of the L. Lilla's piano stood there, and at the moment in which the bell rang Pelham Trent had just lifted his hands from the keyboard and swung round upon the piano-stool.

Lilla said, "That was lovely."

If Lyndall had been going to speak, the sound of footsteps in the hall put it out of her head. Her heart beat a little faster, and without meaning to do so she found herself on her feet, moving towards the part of the room which faced the door. Because it was Philip's step in the hall. She knew it too well not to recognize it now. Not even to herself would she admit how everything in her quickened at the sound. She ought to have stayed with the others—she oughtn't to have come to meet him—there wasn't any reason why she shouldn't come to meet him. These thoughts were all in her mind at the same time, not very clearly defined, and not taking up any time at all. She was shaking a little, she didn't quite know why, and her thoughts were shaken too. She passed out of sight of the two by the piano, and then the door was opening and Philip was coming into the room. Something came in with him—she didn't know what it was. It was like cold air coming into a heated room. But the cold was not physical; she felt it in her mind, and she saw it in Philip's face.

He shut the door behind him, stood back against it, and said,

"Anne's dead."

Lyndall drew in her breath, but she made no sound. It was Lilla who said, "Oh!"

And with that, and with the sudden movement and stir in the part of the room that was out of his sight, it came to Philip Jocelyn that they were not alone. He stood stiffly where he was for a moment. Then he stepped away from the door, opened it, and went out, shutting it behind him. Before Lyndall could follow him he was gone. The clap of the outer door came back to her across the hall.

XXIX

It was just a little earlier than this that Chief Detective Inspector Lamb and Sergeant Abbott emerged from the lift and rang the bell of No. 8 Tenterden Court Mansions, a highsounding name for the block of flats put up at the corner of Tenterden Gardens just before the war. Of the gardens which gave the curving crescent its name there remained no more than a strip of shrubbery, trodden flat since the removal of the railings for salvage, and a few old leafless trees, one of which had been damaged by a bomb splinter. Two of the houses in the middle of the row were empty shells, but the flats were intact.

When Sergeant Abbott had had his finger on the bell for something like a minute he shrugged his shoulders and looked round at his Chief Inspector. They could hear the bell ringing in an empty space, but from inside the flat no other sound struck on the ear.

"No one there, sir."

Lamb frowned.

"She may have cut and run, or she may have slipped out for a bit of shopping. Go along down and ask the porter whether he's seen her go out?"

"And if he hasn't?"

Lamb considered this. He had his search-warrant, but he didn't want to make more talk than he could help. He didn't want to bring the porter into it. No harm in asking whether he'd seen Lady Jocelyn go out. If he had—well, he'd have to think about that.

When Abbott came back to say that the porter hadn't seen Lady Jocelyn all the morning the Chief Inspector frowned again, dipped into his pocket, and produced the latchkey with which he had been furnished.

"Fact is," he said, "I'd have liked it a deal better if Sir Philip had come along and let us in himself—it would have been more regular to my mind. I suppose he's got his feelings, but I'd have preferred it. Fact is, there isn't any room for feelings when you come to this kind of job. Well, there you are—in we go!"

Frank Abbott put the key in the lock and opened the door. They came into a small empty hall with a door to the right, and another facing them. Both doors were half open, as if someone had been going in and out between them, easily. But the flat felt dead empty.

They went directly into the drawing-room. A little pale sunshine slanted through the windows. Everything was neat, everything in order. The chairs were undinted, the cushions plumped up. But the grate had not been done. The charred shell of one of last night's logs lay upon a bed of tumbled ash. Frank Abbott cocked an eyebrow at it.

Lamb grunted, swung round, and went out across the hall to the other open door. It stood a little wider. No need to touch it. No need to cross the threshold in order to find Lady Jocelyn. The room was Philip Jocelyn's study. She lay in a heap beside the writing-table, and both men knew at once that she was dead.

After a brief pause Lamb stepped inside and crossed the room. The woman he had come to arrest would never stand her trial. Whoever she had been, or whatever she had done, she was no longer here. The body lay upon its face with the table telephone dragged down from the desk and lying beside it. There was blood on the bright hair, and on the plain drab carpet.

Lamb bent over her without touching anything.

"Shot from behind at close quarters," he said. "Looks as if she'd been trying to reach the telephone. Well, we'll have to ring up the Yard. We can't use this." He indicated the fallen instrument. "See if there's an extension in a bedroom."

There was—a smart pale blue affair, looking oddly incongruous beside Philip Jocelyn's unmade bed, with his shoes standing about, his brushes on the dressing-table, the general air of a man's room in disorder.

Frank Abbott came back and reported.

"The extension is in his room. The bed hasn't been made."

"Bed?"

"Single. She was along here, next the drawing-room. Her room has been done—bed made, everything tidy."

Lamb gave the grunt which meant that he was thinking.

"Looks as if it had happened first thing. He goes about half past eight, I take it. Looks as if she'd done her room but hadn't had time to do his—he said they had no help. I wonder what about breakfast."

They went together into the small brightly painted kitchen. On a clean checked table-cloth stood the remains of a meal— cups which had held coffee, coffee-pot and milk-jug, rolls and butter untouched and uncut.

"Looks as if nobody had had much appetite for breakfast. Coffee—what's the good of that to start the day on? Give me a rasher and a good strong cup of tea!"

"Who's going to give you the rasher, sir?"

"I know, I know—there's a war on. But I take my bacon ration out at breakfast and try to forget about it. Well, the boys will be here soon. Something queer about it to my mind—breakfasting on a cup of coffee."

"He'd been drugged, and she—well, whoever she was, she'd been living in France, and a cup of coffee and perhaps a roll would be what she was used to."

Chief Inspector Lamb looked heavily disapproving.

"Then you don't want to look much farther for why France came out of the war. Coffee! How do you expect men to fight on coffee?" Then, as the telephone bell rang sharply, "Who's that, I wonder. Go on and see!"

Frank Abbott lifted the pale blue receiver. A distressed voice said, "Who is that? Philip, is that you?"

Frank said, "No," and waited.

It was a very charming voice, soft, and young, and distressed. After a moment's hesitation it resumed.

"I *am* speaking to No. 8 Tenterden Court Mansions?"

"Oh, yes. Who is speaking?"

"Mrs. Perry Jocelyn. Is Lady Jocelyn there? Can I speak to her?"

"I'm afraid not."

"Oh!" The distress deepened. "Oh, please—has anything happened?"

"What makes you think so, Mrs. Jocelyn?"

"Philip said——" Her voice trailed away. "Oh, it isn't true, is it? She isn't dead?"

"Did Sir Philip tell you that Lady Jocelyn was dead?"

"Oh, yes, he did. At least he didn't exactly tell me. He opened the door, and he only saw Lyn—my cousin, Miss Armitage—and he said, 'Anne's dead.' And when I called out he went away again, so we couldn't ask him about it. And I couldn't really believe it, so I thought I had better ring up."

"When was this, Mrs. Jocelyn?"

"It was a quarter to one. But please tell me who you are. Are you the doctor? Won't you tell me what has happened? Was it an accident? Is she really dead?"

"I'm afraid she is."

He hung up the receiver and turned to find Lamb just behind him, his face heavy and frowning.

"That's odd, sir. Could you hear what she said? That was Mrs. Perry Jocelyn, and she says Philip Jocelyn walked in on them a quarter of an hour ago and said his wife was dead. *How did he know?*"

XXX

PHILIP JOCELYN came out into the open air with the unpleasant sense that he had made a fool of himself. Whatever he had had in his coffee last night had left him with a swimming head. He must have been crazy to walk into Lilla's room and say a thing like that without so much as waiting to make sure that he and Lyndall were alone before he blurted it out. "*Anne's dead.*" He hadn't meant to say it. He hadn't even meant to go there. He had just found himself so near that it had seemed all at once an imperative necessity to see her. He had planned nothing. The drug and his disordered thoughts had betrayed him.

As he walked away he had no idea where he was going. Not back to the flat. Not yet—not before he must. Let them get on with it. He became aware that he had had no food all day. A meal would probably stop his head going round. He turned out of a side road into a busy street full of shops and entered the first restaurant he came to.

Half an hour later he walked in at his own front door, and was met by Chief Inspector Lamb.

"This is a bad business, Sir Philip."

"What do you mean?"

"Don't you know?"

"I shouldn't have asked you if I did. She hasn't gone?"

Lamb looked at him out of an expressionless face.

"That's one way of putting it."

Philip's head was steady enough now. He said rather sharply,

"What has happened?"

Lamb said, "This," and moved away from the study door.

Philip came forward a step or two and stood there looking in. There were three men in the room. One of them had a camera. Annie Joyce still lay where she had fallen. Philip thought of her like that—Annie Joyce—not Anne Jocelyn—not his wife. They hadn't moved her yet. He looked at her lying there, and knew that she was dead. He had a brief stab of compunction. Then his face hardened. He stepped back and said in a controlled voice,

"Shot herself? Before you came—or afterwards?"

Lamb shook his head.

"Neither. She didn't shoot herself—someone shot her. There's no weapon."

"Someone shot her?"

"Undoubtedly. We'd better come in here." The Chief Inspector led the way to the living-room. "They're just going to take her away, and I should be glad of a word with you. This is Sergeant Abbott. If you don't mind, he'll take a few notes. We shall want your statement. I suppose you have no objection to making one."

Frank Abbott shut the door and got out his notebook. The sun had left the room. It was cold. They sat down. Lamb said,

"We have been instructed that this is a very confidential affair—a matter of attempting to obtain information for the enemy. But it seems to have turned into a murder case."

Philip said, "Are you sure it isn't suicide?"

"No question about it. Position of the wound—absence of any weapon. Somebody shot her. Now I'm going to ask you straight out—was she alive when you left the flat this morning?"

Philip Jocelyn's eyebrows went up.

"Of course she was!"

Lamb went on in his solid, serious voice, his eyes bulging a little but shrewd, his gaze fixed and unwinking. Not a twitch of the eyelids, not a change of expression in all the big florid face. Above it, the stiff black hair stood up round a bald patch. He had taken off his overcoat, but even without it he filled his chair, sitting rather stiffly upright with a big capable hand on either knee.

"The police surgeon says she's been dead a matter of hours. What time did you leave this morning?"

"Twenty to nine."

Lamb nodded.

"Have any breakfast?"

Philip was as laconic as he.

"Coffee."

Lamb grunted.

"Something about your being drugged last night, wasn't there?" His tone conceded that as a medicament coffee might have its uses.

Philip said, "Yes."

"And whilst you were asleep the case which you had brought back with you from the War Office was opened with your own key and the contents tampered with?"

"Yes."

"Lady Jocelyn's fingerprints——"

Philip interrupted sharply.

"She was neither Lady Jocelyn nor my wife. She was an enemy agent called Annie Joyce."

"But she had been passing as Lady Jocelyn?"

"Yes."

"Her fingerprints were found on your keys and upon the papers inside the case?"

"Yes."

"Were these papers of a secret nature?"

"They appeared to be. They were not actually so. There was a code-book, but the code it contained had been superseded. There was nothing which could be of any value to the enemy."

"Then you suspected that an attempt would be made to tamper with the case?"

"I thought it probable—I wasn't taking any chances. As you know, I put myself in the hands of the Intelligence. I acted under their instructions."

"Did you anticipate that an attempt would be made to drug you?"

"No. But it didn't matter, except that my head is only just beginning to come round. Of course it was on the cards—but I'm a fairly sound sleeper, and she might have chanced it."

"Would she have been in a position to know how soundly you slept?"

"No, she would not."

Frank Abbott wrote, leaning forward over a table with a satin-wood edge, his hair as pale and shining as the polished wood. Everything in the flat shone with polish except the dusty grate with its wreck of last night's fire. He thought, "He's on the spot all right now. If she was alive when he went out, how did he know that she was dead at a quarter to one? He didn't leave the War Office until just before half past twelve. We were in the flat before he could possibly have got here."

Lamb said, "To come back to the deceased. The case was in the papers of course—I mean her coming over from France and claiming to be Lady Jocelyn. May I ask if the accounts which appeared in the Press were substantially correct?"

"I think so. I didn't read them all."

"You accepted her story—you believed her to be Lady Jocelyn?"

"No."

"Will you kindly amplify that?"

"Yes. I didn't think she was my wife. She looked like her, and seemed to know all the things my wife would have known, but I felt she was a stranger. The rest of the family had no doubts at all. They couldn't understand why I should have any."

"The likeness was very strong?"

"Very strong, and—very carefully cultivated."

"How do you account for it?"

"Quite easily. My father succeeded his uncle, Sir Ambrose Jocelyn. Ambrose had an illegitimate son who was the father of Annie Joyce, and a legitimate daughter who was the mother of my wife. The Jocelyns run very much to type, but even so, the likeness was remarkable."

"Annie Joyce and Lady Jocelyn were first cousins?"

"Yes."

Lamb shifted in his chair, leaning forward a little.

"If you believed the deceased woman to be Annie Joyce, why did you allow her to pass as Lady Jocelyn? She was living here under that name, wasn't she?"

Anger and pride cut deeper lines on Philip's face. He answered because he must, because reluctance would betray him, because the only defence he had left was to appear indifferent. He said,

"I came to believe that she was what she claimed to be. The evidence was too strong."

"What evidence, Sir Philip?"

"She appeared to know things that only my wife and I could know. After that I had no choice. I thought I owed it to her to meet her wishes. She wanted to be under my roof."

"So you were convinced of her identity?"

"I was for a time."

"What happened to change your opinion?"

"I learned from an old friend of my wife's, one of her bridesmaids, that she had kept a very intimate and detailed diary. I realized at once that this diary might be the source from which Annie Joyce had drawn the information that had convinced me."

"When did this happen?"

"The day before yesterday."

"Did you then approach the Military Intelligence?"

"No—they approached me. They had received some very damaging information about Annie Joyce. They suggested that I should bring home some faked-up papers and an out-of-date code-book and let her know I had them. She drugged me and went through my case. I took them one or two things she had handled so that they could compare the fingerprints. They found them all over the place."

Lamb sat silent for a moment. Through the silence came the sound of tramping feet. The outer door of the flat shut heavily. The silence fell again. Lamb let it settle. Then he said,

"You needn't answer this unless you wish—but I'm bound to ask you whether you shot her."

Philip's eyebrows lifted.

"*I?* Certainly not! Why should I?"

"You might have waked up and found her tampering with your case."

The eyes under those raised brows gave him back a hard grey stare.

"In which case I should have rung up the police."

"I wonder whether you would, Sir Philip."

"I'm afraid I didn't wake up. I told you I had been drugged."

Lamb grunted.

"You have a revolver, I suppose?"

" Certainly."

"Where is it?"

"In the study—second right-hand drawer of the writing-table."

"Sure it's there?"

"It should be."

"Well, I think we'll just have a look. They've taken her away."

They went in, Philip Jocelyn leading the way, Frank Abbott behind. The room had been straightened, the telephone replaced, but the stain on the carpet showed.

Philip pulled out the drawer with a jerk. Writing-pads and envelopes neatly stacked—nothing else. He frowned, pulled out the next drawer above. No revolver. And so on with all the drawers.

"It isn't here."

"When did you see it last?"

"Last night. I took out a packet of envelopes. It was there then."

He stood frowning down at the table. The packet of envelopes lay where he had left it, away beyond the blotting-pad, the paper band unbroken. He said,

"Do you think it was used to shoot her?"

"It might have been. We can't tell till we get hold of it."

Frank Abbott thought, "If he did it, he's putting on a good act. I can't see why he should shoot her—unless she had the revolver. . . . She might have had it. . . . Say he caught her and grabbed it—she would know where it was. . . . He gets it away from her—she's frightened—she reaches for the telephone, and he shoots. . . Not enough motive—unless there's something we don't know—there generally is. . . . Of course he may just have lost his head and let her have it—but he doesn't look that sort. . . . Quite a brain-wave to get rid of the weapon—you can't prove she was shot with it if it doesn't turn up——"

Lamb was saying, "What time did you get to the War Office this morning, Sir Philip?"

"A few minutes after nine. Why?"

"At what time did you leave?"

"Half past twelve."

Lamb knew that already. He nodded.

"Did you come back here?"

"No."

"Sure?"

"Quite sure."

"Where did you go?"

"First to my cousin Mrs. Jocelyn's flat. I meant to ask her to give me some lunch, but when I found she had a party I didn't stay."

"What did you do?"

"I went and got some lunch, and came on here."

"You didn't have any breakfast, did you—nothing but a cup of coffee? Did you make it yourself?"

"No—Miss Joyce made it."

Lamb grunted. He said,

"There's no proof that she was Annie Joyce, but we'll let that pass. She made the coffee? And she was alive when you left the flat?"

"Yes."

"Then how do you account for the fact that you knew she was dead when you walked in at Mrs. Perry Jocelyn's?"

Philip stared. He said,

"But I didn't know. How could I?"

Lamb gave him back his look.

"That's not for me to say. But you walked in on Mrs. Jocelyn and her party and said, 'Anne's dead,' and walked out again."

Philip stiffened. He tried to remember just what he had said. He hadn't seen anyone but Lyn, hadn't thought of anyone. He had said "Anne's dead " because it was on his mind. He had said it to Lyn. And then Lilla had called out—someone moved. And he had just turned round and gone out again. He frowned a little and said,

"You've got it wrong. I wasn't speaking about Annie Joyce. I didn't know that she was dead—she wasn't in my mind at all. I was thinking about my wife."

"Your wife? " The Chief Inspector's voice sounded solidly unconvinced.

Philip felt a cold rage. Why should anything that was true sound as thin as what he had just said? Even to himself it carried no weight. He said,

"That's true. If this woman was Annie Joyce, my wife was dead—had been dead for three and a half years. The fact that my case had been tampered with was an absolute proof of that as far as I was concerned. When I walked into Mrs. Jocelyn's flat I didn't know that there were other people there —I said what was uppermost in my mind. When I found that we were not alone I walked out again. It wasn't the sort of thing I could discuss in front of strangers."

Frank Abbott wrote. The words were down in his notebook now. As his hand travelled, his slightly cynical expression became modified. "Might be—you never can tell," he concluded. "The Armitage girl comes into it somewhere. The old game—spot the lady. He was in a bit of a hurry to tell her his wife was dead. And he hasn't mentioned her now. I suppose the Chief is on to that—he doesn't miss much."

He shut up his notebook as the telephone bell rang.

XXXI

FRANK ABBOTT removed the receiver from his ear, covered the mouthpiece with his hand, and said,

"It's Miss Silver, sir."

The Chief Inspector's colour deepened, his eyes bulged. The simile of the peppermint bullseye recurred irreverently to his Sergeant.

"Miss Silver?" His voice had a note of exasperation.

Frank nodded.

"What do I say?"

"Who did she ask for?"

"Lady Jocelyn."

The deepened colour became purple.

"What's she doing in this? You can't move for her! I suppose she's recognized your voice! Ask her what she wants!"

"Do I tell her what's happened?"

Lamb grunted.

"Ask her first!"

Frank addressed himself to the telephone mellifluously.

"So sorry to keep you waiting. The Chief wondered whether you would mind telling him what you wanted with Lady Jocelyn."

Miss Silver's slight reproving cough came to them distinctly. The words which followed were only a murmur as far as Lamb and Philip were concerned.

Frank said, "Yes, I'll ask him." He turned again. "She wants to come and see you, sir."

Lamb jerked his big head.

"Well, I haven't got time to see her—just tell her that! You needn't wrap it up too carefully either—I haven't got time. You can tell her it's a murder case. Genuine this time. None of her mare's nests. And I'll be glad if she'll keep out of my way and let me get on with the job."

Trusting that his palm had been sound-proof, Sergeant Abbott proceeded to translate.

"The Chief's very busy. The fact is there's a bit of a mess-up here. She's been shot. . . . Yes, dead. . . . No, not suicide. . . . Yes, we're up to our necks in it. So you see——"

At the other end of the line Miss Silver coughed in a very firm and determined manner.

"I have something of the utmost importance to communicate. Will you tell the Chief Inspector that I hope to be with him in twenty minutes."

Frank turned back to the room.

"She's hung up, sir. She's coming round. She says she's got something important. She generally has, you know."

The Chief Inspector came nearer to swearing than he had done for a good many years. He was a chapel member in good standing, but the strain was considerable.

Nevertheless when Miss Maud Silver arrived the meeting between them was attended by all the rites of old acquaintance and mutual respect. They shook hands. She enquired after his health, after Mrs. Lamb's health, after his three daughters, for whom he had a heart as soft as butter. She remembered which of them was in the A.T.S., the Wrens, the W.A.A.F.s. She remembered that it was Lily who was engaged to be married.

Under this soothing treatment Frank Abbott observed his Chief relax. "And the marvellous part is that it isn't put on. She's really interested. She really wants to know about Lily's young man, and whether Violet is going to get a commission. He'd see through it like a flash if she was putting it on. But she isn't, she doesn't—she really wants to know. Astounding woman, Maudie."

Lamb put a period to the compliments by saying,

"Well, I've got my hands rather full, Miss Silver. What did you want to see me about?"

They were alone in the flat. Philip Jocelyn had gone back to the War Office. Miss Silver selected a small upright chair and sat down. The two men followed her example.

Frank Abbott, who could make himself a great deal more useful than anyone would have supposed, had tidied up the hearth. He had also lighted the fire. Miss Silver regarded it with approbation, and remarked that the weather was really very cold for the time of year, after which she coughed and addressed herself to Lamb.

"I was very much shocked to hear of this new fatality. I feared that she was in danger, but I had, of course, no idea that a catastrophe was imminent."

"Well, I don't know about a catastrophe, Miss Silver. She

wasn't up to any good, you know. Or perhaps, for once, there's something *you* don't know. Just between you and me and Frank here—I know I can trust you not to talk—she was an enemy agent."

"Dear me! How extremely shocking! I suspected something of the sort, but of course there was no proof."

"Oh, you suspected it, did you? Why!"

To Frank Abbott Miss Silver's manner indicated that she considered the Chief Inspector to be lacking in what might be called the finer shades of courtesy. She said a little primly,

"It is difficult to say just how an impression is received. As I said, there was no proof at all, but I thought she must have had some guilty knowledge in the matter of poor Miss Collins——"

"Accident," interjected Lamb—"pure accident."

Miss Silver coughed.

"I think not. It occurred to me that Lady Jocelyn——"

Lamb interrupted again.

"Sir Philip says she wasn't Lady Jocelyn—says she wasn't his wife—says she was the other woman there was all the talk about, Annie Joyce."

"That does not surprise me. Lady Jocelyn could have no interest in the death of Nellie Collins. Annie Joyce might have had a very vital interest. Miss Collins undoubtedly knew of some distinguishing mark which would have enabled her to recognize the child she had brought up. This would give Annie Joyce a very strong motive."

Lamb gave one of his grunts.

"I don't know—you may be right. I'll tell the police surgeon to look out for distinguishing marks. Well, you haven't said how you got your 'impression'."

"From the whole circumstances, I think. I formed the opinion that an impersonation was probably taking place, and it struck me that it would have been very difficult for Annie Joyce to have planned it and carried it out without assistance. How did she know that Sir Philip was in England? She did know, because she rang up Jocelyn's Holt from Westhaven and asked for him. After Miss Collins' death I looked up the accounts in the Press again. I was struck by the coincidence of a lost wife turning up from occupied France just as Sir Philip was about to take up a confidential post at the War Office. His work is, I believe, very confidential."

"And who told you that?" said Lamb.

Miss Silver smiled at him.

"You do not really expect an answer, do you? . . . To return to what I was saying. I could not help thinking that it would be very useful to the Germans if they could plant an agent in Sir Philip Jocelyn's household. In fact, I thought her appearance a little too well timed."

Lamb sat looking at her. She wore the old black jacket with its narrow shoulders and worn fur collar, the neat dowdy felt hat with its small bunch of purple pansies on the left-hand side. Her hands in their shabby black kid gloves were folded in her lap. He was thinking, "Looks as if ten bob would buy her up, but there's something about her—you can't get from it." He said,

"Well, that's that—she was an enemy agent all right. She drugged Sir Philip last night and went through his papers. Seems he suspected her, and they were a fake lot. Military Intelligence went through them for fingerprints and found hers all over the place. We come in to arrest her, and there she is, by the table in the study, shot through the head. The question is, did Sir Philip catch her at his case and shoot her out of hand? Some men might. I'm bound to say he doesn't look that kind to me."

Miss Silver coughed.

"If the papers were not genuine, there would be very little motive for his shooting her. He might have done so if he had suddenly discovered that she was an enemy agent, but not if, as I understand, he knew that already and was a party to the trap which had been laid for her."

"Um—that's a point. Yes, there's something in that. Anyhow he says he left her alive. They both had coffee—her bedroom was done but not his—the grate in here was all in a mess. The police surgeon says she'd been dead some hours at least. We'll know more about that later. Well, Sir Philip starts out at twenty to nine. The porter saw him go. Says he'd just looked at his watch because he was expecting workmen round to see to the skylight on this floor—it was warped, and the black-out wouldn't stay put—so he was about and taking notice at the time. He says Sir Philip went off at twenty to, and he says he was looking queer. The men he was expecting came in at nine o'clock and went upstairs. From then on, there they were until half past twelve, right outside this flat—nobody could go in or out without their seeing them, and nobody did go in or out. We got on to the men, and they're positive about that."

Miss Silver said, "Dear me——" in a meditative manner.

Frank Abbott considered his Chief's superior tone a little overdone as he continued.

"That narrows things down a bit—you'll admit that, I suppose. She must have been dead before the men came at nine. That gives twenty minutes after Sir Philip left for someone to have got in and shot her and got away again. The porter was hanging about looking out for his men, and he says he didn't see anyone."

Miss Silver coughed.

"No doubt you pressed him on this point. People are very apt to say they haven't seen anyone, when what they really mean is that they have not seen anyone whom it would occur to them to suspect."

"Quite so. And, as you say, I pressed him. Actually, three people went up and came down again whilst he was waiting for the workmen—the postman, whom he knows personally, a boy delivering milk, and a man from the laundry."

"Had the milk been taken in?"

"No, it hadn't. That looks as if she was dead by the time it came."

"For which flat was the laundry?"

"He doesn't know. It was just after Sir Philip went, and he was at the back of the hall. The man went past with the laundry-basket on his head—he didn't take any more notice than that. Three of the flats have new tenants—he doesn't know where they go for their laundry."

Miss Silver coughed and said, "Quite so."

Lamb banged his knee.

"Look here, you don't suggest that a perfectly strange laundry-man comes in here, knows just where to put his hand on Sir Philip's revolver, shoots the woman, and goes off again with the weapon, all inside of five or six minutes?"

Miss Silver coughed again.

"It does not take very long to shoot anyone. Sir Philip's revolver may not have been used. If she considered herself to be in danger she may have tried to get hold of it—she would, of course, know where it was. After committing the crime it would, perhaps, occur to the murderer that he might throw suspicion on Sir Philip by removing it. This is, however, mere speculation."

Lamb gave his robust laugh.

"I'm glad you admit that!"

"I would like to know whether the laundry-man was seen coming down again."

"Yes, he was. The porter was answering a 'phone call, so he only saw him out of the tail of his eye."

"Had he still got the laundry-basket on his head?"

"Well, he would have, wouldn't he? He'd bring back the clean clothes and take away the dirty ones. And it's no good asking me any more about it, because that's all I know. You can ask the porter, but you won't find he knows any more either. No—the way it looks to me, the one that had the motive and the opportunity is Sir Philip. You may say that the motive isn't strong enough—and there's something in that. But the circumstances are all very suspicious. Here's one of them. He was at the War Office from nine to halfpast twelve—we've checked up on that—but he walks in at Mrs. Perry Jocelyn's flat at a quarter to one, sees Miss Armitage, doesn't see anyone else—it's one of those L-shaped rooms, and they're round the corner—and says 'Anne's dead.' Doesn't say any more because he realizes there are other people there, just turns round and walks out again. Now unless she was dead before he left this flat he couldn't have known about it. His explanation is that he meant something quite different—meant, in fact, that he was now certain that it was his wife who had died three years ago. What do you think of that?"

"He said it to Miss Armitage, thinking that they were alone?"

"So I understand. Mind you, he didn't say so—he left Miss Armitage out of it. I'm putting in what Mrs. Jocelyn said. She rang up to ask what had happened. It was she who mentioned Miss Armitage."

Miss Silver coughed.

"It must have given her a great shock, poor girl. She does not look at all strong."

"Do you know her?"

"I have met her. A very charming girl."

"Do you mean there's something between her and Sir Philip? Looks as if there might be, his running off to her like that. Look here, if that's the case, he'd have a very serious motive. Say he's tied up to this woman—doesn't know if she's his wife or not, but can't prove she isn't—there would be a very serious motive there." He paused, and added, "His revolver's gone. He admits it was there last night. What do you make of that?"

Miss Silver declined to make anything of it at all. She opined that it was a very interesting case, and that it was without doubt in the most capable of hands. Having permitted a perfectly genuine note of admiration to appear in her voice, she gave him a friendly smile and said,

"It is so good of you to let me know just how matters stand. I am really very much interested, especially after the rather curious thing which happened yesterday."

Frank Abbott felt a lively curiosity. What sort of rabbit was Maudie going to bring out of the hat? He had an inward spasm as he thought how much the simile would have shocked her. Or would it? You never knew with Maudie.

If Lamb felt any curiosity he didn't show it. His tone was off-hand and casual as he said,

"Oh, yes—there's something you wanted to tell me."

Miss Silver's manner became faintly tinged with reproof.

"There was something I felt it my duty to tell you."

"Well, let's have it. I'll have to be getting along."

The reproof became a little more definite. The Chief Inspector had the fleeting illusion that he was back in school and was perhaps about to be rebuked. It was so strong that for a moment he saw quite plainly the village schoolroom where he had learned the three Rs—the long bare room, the rows of forms, the red-cheeked country children, the small-paned windows standing open to a summer sky and the buzz of bees, the blackboard, the teacher's face. . . . Old Miss Payne—he hadn't thought of her for years. . . . It came and went in a flash, but he found himself sitting up and looking respectfully at Miss Silver, who was addressing him.

". . . yesterday afternoon. The sun came through for a moment, and I went over to the window and looked out. Lady Jocelyn—I will call her that for convenience—was coming down the street."

"What?"

Miss Silver inclined her head.

"She stopped on the opposite pavement and stood there looking up at Montague Mansions. She remained like that for some time, just standing there and looking up. She could not see me of course, as I took care to stand behind the curtain. I do not know whether she had the half-formed intention of coming in. If she had done so she might still be alive. She may have been too deeply implicated, or she may have thought that her danger was not so pressing as it has proved to have been. But I have ascertained that she had rung up Mrs. Garth Albany—you will remember her as Janice Meade—and obtained my address. Garth Albany is a connection. It was in their house that I met Miss Armitage."

Lamb was looking at her with a kind of frowning intensity. "Is that all?"

"By no means. Lady Jocelyn had been followed."

Lamb said, "What!" again, this time more sharply.

"By a girl in a shabby brown coat with a brown and purple scarf tied over her head. She was quite young, not over seventeen years of age I should say, and she had come out in a hurry, because she was wearing indoor shoes. She went up into the porch of one of the opposite houses and watched Lady Jocelyn from there."

"Look here, how do you know it was Lady Jocelyn?"

"Reproductions of her portrait by Amory were in all the papers at the time of her return from France. Her identity is really not in question. Apart from everything else, her manner when I spoke to her of the occurrence——"

"You spoke to her?"

"On the telephone—but I will come to that presently. As I knew that the police were now satisfied that Miss Collins' death was due to a road accident, and that they were no longer interested in Lady Jocelyn, the fact that she was being followed attracted my attention. In any case, the young girl I had seen would not have been employed in a police case. I thought the matter curious and somewhat alarming. My valued maid, Emma Meadows, was on the point of going out to the post. I asked her to follow the girl, and if possible to find out where she went."

"Well?"

"She kept both her and Lady Jocelyn in sight until the latter hailed a passing taxi. I think there is no doubt that she came straight back to this flat. The girl turned round and retraced her steps. Emma followed her, but unfortunately lost sight of her a little later at a crowded corner. When she got through the crowd herself—she is elderly and rather stout—the girl was nowhere to be seen. She may have gone into a shop, or she may have got on a bus."

"What street was this?"

Miss Silver told him, and Frank Abbott wrote it down. She continued,

"Later on, after tea, I rang Lady Jocelyn up."

"Why did you do that?"

"On thinking the matter over carefully I had come to the conclusion that if she was being shadowed, it was in all probability at the instance of someone other than the police. When I asked myself to whose interest it would be to keep her under observation, the answer was quite simple. I had reason to believe that she had illegal associates—I found it quite impossible to accept the conclusions of the police with regard to the death of Miss Collins—and it occurred to me that if her associates, already sufficiently distrustful to have her watched, were to believe that she had formed the intention of approaching me, she would be in very grave danger. My name is not known to the public, but, especially since the Harsch case, it may have become known to those with whom Lady Jocelyn was entangled. After thinking the matter over I decided to warn her. If she had any intention of abandoning her associates, I felt that she should be encouraged to do so."

"Well, you rang her up. What did she say?"

Miss Silver shook her head gravely.

"Her mood had altered. She assumed a confident tone and declared that she did not know what I was talking about. I offered to come and see her, and there was, I believe, a moment when she hesitated, but in the end she rang off quickly. I think she was afraid, but I think she had made up her mind to go through with what she was doing."

Lamb got to his feet with a grunt.

"Well, it doesn't get us much farther, does it?"

XXXII

LILLA JOCELYN went out after lunch to the canteen at which she worked as a voluntary helper. Pelham Trent, after seeing her off, came back into the room.

"Do you mind if I stay for a minute or two?"

Lyndall said, "No," and didn't know whether she was telling the truth or not. She wanted to be alone, and she was afraid of being alone. She wanted to mourn for Anne who was dead, but she didn't know just how truly she could mourn. If she was alone she could think herself back to the old days when Anne was one of the three people she loved most on earth. A warm feeling of sorrow welled up in her, melting away the cold sense of shock. Yes, she must be alone. She lifted her eyes to Pelham Trent, and he saw that they were bright with tears.

"You ought to rest," he said quickly. "You won't try and go out or do anything, will you? I'm sure you ought to rest."

She said, "Yes, I will." And then, "I wish we knew something more. Lilla doesn't know who she was speaking to, and the man who answered didn't tell her anything—only that Anne was dead. Do you think it was an accident? I had tea with her the day before yesterday—she was quite well then." She kept her eyes on him as she spoke, the tears shining, something strained and piteous about her look.

He said, "My dear—I'm sorry—it's been a shock. Would you like me to go round and find out for you? It's only five minutes' walk."

"I don't know. . . . No—Philip mightn't like it." She put up a hand and pushed back her hair. "You're very kind."

He shook his head.

"I needn't go up to the flat, you know. If Jocelyn's there he won't want to be bothered. I could ask the porter—but no—that wouldn't do."

Lyndall said, "No." And then, "I'll ring up. We are relations—we've got a right to know. Philip wouldn't mind."

It was Sergeant Abbott who answered her ring, but she wasn't to know that. He was just a voice—the sort of voice that might have belonged to any of Philip's friends. He said, "Just a moment, Miss Armitage." She heard his steps going away, then men's voices, and the steps coming back.

"Are you speaking from Mrs. Jocelyn's flat?"

"Yes—she had to go out. Will you please tell me what has happened to Anne? It's so dreadful not knowing."

Frank Abbot reflected cynically that it might be a great deal more dreadful to know. He said,

"You know she's dead?"

"Yes."

"Sir Philip Jocelyn told you that?"

"Yes—but not how it happened—*please*——"

"I am afraid you must be prepared for a shock. She was found shot."

"Oh——" It was just a long, soft breath. And then, "Did she—shoot herself?"

"No—someone shot her."

"Who?"

"We don't know."

She said, "Who are you?" in a wondering voice.

"Detective Sergeant Abbott. The police are in charge here."

After a pause she said, "Is Philip there?"

"No, he hasn't turned up yet."

She said, "Oh——" again.

After a moment she hung up the receiver and turned round to Pelham Trent, her face quite drained of colour.

"Pelham——"

"I know—I heard what he said. What a dreadful thing! Here, come and sit down."

She let him put her into a chair and leaned back in it. After a moment she said,

"Dreadful for Philip—dreadful for her—poor Anne——" Her voice went, a violent shudder ran over her.

After looking at her with frowning intensity Trent walked away to the far end of the room.

As far as she could feel anything just then, she felt relief. She had the shocked creature's desire to creep away into a dark place and be alone. But she couldn't do that. Behind the sense of shock she was aware of Philip. What she did and what she said now was going to matter to Philip. She had a sense of fear for him, and a great longing to help. She tried to focus her mind, to get things clear. This absorbed her so deeply that she did not notice Pelham Trent's return until she heard his voice.

"Lyn—you're all right—you're not faint!"

"I'm all right——" Her tone was vague. She was coming back from a long way off.

He took a chair, pulled it close to her, and sat down.

"Lyndall, will you please listen. I hate to bother you now, but we can't count on your being left alone. If this is murder, the police may be here at any moment. It was most unfortunate that Lilla should have mentioned Jocelyn's coming here and saying what he did. And it's doubly unfortunate that she should have told the police it was said to you. They'll want to know why he came here—why he told *you* his wife was dead— why he went away in a hurry as soon as he found that Lilla and I were here. I'm bound to tell you that in a case of this sort a husband or wife is always under suspicion. At the very least there will be talk, publicity. You've got to be kept clear of it, for Jocelyn's sake as well as your own. This murder coming on the top of all the talk about Anne Jocelyn's return—well, my dear, you can see for yourself. If the police get it into their heads that Philip Jocelyn is fond of you, or that there's anything between you, it will be just about the most disastrous thing that could happen—for him. You've got to be very careful indeed. Philip and Anne Jocelyn were your cousins, and you were very fond of them both—that's your line. You were her bridesmaid—remember to bring that in. And—oh, my dear, don't look at them the way you're looking at me!"

"No—I won't. I'm sorry——"

He put reassurance into his voice.

"You'll be all right. Don't say a word more than you're obliged to. Don't tell anyone anything. Don't discuss anything with anyone. I'm your lawyer, you know, and that's sound legal advice. And here's some more, only I'm afraid you won't like it. Don't see Jocelyn—or if you do, don't discuss anything."

Her eyes darkened, the lashes screening them. He felt her withdrawn, resisting. He concentrated all that he had upon convincing her.

"You don't know what getting mixed up in a case like this may mean. You don't know what you are up against. You don't know what harm you may do with a word. You don't know how easy it is to let something slip. They'll question you. You must remember only to answer their questions. Say yes, or say no. Don't go farther than that."

"Do you think I would say anything that would hurt Philip?"

"That is not for you to say. You might not know what would hurt him. You'd better keep out of it. Don't let him tell you anything. The less you know the better." He had been speaking in a low, tense voice that was almost a whisper. Now it changed, lightened, and resumed its normal pitch. "There —that's all. Just be sensible and keep a still tongue, and everything will be quite all right. Jocelyn ought to get into touch with Codrington at once—he may have done so already. If he does ring you up or come here again, just push him off to the office. And remember—not one unnecessary word."

Her eyes had closed. She opened them now with an effort and said,

"Thank you." And then, "Pelham, will you go now? I don't think I can talk about it any more."

He had a word of approbation for this.

"Stick to that and everything will be quite all right. And don't worry. I didn't mean to frighten you about Jocelyn. If he was at the War Office he's probably got an absolutely water-tight alibi. What we do want to avoid is raking up anything like the question of Anne Jocelyn's identity, and having the Press get hold of it, or of any other bit of scandal."

When he was gone Lyndall sat up, her hands linked tightly in her lap, her face white and set, her eyes intent. She did not move for a long time, but in the end she got up, went over to the telephone, and dialled Janice Albany's number.

XXXIII

MISS SILVER looked up from her knitting at the sound of her front door bell. The hands of the clock on the mantelpiece stood at half past three. She was not expecting anyone, and had sat down by the fire to knit, and to consider with regretful interest the tragic fate of Lady Jocelyn, who was not in her opinion Lady Jocelyn at all, but Annie Joyce.

Following upon the ring she heard Emma's rather deep tones, after which the sitting-room door was opened.

"Will you see Miss Armitage?"

Miss Silver placed her knitting carefully on the arm of her chair and rose to receive her visitor. There came in the girl with whom she had talked at Janice Albany's. She wore the same dark green coat and hat, but she looked decidedly paler and more frail than she had done on that occasion. The big grey eyes with their dark lashes were fixed with painful intensity upon Miss Silver's face as she said,

"Janice told me you were kind——"

"I hope so, my dear. Won't you sit down? Now would you like to have a cup of tea with me first, or would you rather tell me what I can do for you? Emma could get the tea in a moment."

Lyndall shook her head.

"Janice said to come and see you. She doesn't know why. She only knows that we're in trouble because—Anne is dead."

Miss Silver had resumed her seat and her knitting. The needles clicked in a gentle and soothing manner.

"Yes, my dear, I know. You are referring, of course, to Lady Jocelyn."

The faint colour of surprise tinged the transparent skin for an instant.

"How did you know—but Janice said you knew everything. Did you know that she had been shot?"

Miss Silver gave her a clear, kind glance.

"Yes, I knew."

"That she was murdered?"

"Yes."

With a hastily drawn breath Lyndall went on.

"Then can you tell me what I ought to do? Janice said——" The breath failed, the colour was all gone again.

"What did she say?"

Lyndall shook her head as if she couldn't explain. Then she said,

"If I told you anything—would you have to tell the police?"

Miss Silver coughed.

"That would depend upon what it was."

Lyndall sat looking at her. The grey eyes were asking questions. Presently she said,

"Do they know who did it?"

"No, If there is anything that you know, Miss Armitage—anything that would help to identify the criminal—you ought not to hold it back. I think you do know something or you would not be here."

"I don't know whether it would help. That's why I came—I thought you would help me to know—but it's so difficult —— I'm afraid——" Her voice went again suddenly.

Miss Silver had stopped knitting. She looked at her gravely. Then she said,

"Miss Armitage, I will tell you something. Yesterday afternoon Lady Jocelyn came and stood on the pavement opposite these flats. She remained there for some time looking up. I believe that she was trying to decide whether she would break with some dangerous past associations. I believe she had the half-formed intention of coming to see me, and I believe that if she had done so she would not now be lying dead. Afterwards I rang her up to warn her, but she had by then decided upon her course."

Lyndall put a hand up to her throat. She said in a whisper, "Was it something about Miss Collins?"

"Miss Armitage, if what you know has anything to do with the death of Nellie Collins, I beg that you will tell me what it is. There have been two deaths already. What you know may be as dangerous to you as it was to Miss Collins and to Lady Jocelyn."

Lyndall's hand dropped into her lap again.

"It's not because I'm afraid," she said, speaking like a child. "It's because of Philip. It's so dreadful for him already, that anything about Anne—*anything*——"

Miss Silver gave her the smile which had induced so many confidences. It had an extraordinarily encouraging, heartening, and bracing effect.

"My dear, the truth is sometimes painful, but it is salutary. Well-meant deceptions and the withholding of evidence are extremely dangerous in a criminal case. We all have to face pain sometimes—I fear that Sir Philip Jocelyn may have to face a good deal of it. You will not help him by withholding anything which might bring a dangerous criminal to justice."

Lyndall gave her a straight look.

"Pelham said they might suspect Philip. Do they suspect him?"

Miss Silver did not answer the question. She coughed and said,

"Who is Pelham?"

"He is a partner in the firm of Philip's solicitors. There is just him and Mr. Codrington now. He was there when Philip came in and said that Anne was dead, and he said I oughtn't to talk to anyone or say anything, because Philip might be suspected. He talked to me for a long time after Lilla went out."

"Was he aware that you knew something?"

"Oh, no—how could he be?"

"You are sure he did not know? Did anyone know?"

"Anne knew."

"You told her?"

"Yes."

"Because it was something to do with Miss Collins?"

"Yes."

"What did she say?"

"She said it would hurt Philip——" Her voice faltered piteously. "I—promised—I wouldn't say anything."

After a little pause Miss Silver said,

"I do not think that you can keep that promise now."

Again Lyndall gave that slight shake of the head.

"No—I can't keep it now. I thought for a long time after Pelham had gone away, and then I rang up Janice and asked her about you. She said you would be fair, and kind, and she said I could trust you—I'm going to trust you. This is what happened. It was before Philip and Anne came up to town. I think it was on the twelfth—yes, Wednesday the twelfth. Someone said there was a shop that had enamelled saucepans, so I went to see, for Lilla, but they hadn't got any. When I was coming back I saw Anne—at least I thought it was Anne. She had her back to me, and she was just going into a shop— a hairdresser's shop called Félise."

Miss Silver said brightly, "In Charlotte Street?"

Colour ran up into Lyndall's face.

"How did you know?"

Miss Silver coughed.

"Pray proceed, Miss Armitage. I am most interested."

Lyndall thought, " She really does know everything."

Oddly enough, this did not frighten her. It provided a sense of support. If she made a mistake, Miss Silver would be able to put it right. She went on with less effort.

"I wasn't sure that it was Anne. I wasn't sure if she had seen me. I didn't want her to think—— I followed her into the shop. She wasn't there. The girl behind the counter was busy—she didn't see me. I went through to see if Anne was in one of the cubicles, and she wasn't. There was a door at the end—a looking-glass door. I opened it, and there was a dark passage, quite small, and a stair going up, and a door at the end. The door wasn't quite shut—there was a little line of light all down the edge. And I heard Anne say, 'You might as well let me write to Nellie Collins. She's quite harmless.' And a man said—a man said——"

"Go on, my dear."

Lyndall stared back at her, her eyes fixed blindly upon a face she could no longer see. Her lips only just moved.

"He said, 'That is not for you to say'."

"And then?"

"I ran away." She gave a deep sigh and seemed to come awake again. "I was frightened—I don't think I've ever been so frightened in my life. It was stupid——"

Miss Silver coughed.

"I do not think so."

There was a silence. Lyndall leaned back and closed her eyes. She felt as if she had been climbing a long, steep hill. Now that she was come to the top, there was no breath in her. And she was afraid to look over the edge and see what lay beyond.

Miss Silver's voice broke in upon her thoughts.

"You told Lady Jocelyn what you had overheard. When did you do so?"

She opened her eyes.

"When I saw about Miss Collins in the papers."

"Will you tell me just what she said?"

Lyndall told her, speaking only just above her breath, with the picture in her mind of Anne pouring out tea, Anne kneeling by the fire, Anne asking her not to hurt Philip.

"She said I'd made a mistake. She said it might hurt Philip, so I promised."

"I see. Miss Armitage, how well did you know Lady Jocelyn? I do not mean since her return, but before she went to France."

She was startled by the change of subject. She sat up.

"We were at Jocelyn's Holt together when she came there to stay after her mother died. None of us knew her till then. She was grown up, and I wasn't. She was marvellous to me. I loved her—terribly. When she and Philip got engaged I thought it was wonderful. I was one of her bridesmaids."

"If you were girls together in the same house you would have been in and out of each other's rooms, dressed and undressed together. Can you tell me whether Lady Jocelyn had any mark by which she could have been identified?"

"Oh, no, she hadn't. All the relations asked me that when she came back. There wasn't anything."

She met a very penetrating gaze.

"If she had had a brown mole the size of a sixpence just above her left knee, you would have noticed it?"

"Of course. But she hadn't anything like that."

"You are quite sure? It is very important."

"Yes, I am quite, quite sure."

"You would be able to swear to it? You will, I think, be called upon to do so."

Lyndall pressed her hands together in her lap. She said, "Yes." And then, slowly, "I don't understand. Will you please tell me?"

Miss Silver said gravely,

"The woman who died today had a mole such as I have described. I think Miss Collins knew that Annie Joyce had such a mole. I think Lady Jocelyn died more than three years ago."

XXXIV

"I WANT police protection for her," said Miss Silver firmly.

The Chief Inspector, at the other end of the telephone, drew out a handkerchief and blew his nose with an exasperated sound.

"Now, Miss Silver——"

She coughed and proceeded.

"I consider it most desirable. I will give you the address of the hairdressing establishment. It is Félise, Charlotte Street. . . . I beg your pardon?" An exclamation of surprise had reached her along the wire. "Is the name familiar to you?"

"I don't know about familiar. Sir Philip says his wife had an appointment there to have her hair done yesterday afternoon. We were asking him about her movements on the previous day, and he mentioned having heard her make this appointment. Says he heard the name as he was letting himself into the flat, and she explained it was her hairdresser. Quite a good cover-up."

"It is a genuine hairdressing establishment. It stands three doors from the corner where Emma Meadows lost sight of the girl who had been following Lady Jocelyn—or, as I think we may now call her, Annie Joyce."

The Chief Inspector blew his nose, meditatively this time.

"Well, you'd better keep Miss Armitage. I'll send Frank round. Just leave him to form his own conclusions, will you? He's a bit too much inclined to take all you say for gospel, if you don't mind my saying so."

Deprecation of his tone was evident as Miss Silver replied, "I do not consider that Sergeant Abbott is so easily influenced—except, as we should all be, by the facts of a case." The stress laid upon the word "facts" accentuated the reproof.

Lamb turned it off with a laugh.

"Well, we won't quarrel about that. If Frank is satisfied, the people at the shop will be put through it. I'll get someone on to finding out about them straight away."

Sergeant Abbott, arriving at Montague Mansions, was duly acquainted with Miss Lyndall Armitage's story.

"Where is she, Miss Silver?"

Miss Silver, well on the way to completing Johnny's second pair of stockings, replied that Miss Armitage was lying down —"in my bedroom next door. She is far from strong, and it has shaken her a good deal."

Frank regarded her with admiration.

"Tucked up under an eiderdown with a hot-water bottle, I don't mind betting. Will you be angry if I quote Wordsworth instead of Tennyson?

> 'A perfect Woman, nobly planned,
> To warn, to comfort, and command.' "

Miss Silver smiled indulgently. If she detected a faintly sardonic flavour in tone and look she gave no sign of resenting it, but said soberly,

"We have no time just now to discuss the poets, my dear Frank. I have kept Miss Armitage here because I do not feel justified in allowing her to return to her flat without protection. She tells me that her cousin, Mrs. Perry Jocelyn, is unlikely to be home much before eleven, and that they have a daily maid who leaves at three o'clock. I think, in the circumstances, that it would be extremely dangerous to leave her alone and unprotected."

"What makes you think she is in danger?"

"My dear Frank! The day before yesterday at tea-time she acquainted Annie Joyce with the fact that she had overheard part of a conversation between her and the man from whom she was taking her orders. Only two sentences, it is true, but could anything be more compromising?—'You might as well let me write to Nellie Collins. She is quite harmless,' and, 'That is not for you to say.' They supply clear evidence of a connection with Miss Collins, they imply that Annie Joyce was not permitted herself to answer the letter she had received from her, and they make it clear that she was not a principal, but an agent acting under the orders of this man whom she had come to see. Annie Joyce could have been under no illusion as to the importance of what Miss Armitage had overheard. She did, in fact, do all she could to ensure her silence. She assured her that the whole thing was a mistake, that she must have imagined having overheard the name of Nellie Collins, and she appealed to her affection and family feeling not to repeat anything which might revive the publicity from which they, and especially Sir Philip, had already suffered so much."

"This was the day before yesterday?"

"Yes. And yesterday afternoon she kept another appointment with the man from whom she took her orders. It is, I suppose, possible, but I do not think it is at all likely, that she did not acquaint him with what Miss Armitage had told her. There is some evidence that the interview disquieted him, since he had her followed when she came away from it. If she told him that a previous interview had been overheard, he may have decided that her usefulness as an agent was seriously compromised. The German secret service has never hesitated to sacrifice an agent who might prove to be more of a liability than an asset. If she told him that it was Miss Armitage who had overheard them, you will, I think, agree that she may be in very serious danger, and that until this man is under arrest she should be given the very fullest possible measure of protection."

Frank Abbott ran his hand back over his hair.

"All right, we'll look after her. But, you know, the Chief thinks you're trailing a red herring. He thinks Jocelyn shot the woman. There's some evidence—no, not evidence—there's some indication of a personal motive. Suppose he was in love with this Armitage girl. I know some people who live near Jocelyn's Holt. They tell me everyone was expecting the engagement to be given out, when Annie Joyce bobbed up as Lady Jocelyn. Rather a nasty strain on the temper, you know, especially as local talk had it that Philip Jocelyn stuck to it for as long as he could that he didn't recognize her, and she wasn't his wife. Well, he seems to have been convinced in the end, and they set up house together on strictly detached lines. Then something happened which upset his conviction, and at the same time Military Intelligence suggest to him she's an emeny agent. Pretty galling, don't you think? And then he finds her with her fingers in his papers. Don't you think he might fly off the handle and shoot? Murder's been done for a good deal less than that. Anyhow, the Chief thinks that's what happened —and he doesn't know the gossipy bits I've just imparted to you, which are strictly off the record and *entre nous*. The time question narrows it down, you see. Jocelyn went off at twenty to nine, the laundryman came and went immediately after that, the postman and the boy with the milk one after the other just before nine, and the workmen had camped down on the landing by nine o'clock."

Miss Silver's needles clicked rapidly, the long grey stocking revolved.

"Have you traced any delivery of laundry?"

He shook his head.

"Two lots of tenants are away. The man may simply have gone up, found he couldn't get in, and gone away again."

Miss Silver gave a small sceptical cough.

"Oh, no, he would not do that. He would have left the basket with the porter."

"Well, he might. But the porter says people aren't very trusting with new tenants nowadays—they like payment on delivery." He cocked an eyebrow. "I see you've set your heart on the laundryman." He got up, looking very tall and slim. "Well, I must see Miss Armitage, and then I'll go and deal with the hairdresser. Wish me luck!"

XXXV

LYNDALL was presently seen home by a large constable with a benevolent face and a slow, persevering manner of speech. In the twenty minutes or so which it took them to arrive at Lilla Jocelyn's flat he had told her all about his wife, whose name was Daisy and who had been an upholstress before they were married, and their three children—Ernie, turned seven, who was a wonder at his lessons, Ellie aged four, and Stanley who would be six months old next week. In moments of strain small irrelevant things may pass quite unnoticed, but they may also become idelibly impressed upon the memory. Lyndall was never to forget that Ernie could read when he was four, or that little Ellie screamed whenever she saw a cat. The constable appeared to be rather proud of this idiosyncrasy, but informed her that his wife said it wouldn't do to let it go on, and she was going to get a kitten and break her of being so soft.

Later, when she had ensconced him in front of the kitchen fire and provided him with the papers, she sat down by herself in the L-shaped living-room and thought what a long time it would be before Lilla came home.

It was some time after this that Frank Abbott rang up his Chief.

"Well, sir, I saw Miss Armitage. She's quite clear about what she heard. The snag is that at the time she wasn't at all sure whether the woman she followed into the hairdresser's shop was the so-called Lady Jocelyn or not, because she only saw her back. In fact, what she saw was the right coloured hair, the right sort of coat, and the right coloured dress. But there aren't so many mink coats walking round London or women with the right hair and just that shade of blue dress. They are the clothes of the Amory portrait and fairly noticeable, you know. Anyhow she wasn't sure at the time. That's why she followed her in—she wanted to make sure. And she won't swear to the voice which she heard on the other side of an unlatched door, but she thought it was Lady Jocelyn's voice. What she will swear to through thick and thin is what she heard—what the woman said, 'You might as well let me write to Nellie Collins. She is quite harmless.' And the man's answer, 'That is not for you to say.' That is what she heard, and that is what she repeated to Annie Joyce. It would certainly make her sit up and take notice, and if she repeated it to her employer, I agree with Maudie that we'd better keep an eye on the Armitage girl."

Lamb grunted.

"You always do agree with her—that's nothing new."

"Oh, no, sir—not always—only when the brain is waving rather brightly." Then, before Lamb had time to disentangle this, "Well, I'm talking from the hairdresser's—telephone in the room across the passage described by Miss Armitage.

Clarke is shepherding the staff in the shop. Proprietress, stout Frenchwoman called Dupont, very angry, very abusive—says she's never been so insulted in her life. Says Lady Jocelyn was a client—oh, but certainly—her hair was much impoverished and needed frequent attention. Her husband M. Felix Dupont —that's where they get the Félise from—occasionally saw special clients in the office. He had probably seen Lady Jocelyn there—she was a very special client. But she couldn't have seen him yesterday, or any day this week, because he had been in bed, very ill, very suffering—wounds of the last war. I must understand that he is an invalid, and that only occasionally can he come to the shop and give his valuable advice. For all the rest of the time it is she who has to do everything and nurse her husband as well, and a lot more on those lines, all very rapid and French. But you remember what Maudie said about the girl who followed Annie Joyce—said she had on a brown coat and a brown and purple scarf over her head—well, one of the girls here has got a brown coat and a brown and purple scarf, so that hooks up all right. As you know, Maudie's Emma went after the girl she saw, and lost her only just round the corner from here."

Lamb grunted.

"We'll have to see if they can pick this girl out."

"It won't be necessary, sir. I've had her in alone, and she owned up. She's only about sixteen, and she's all of a doodah. Said she didn't know she was doing anything wrong. Mr. Felix told her to put on her coat and see where Lady Jocelyn went, and he gave her half-a-crown when she got back. And when I said, 'You mean M. Felix Dupont, Madame's husband?' she said, 'Oh, no, it wasn't him—it was the other gentleman.' "

The wire vibrated with the Chief Inspector's "*What!*"

"Yes, sir. Continuing our interesting conversation—I elicited the following facts. M. Felix did come down occasionally. He was a very clever hairdresser, and he only saw special clients, but he was often too ill to come at all. Mr. Felix also saw special clients. He came in by a back way, never through the shop. They had to take messages for him and make appointments. If Madame was in she answered the telephone herself. If she was out, they had to write the message down, and she would attend to it later. Now comes the *pièce de résistance*——"

178

The Chief Inspector was heard to thump his office table.

"If you don't know enough English to speak your own language you'd better go back to school and learn how!"

"Sorry, Chief—my mistake—I should have said titbit. Anyhow, here it is. None of the girls ever saw Mr. Felix. He came and went by the back way, and he never set foot in the shop. M. Felix Dupont used the shop entrance—they all saw him whenever he came. But nobody ever saw Mr. Felix except Madame and the ladies who came by appointment."

"What about his sending her after Lady Jocelyn?"

"Yes, I asked her that, and she said it was Madame who told her that Mr. Felix would like her to go after Lady Jocelyn, and it was Madame who gave her the half-crown and told her not to talk about it, because, she said, it wouldn't sound very nice, but he had given her a very special treatment, and he wanted to know whether she did what he told her and went straight home. He said it wouldn't be good for her if she didn't."

"Think she swallowed that?"

"I don't suppose she bothered. All in the day's work, so to speak. You know how it is with a girl like that—customers are just work. What really matters is who is going to take them to the pictures, or part with some coupons so that they can get another pair of alleged silk stockings."

Chief Inspector Lamb was heard to thank God that his girls had been differently brought up to that.

"Yes, sir—they would be. But I think this kid is all right. Too scared, and talking too freely to be in on any games they've been up to here. I think we ought to pull Madame in. And then I thought I'll go along and see her interesting invalid. . . ."

XXXVI

THE time went very slowly by. Lyndall found, as innumerable women have found before her, that she could do nothing to hasten it. She couldn't read, or sew, or listen to the wireless, because to do any of these things you must be in control of your own thoughts, and she was not in control of hers. Whilst she was talking to Miss Silver and Sergeant Abbott, whilst the constable had talked about his family, there had been a varying degree of constraint upon her mind, and in a varying degree it had responded. But as soon as she was alone it turned again to the point from which she now found herself unable to deflect it. There are things which are so shocking that they are believed at once, the very force of the shock pressing in past all the normal barriers. There are things so shocking that they cannot be believed at all, but you can't forget them, you can't get them out of your mind. Lyndall could not have said that she was in either of these two states. There had been so great an initial shock as to render her incapable of either belief or judgment, but now as time went slowly by she found herself believing something which chilled her body almost as much as it froze her mind.

She got up once and went to the telephone, but after standing for a long half minute with her finger on the first number she would have to dial she turned away and went back to the chair from which she had risen. She couldn't do it. Perhaps tomorrow when her mind didn't feel so sore and stiff and she could think again. Not tonight—not now. Once you have said a thing you can never take it back.

When about five minutes later the telephone bell rang she went to answer it with shuddering reluctance. Philip's voice said her name.

"Lyn—is that you?"

"Yes——" The word wouldn't sound the first time. She had to try it again.

"Are you alone? I want to see you—very badly. I'll come straight round."

He hung up on that, but she stayed where she was until it came to her that Philip would be arriving and she must be ready to let him in. As she passed through the hall she stopped at the half open kitchen door to say, "My cousin is coming round to see me—Sir Philip Jocelyn."

It was hardly said before the door bell rang. She opened it with a finger on her lips and a gesture in the direction of that half open door.

Philip looked surprised. He took off his coat and hung it up. Then when they were in the living-room he asked,

"What was all that for? Who's here?"

"A policeman in the kitchen."

"Why?"

"Because I overheard something, and they don't know if she—if Anne——"

He said, interrupting her, "She wasn't Anne—that's certain now. She was Annie Joyce." Then, after a curious pause, "I've found Anne's diary."

"Her diary?"

"Yes. Of course I knew she kept one—I suppose you did too. What I didn't know until a couple of days ago was that she put down everything——" He broke off. "Lyn, it's quite incredible! I didn't want to read it—I don't intend to read it. What I've had to do is to see whether the things she told me—the things which convinced me against every instinct I've got —whether they were there. And they are. What I said when I asked her to marry me—things that happened on our honeymoon—things it seemed impossible that anybody else should know—she had written them all down. And Annie Joyce had got them by heart."

Lyndall looked at him in a bewildered rush of feeling. The stranger who had stood between them had gone and she had never been Anne. Presently she would be able to go back to remembering that she had loved Anne very much. Just now she could only listen.

Philip was telling her about finding the diary.

"I made sure she would have it with her. However carefully she had learned it all up she would be bound to keep it handy. Well, I found it—two volumes sewn into the mattress on her bed—good long stitches so that it wouldn't have taken a minute to rip them out if she wanted it. That's what caught my eye—when I'd looked everywhere else. That settled the matter as far as I was concerned. She never convinced anything except my brain, and the diary lets that out. Anne's been dead for three and a half years. You've got to believe that, Lyn."

She wanted to with all her heart. But she couldn't find words. She didn't even know that she could find thoughts to answer him. Her mind swung back on the fixed point to which it had been held. She heard him say,

"Lyn, that's what I meant when I came here this morning. Annie Joyce was a spy, you know—planted on me. It wasn't just an ordinary impersonation. It was all very carefully planned. She was an enemy agent with a very definite job. She drugged me last night and went through my papers."

"Philip!"

"They were spoof papers, and an old code-book. We'd been doing a bit of planning too. My guess is that she was working under orders, and someone came along to collect. Whoever it was knew enough to realize she'd been had. That meant she was for it from us, if not from them. At the best, she wouldn't be of any more use—at the worst, we might get something out of her. They are quite ruthless over that sort of thing, and I think that whoever it was just shot her out of hand—possibly with my revolver, or possibly not. Anyhow it probably seemed a good idea to remove mine and hope the police would think I'd shot her—which they do."

She said his name again.

"Philip!" And then, with a rush, "They don't—they can't!"

He put an arm round her.

"Wake up, Lyn! They do, and they can. Wake up and face it! I'm in a mess. Codrington says I'd better keep away from you. I will after this. But I had to see you first—I couldn't risk your thinking it was worse than it is. They think it looks bad, my coming straight here from the War Office and saying Anne was dead when I couldn't have known about the murder unless it had happened before I left the flat. But when I said Anne I meant my wife, Anne Jocelyn, and not Annie Joyce at all. I meant that I was convinced of Anne's death—not that I knew Annie Joyce had been shot. Lyn—you've got to believe me!"

"Of course I believe you."

She began to tell him about seeing Anne—no, Annie—going into the hairdresser's shop, and what she had overheard in the dark passage with the line of light just showing at the edge of an unlatched door.

His manner changed abruptly.

"You heard that? You're sure?"

"Yes—I told Miss Silver."

"Who is she?"

She explained Miss Silver.

"And then Sergeant Abbott came, and I told him, and I think he's gone to arrest the people at the shop."

"Well, that's something." Then, "I suppose you know how important this is?"

"Yes. Philip, I told Anne—I mean Annie—about it."

He stared.

"You didn't!"

"Yes, I did. I felt as if I had to. I told her the day before yesterday."

"*Lyn*—you little fool! Suppose she told him—this man!"

Lyndall nodded.

"That's what Miss Silver said. So they sent me home with a policeman. He's in the kitchen doing a crossword."

He had just begun to say in a tone of relief, "Well, somebody's got some sense," when the front door buzzer went again. Lyndall felt the sound of it go tingling through her. Perhaps it was what she had been waiting for.

Philip's arm dropped from her shoulders. He wore a look of frowning pallor.

"I ought not to be seen here. Who is it likely to be? Get rid of them if you can!"

She nodded without speaking. The buzzer went again as she crossed the room, but she took her time—time to open Lilla's panelled chest and let Philip's coat down on the spare blankets, time to pull the kitchen door to so as not to show the lighted room beyond.

Then she opened the outer door and saw Pelham Trent. He came in at once, easy and friendly as he had always been.

"Are you alone, Lyn? I wanted to see you. Lilla isn't home yet?"

"No. It's her late night. She isn't home."

They were standing just inside the door. As he turned to shut it, she said,

"I wanted to see you too. I wanted to ask you something."

He turned back, a little surprised.

"Well, let's go into the drawing-room. I can't stay, so I won't take my coat off."

She stood between him and the door of the room where Philip was.

"Do you know a shop called Félise?"

Surprise became astonishment.

"My dear Lyn! What is this—a guessing game? I really wanted to say something——"

She came in with a sort of quiet determination.

"I think you do know it."

"What do you mean?"

She said in a clear, steady tone,

"I followed her, you know. Not because I thought there was anything wrong. I just didn't want her to think—that doesn't matter now, does it. I heard her say, 'You might as well let me write to Nellie Collins. She is quite harmless.' And you said, 'That is not for you to say.' "

He stood where he was, looking at her aghast.

"Lyn—have you gone mad?"

She shook her head gently,

"I didn't know it was you at the time—I didn't know until this afternoon when you said the same thing again. You said it to me—in the same kind of whispering voice, 'That is not for you to say'. I guessed then. Afterwards I was sure. I told Miss Silver and the police about what I heard, but I didn't tell them about you. I shall have to tell them, but I thought I would tell you first, because we have been friends."

As soon as she had said the last word she knew that it wasn't true. This man had never been a friend. He was a stranger, and dangerous—she was in very great danger. Through all that had happened in the last few hours thought had been fixed and rigid. Now, under the impact of danger, it swung free. She cried out, and her cry was loud enough to bring Philip Jocelyn round the corner of the L to the half open door, and to arouse the large constable from the consideration of what a word of four letters suggesting a light could be. He got himself out of his chair and opened the door, to see a strange man in an overcoat holding Miss Armitage by the shoulder with his left hand, whilst with the other he held a revolver to her head.

The same spectacle had halted Philip Jocelyn. Pelham Trent, looking in that direction, was aware of him, but not of the constable, his attention being a good deal taken up by the emergency and the brilliant ideas which it suggested. He said harshly to Philip,

"Jocelyn, if you move, I'll shoot her—and with your revolver! You damned fool—to think that you could lay a trap like this for me! You've just played into my hands, the two of you, and this is what is going to happen. I'd like you just to know, because I've had it in for you for quite a time. You think a lot of yourself, don't you? You think a lot of your name and your family. Well, you're going to be a headline in every dirty rag in the country—'Suicide Pact in a Flat—Sir Philip Jocelyn and Girl Friend.' Perhaps you can imagine the letterpress for yourself. I must just get a little closer to you to make it really convicing. Come along, Lyn!"

He began to walk across the hall, pushing her before him. She could feel the cold muzzle of the revolver against her right temple.

This was on the outside. She knew about it, but it had very little to do with what was in her mind. There, in a very clear light, she saw and knew that she and Philip were on the edge of death, that if she moved or tried to pull away she would be dead at once. And then he would shoot Philip. But he wouldn't shoot her first if he could help it, because the moment he fired Philip would rush him. She didn't know what the constable was doing. She couldn't see the kitchen door. Even if he had heard her call out, she would be dead before he reached them.

She saw all these things together in the bright light and without any passage of time. She wasn't frightened, because it was rather like being dead already. From somewhere outside time she saw that there would be a moment when the revolver would swing away from her and aim at Philip. She held herself like a coiled spring and waited for that moment.

When it came, she caught with both her hands at Pelham Trent's right arm, dragging it down, and in the same instant Philip sprang. There was the cracking sound of a shot, very loud in the little hall. Glass splintered somewhere, a loose rug slid under Pelham's feet, and they were all down together. Lyndall crawled out between flailing arms and legs, stumbled up to her feet, and saw the constable kneeling on Pelham's chest whilst Philip held his ankles. The revolver stuck out from a rolled-up corner of the rug. Lyndall went and picked it up. Her knees were dithering and her mind shook. The mirror over the blanket-chest was broken, and there were little bright bits of glass everywhere.

She went into the drawing-room and pushed the revolver down behind one of the sofa cushions. When she came back Philip looked over his shoulder and said,

"We want something to tie him up with. Those things that loop the curtains back will do. Hurry!"

XXXVII

THE Chief Inspector looked at Miss Silver across his office table. His manner combined modest self-satisfaction and honest pride with just a dash of official dignity. His florid complexion glowed. He said in a hearty voice,

"Well, Miss Silver, I thought you'd like to know that we've got it all cleared up—no untidy ends."

Miss Silver, sitting rather primly upright with her hands in a small round muff of the same date as her fur tie, gave a slight cough and said,

"That must be extremely satisfactory to you."

"Well, I like to get a job finished up. And I won't say you haven't been quite a help. I wouldn't have liked anything to have happened to that girl—she's a plucky little thing. And I don't mind saying I shouldn't have thought of giving her police protection if you hadn't put me up to it. You see, you've got a pull on us poor policemen. Young ladies don't come and cry on our shoulders and tell us all their secrets like they seem to do with you—though I have got daughters of my own."

Sergeant Abbott, propping the mantelpiece and keeping most of the fire off the room, was understood to suggest that Miss Silver should impart her recipe. He got a frown from his Chief Inspector and a recommendation to use the good old English word receipt, if that was what he meant.

"That's what my mother called it, and what was good enough for me is good enough for you, my lad, and don't you forget it! Frenchified words may be all very well in France, but I won't have them here in my office! And I'll tell you what I've come to notice—that you give way to using them when you're a bit above yourself. I don't say you haven't done a good job of work over this case, because you have—but no need to go up in the air and talk like a foreigner. And now, if you'll stop interrupting, I'll get on with telling Miss Silver what we've turned up."

Miss Silver inclined her head.

"I should be most grateful, Chief Inspector."

Solidly filling his chair, a hand on either knee, Lamb spoke.

"He'd covered his tracks very cleverly of course—these gentry do. And there must have been people helping him we haven't got hold of, and can't get hold of. As a matter of fact we shouldn't have got hold of him if Miss Lyndall Armitage hadn't recognized his voice when he used the same words to her that she'd heard him use to Annie Joyce. And that was a thing she didn't tell you, did she?"

Miss Silver coughed.

"No—she kept that back. She has told me about it since. It was extremely unwise of her, and it very nearly cost her her life—and Sir Philip's. But when I saw her she was, I think, still resisting her own conviction. You see, he had been a friend—a very trusted friend. I think she had some lingering hope that when she put it to him he would be able to restore that trust. It is not easy for a girl to give a friend up to the police, but she ran a most terrible risk. I am glad that the constable was there, and that he was so prompt and helpful—though it was, I understand, Miss Armitage's own presence of mind which saved them all. But pray continue."

"Well, we traced his back history. An uncle of his was Mr. Codrington's partner—that's how Mr. Codrington came to take him on. He's a qualified solicitor of course. Got bitten with Fascist ideas when they were all the go, but dropped them—or I should say appeared to drop them—when Hitler was showing his hand and they weren't so popular. He used to go off hiking in Germany. Lots of people did, and no harm in it, but if you wanted a cover-up for any funny business it was quite a good one. Just when he definitely started working for the Nazis, we don't know, and we're not likely to, but he must have been playing their game for years. We've got Madame Dupont identified. Her name's Marie Rozen, and she's a nasty bit of work. I think her husband is just what she said he was—a clever hairdresser, badly broken in health and not in this Nazi business at all. They were only married just before the war. She got in here under his first wife's name. To get back to Trent. Besides the very respectable rooms where he lodged, he kept a room over a garage in one of those streets off the Vauxhall Bridge Road. He'd an envelope on him addressed there in the name of Thomson, and the people have identified him. That's where he changed when he wanted to be Mr. Felix or anybody else. We found a couple of wigs, one red and one grey, and all sorts of clothes, some of them very shabby, and a big loose overcoat. With that and the red wig, I don't suppose his best friend would have known him.

He kept a battered old taxi in the garage, and passed as a driver who had been called up for Fire Service. I don't think there's much doubt that he met Miss Nellie Collins at Waterloo and told her he was taking her to see Lady Jocelyn. She may have thought she was being driven to Jocelyn's Holt. He could have made a long way round of it to the lane where she was found. There are plenty of ways you can waste time if you put your mind to it, and she wouldn't think she had any reason to be suspicious, poor lady. Then, when he'd got her where he wanted, he'd make some excuse to get her out of the car and just run her down. See?"

Miss Silver coughed.

"Dear me—how extremely shocking!"

Frank Abbott put up a hand to his mouth for a moment. A gleam of cynical amusement might have been observed by his companions, had either of them been looking in his direction. His thoughts were of a lively irreverence. "The old fox! He's cribbed most of that from Maudie, and she's letting him get away with it—she always does. Now just how far is he really kidding himself, and just how far does he think he is kidding Maudie—and me?" His conclusion being that it was as good as a play, he resumed the enjoyable pose of listener. His Miss Silver had just proffered a neat little bouquet of compliments. His Chief Inspector was accepting it heartily, if not with grace. The atmosphere was genial.

Lamb fairly shone with satisfaction as he said,

"Well, there it is—the police do earn their pay sometimes! Oh, by the way, we found the laundry-basket. It was in the corner of his garage. Nothing inside but a lot of crumpled-up paper. I should say there's no doubt he took it along in the taxi and waited till he saw Sir Philip come out. Then he'd only to put the basket on his head and walk in and up the stairs. It sounds a lot more risky than it was. If he had both his hands up steadying the basket, it would be easy enough to tip it so that anyone he met wouldn't see his face."

"You put it so clearly." Miss Silver's voice held an admiring note.

The Chief Inspector beamed.

"Oh, well—it's guess-work. But we've got it pretty well figured out. This Annie Joyce would be acting under his instructions. I think we may take it that she'd been told to drug Sir Philip and go through his papers, but meanwhile she had

aid or done something to make Trent suspect her. He had
her followed. He knew she had got at any rate as far as thinking about coming to see you. It's long odds she had told him
what Miss Armitage had overheard. I think she'd be fright-
ned to keep it to herself. What do you say?"

Miss Silver said gravely,

"I think she told him. From one or two things Miss Armitage said, I think Annie Joyce had a grudge against her. Miss
Armitage had been very devoted to the real Lady Jocelyn. In
a terribly difficult situation, she was trying very hard to main-
tain the old friendship and affection, but without success. I
will give you her own words. They were spoken, I am sure,
in deep sincerity. She said, 'I loved her so much, but after she
came back she wouldn't let me. It didn't even seem as if she
liked me.' "

Lamb nodded.

"That would be about the size of it. Well, let's take it
Trent knew they had been overheard. That would give him a
very strong motive for getting rid of Annie Joyce. She may,
or may not, have known who he really was."

Miss Silver coughed.

"From the enquiries I have made since his arrest, I do not
find that he and the so-called Lady Jocelyn had ever met. I
think he would be very careful not to expose his identity. He
undoubtedly disguised himself to keep those appointments at
the hairdresser's shop, and from what Sergeant Abbott has
told me of the lighting arrangements in the office there, it is
clear that the heavily shaded reading-lamp could have been
so disposed as to leave him in shadow whilst turning all the
light upon a visitor."

"Yes, that's the way it would be—and his voice kept down
to a whisper like Miss Armitage says. It's a queer thing, itsn't
it, that he should have given himself away by falling into the
very trick he had used as a safeguard. If he hadn't said those
same words to Miss Armitage in the same whispering voice that
she'd heard on the other side of that door, he might have got
clear away. Madame Dupont only knew him as Mr. Felix.
With that connection cut and Annie Joyce dead, there wouldn't
have been a single clue to lead to Mr. Pelham Trent. You
could get quite a moral out of that—couldn't you?"

Miss Silver said, "Yes, indeed."

The Chief Inspector resumed.

"Well, there we are—he goes up with the laundry-basket and she lets him in. She may have been expecting him—we can't know about that—but she'd be pleased enough to see him, because she'd think she had got what he wanted. There's no doubt, from the finger-prints, that she had been all through that code-book—copying it, no doubt. You may call it a guess, but it's a pretty safe one. As you know, the code was out of date—part of the trap to catch her. A man in Trent's position would know enough to know that. He may have meant to kill her anyhow, but if she had let herself be trapped he just couldn't afford to leave her alive and risk what she might be able to give away. She took fright and tried to get to the telephone. He shot her down. Then he had a look for Sir Philip's revolver and took it away with him. He may not have had to look—she may have tried to get it—we can't know. He didn't leave any fingerprints, so he must have worn gloves in the flat—probably slipped them on when he was waiting for her to open the door. He had the revolver on him, as you know, when he was arrested. It's a perfectly water-tight case, and a good riddance of three dangerous people—more, maybe, if Madame Dupont talks. Well, that's about all there is to it. Excuse me, will you—I've got to see the Assistant Commissioner."

When he had gone after a cordial handshake, Sergeant Abbott came over to lean against the table and looked down at his "revered preceptress."

"Well?" he said. "What are you thinking about?"

She gave a slight hesitant cough.

"I was thinking of what the Chief Inspector said."

Frank laughed.

"He said quite a lot, didn't he?"

"At the end," said Miss Silver—"when he said, 'That is all there is to it.' Because there are no circumstances in which that can be true."

"And how?"

She looked at him simply and gravely.

"It goes so far back. I have been talking to the Jocelyns, and they have told me a good deal. It goes back to Sir Ambrose Jocelyn, who made no provision for the woman he had lived with, or for their son. Sir Philip's father made her a small allowance. The bread of charity is not really sweetened to the recipient by the fact that it is paid for out of a purse which ight have been his own. Roger Joyce was a weak and in-ffectual person. From what poor Miss Collins told me, it was ear that his daughter had been brought up to consider her-lf wronged and defrauded. When he died she was fifteen. iss Theresa Jocelyn took her up, and after making a very nwise attempt to force her upon the rest of the family went road with her. A girl of that age is very sensible to slights. e stayed a week at Jocelyn's Holt, and saw all the things hich she might have had if her father had been a legitimate stead of an illegitimate son. She went away with what must ave been very bitter feelings. Ten years later Miss Jocelyn, ho had made a will in her favour, suddenly changed her ind. She was an erratic and impulsive woman, and just as n years before she had taken a sudden fancy to Annie Joyce, e now took an equally sudden fancy to Anne Jocelyn, and nnounced that she was making a will in her favour." Miss lver paused and coughed. "Such lack of principle is very ifficult to understand. It began immediately to produce the oubles which want of principle always does produce. Sir hilip had a serious quarrel with his wife. He forbade her to ke the money, expressing himself with considerable vehe-ence, whilst she asserted her right to take it if she chose. he was, as you probably know, already a considerable heiress. he defied her husband and joined Miss Jocelyn in France. he effect upon Annie Joyce may be imagined. Her father nd Lady Jocelyn's mother were half-brother and sister, one oor and disowned, the other rich and prosperous. Lady ocelyn had everything that Annie Joyce had not—rank, posi-on, money, the family estate, the family name. They lived or three months under the same roof. Can you doubt that uring those three months the bitterness and resentment in hich Annie Joyce had been brought up became very greatly tensified? We have no means of knowing more than Sir hilip has told us of what happened on the beach when he was ttempting to get the two girls away. Annie may have realized t the time that Anne had been fatally injured, or she may have emained in ignorance for quite a long while. It seems certain nat she returned to the château and lived there as Annie oyce, that she came more and more under German influence, nd that there came a time when they decided to make use of er. She must herself have informed them of her likeness to ady Jocelyn. Sir Philip tells me that his cousin, Miss Theresa

191

Jocelyn, had a very large collection of family photograph
They would be able to judge of the resemblance for themselve
Up-to-date information about the family was undoubted!
obtained from Mr. Trent. I may say that I had all along a fee
ing that the person directing the so-called Lady Jocelyn wa
likely to be someone closely associated with the family. D
tails which no stranger could have known were essential to th
success of the impersonation. The diary accounts for a gre
deal, but it did not supply the current knowledge of S
Philip's affairs, nor had it any share in the careful timing of th
—supposed—return of his wife."

Frank Abbott had been listening with respectful attentio
If there was a moment during which the irreverent phras
"Moralizings of Maudie", flickered across his mind—if h
rather light eyes never entirely lost a faintly cynical spark, h
still felt, as he always did, an affectionate respect which had on!
ceased to surprise him because it was now of quite long stan(
ing. As she rose to her feet, he straightened up.

"I see Jocelyn has a notice of his wife's death in all th
papers—with the date." He picked up *The Times* from th
table behind him and ran his eye down the column. "Here w
are—'On June 26, 1940, by enemy action, Anne, wife of S
Philip Jocelyn——' Well, I suppose we shall be seeing h
name in the Marriages next."

Miss Silver coughed, a thought reprovingly. She said,
"I hope so."

THE END